WAKE UP
and
DIE RIGHT

Kerrigan Rhea

Outskirts Press, Inc.
Denver, Colorado

This is a work of fiction. The events and characters described herein are imaginary and are not intended to refer to specific places or living persons. The opinions expressed in this manuscript are solely the opinions of the author and do not represent the opinions or thoughts of the publisher.

Wake Up and Die Right
All Rights Reserved.
Copyright © 2009 Kerrigan Rhea
V5.0

Cover Photo © 2009 JupiterImages Corporation. All rights reserved - used with permission.

This book may not be reproduced, transmitted, or stored in whole or in part by any means, including graphic, electronic, or mechanical without the express written consent of the publisher except in the case of brief quotations embodied in critical articles and reviews.

Outskirts Press, Inc.
http://www.outskirtspress.com

ISBN: 978-1-4327-2168-8

Outskirts Press and the "OP" logo are trademarks belonging to Outskirts Press, Inc.

PRINTED IN THE UNITED STATES OF AMERICA

Table of Contents

Chapter 1
Dirty Little Secrets   1

Chapter 2
Not Daddy's Girl   25

Chapter 3
The Children's Home   60

Chapter 4
The Day I Misplaced The Corpse   84

Chapter 5
To Serve My Country   98

Chapter 6
Lady In Blue   149

Chapter 7
Good Cop/Bad Cop/Dead Cop   219

Chapter 8
Starting Over   261

Wake Up and Die Right is a fictional narrative that is sensitive as well as an emotional roller coaster. Born in a second-generation dysfunctional family, Svetlana "Loni" Chekov takes on the challenges of her past destructive relationships, refuses to become another professional victim. Her decisions left her bartering with survival most of her existence.

When she became a police officer, a new nightmare begins along with one of the South's most corrupt police departments. After her partner is, murdered for knowing too much, Loni fears for her own life as Georgia's *"Good Ole Boys"* control more than what is going on within the department. They surely aren't going to let their *token* female officer do her job without a little havoc, *Southern Style*. Her extraordinary life behind the badge is the saga of the Crestview Police Department.

Wake Up and Die Right tell the secrets hidden behind closed doors.
Based on a true story.

Dedication

This book is dedicated to some special people who made lasting recollections in my life.

In memory of my mother, I feel her presence when I remember her words "Wake up and die right!" She told me this as a child when I was going through some hard times. It took me 40 years, but now I understand that when something is wrong in my life, I should just stand back and look at the situation, then work the problem to my advantage. She is one of the reasons I am writing this book.

To my grandparents, who always gave me a secure sanction. They were always proud of me and I have tried to live up to their expectations.

To my little sister and my little brother, our childhood memories are so different. Each of us focused on certain unforgettable moments that led us to take the paths we made as adults. Each memory played a part in making us what we are today.

To my husband Tom and my wonderful mother-in-law Gloria, thank you for your support. You made me stronger and fearless to take chances.

To Rosemarie Urista and Vanessa Smith, thank you for taking the time to read and edit my book to disguise my dyslexia so it isn't too obvious to others.

Marti Smith, you are a very strong willed lady. You give me strength as I see you fight cancer by never giving up.

In memory of Mitch, my police partner and friend helped me through the police academy. His death was not in vain. The only thing that gives me comfort in his demise is to know that even though the people responsible for his death may have gotten away with it in this lifetime; they won't be able to do so in their next lifetime. The names have been changed to protect the Guilty.

Chapter 1

Dirty Little Secret

It was a warm spring evening when I first came into the world. Not that I can remember that particular day, but I recall my mother telling me about the day she first became a mother. She recalled the twenty-eight hours of labor as love.

My mother Emily was of English descent. Looking at photos of her about the time I was born, I could tell she was a beautiful woman. She was tall and statuesque. Standing 5'9", she had long wavy auburn hair that shined in the sunlight like gold Christmas tinsel. Her eyes were deep blue, which can only compare to the most precious blue sapphires. I can clearly remember my mother's smile as that of an angel.

Emily didn't always have much of a reason to smile, growing up in an orphanage. My grandmother loved her with all her heart but had to make a decision that she thought was the best for Emily.

It was during the Depression and Emily was only five years old. Her mother Mildred was married to Lou Fennimore, whose family was very wealthy. Lou's weaknesses were horse racing, women and booze. Often, no one heard from him for weeks at a time. When Lou did come home from one of his escapades, he was in a drunken fit of anger and verbally abusive toward Mildred and their daughter.

On a warm spring day, he saw Emily playing in a two-foot-high box filled with puppies from the family dog. Her long curls were hanging over the raw edges of the box as she sat surrounded by yipping puppies licking her face. Lou yanked Emily by her long curls, dangling the small-framed tyke twelve inches over the puppy-filled box. After his exhibition of cruelty, it accelerated the already doomed marriage to end. Christian-raised, Mildred could no longer watch Lou flaunt his infidelity while they suffered for his indiscretions. She divorced him soon after the incident with the puppies.

The Fennimore family was not only wealthy, but also influential in the political and judicial realm. Mildred was granted a divorce but only awarded TEN DOLLARS a month for child support. Lou didn't attempt to pay the meager amount or to see his only child until she was grown.

Mildred found it difficult to support the two of them with no one to look after her precious child as she washed and ironed the clothes of affluent employers for $2.50 a week. She did what so many heartbroken families had to do during the Depression. Mildred placed Emily in an orphanage so she could earn enough money to have a place they could call their own. So many times, I remember my grandmother telling me stories of the days she worked long hours so that she could earn enough money for food and save for a weekly bus ride to the orphanage to see Emily. Mildred would walk TEN miles each way from where the bus dropped her off just to see her beautiful auburn haired daughter. In the winter, the long walk made her feet numb from the cold, which was the only relief from the aching of large blisters on her feet from her worn out shoes.

Mildred told me of the heartache she endured because she couldn't take Emily home. It was hard to see her child cry as though she were in physical pain when leaving her behind. Emily would stare with swollen, glazed eyes as her mother walked in three-foot snowdrifts down the winding road leaving the orphanage. She looked intently as the shadowy figure of her mother faded from her sight.

Emily ran after her in the winter chill without a jacket, diligently placing her tiny feet in the footprints in the snow left behind by her mother. Tears froze to Emily's rosy cheeks before one of the matrons would catch a glimpse of her through the frosted windows of the main office.

Emily was depressed over her abandonment. Time seemed to stand still as it took ten and a half years before she was no longer a ward of the state of Tennessee. She cautiously looked forward to returning home to Mildred, pondering whether she could ever forgive her mother for deserting her.

Emily hadn't changed much over the years. She was still shy, quiet and later became awkwardly taller than the other children her age. This seemed to be an open invitation for other children to taunt and tease her. Not having much self-confidence, she would sob herself to sleep. Her pillow saturated as she kept her sorrow to herself.

As a young teenager, Emily was irate with distrust and anger. She had the feeling of abandonment by both her father and her mother. In those teen years, Mildred had met and married an older man by the name of Nigel Forester. Nigel came to America from England. In his late forties, he married Mildred. Even though he was a hard-working man and good to Emily, adolescent emotions made it difficult for her to see his good intentions. No one seems to be able to reach the lost little girl who was still inside her, wanting help.

Emily ran away from the loving home that Mildred and Nigel provided for her, looking for something to fill the void. She even sought the comfort of her biological father she never had a chance to know.

Lou had been married and divorced several times before his meeting with his only offspring. Thrilled to see his long-lost daughter, he invited her to stay with him on the family horse-breeding ranch. By the time Emily was reunited with her father, she had outgrown the skinny, awkward teenager, she once was. She was more beautiful than imaginable.

There was a strong feeling of jealousy between her new stepmother Nellie and stepsister Ruthie. Lou's latest wife felt somewhat threatened by Emily's presence. Perhaps she thought she would have to share her riches or conceivably, she was a true "Wicked Stepmother" in every sense of the word.

In comparison to Emily, Ruthie was a true redhead, almost to the point of being orange. Her hair was shoulder length, dry and brittle, it looked as though she had a bad perm. Her skin was ruddy and covered with acne. She was flat chest and with no waist resembled more a teenage boy. In contrast, Emily looked as though she had walked out of a high fashion magazine. She was tall and buxom with milky white skin. Her auburn locks flowed past her waist with every hair in place.

Ruthie despised her stepsister and did everything she could to get Emily in trouble. She had explosive tantrums and whining to Nellie falsely accusing Emily of hitting her or that she took her jewelry. Ruthie was systematically placing her precious jewels in Emily's dresser drawer to blame her for stealing them.

Nellie established that she, too, could be nasty. Fueled by Ruthie's fits, Nellie took Emily out to the barn and beat her methodically. She typically used a buggy whip, the same whip she used on her horses when she was displeased with their performance during a race.

(There were still faint scars that could be seen on Emily's back the day she died.)

Lou's bad habits hadn't changed since he was married to Mildred. His drinking was worse and his infidelity was the same, but this time he was going to include Emily as one of his conquests.

Emily remained in her room most of two weeks, healing from wounds inflicted by Nellie's rage. Lou had been out of town on business and came home late one night. In his drunken state, he stumbled into Emily's room. She was still weak and unable to move as her father crawled into her bed. Petrified with fear, she tried to get out of the bed as her father reached for her breast. She prayed that Lou would be so drunk that he would pass out. Her prayers were answered. The next morning Lou awoke, perplexed to find himself in his daughter's bed.

Emily moved back home with Mildred and Nigel. Even though she had recuperated from her physical wounds, her emotional wounds festered. While Mildred was a very good and loving mother, Emily was unfeeling towards her. Mildred and Nigel tried desperately to convince her that there was a new beginning for all of them. Confused by her adolescent immaturity, she withdrew from her parents and sadly, the one thing that she always wanted, love and attention.

As school started and the football games began,

Wake Up and Die Right

Emily noticed she was drawing attention from the opposite sex. More important, Mildred noticed it first! Mildred was not going to stand for it.

One cool fall evening the newspaper boy decided to make a stop on his route to hand deliver the Foresters' newspaper. He could see Emily sitting on the porch swing wearing a pale pink sweater dotted with tiny white pearls draped over her shoulders. Apprehensively, he approached the front porch. Emily saw the cotton top haired boy with blemished skin trembling as he took his first step onto the porch. His Adam's apple bobbed up and down as he nervously swallowed. He spoke to her briefly, introducing himself as Stanley Fenster. Emily smiled; she said she knew who he was. She told him she had seen him in the halls of their school. When Stanley smiled back at her, his braces shined almost as much as Emily's hair glistened in the moonlight.

Stanley bravely sat on the swing next to Emily. They talked about school and the dance that was coming up at the recreation hall in the town square. Stanley decided that he needed to get back on his route and gently leaned over to kiss Emily on the lips. Just as he was sealing his date with a kiss, Mildred walked out onto the veranda. She made her presence known by slamming the warped screen door. Both Stanley and Emily jumped as the startling noise broke their concentration. Before Mildred could utter a word to Stanley, he jumped the porch railing, leaping over the magnolia bushes and ran down the street as if his pants were on fire.

Mildred gave Emily an uncompromising look. She knew it was time to explain the birds and the bees to her shapely sixteen-year-old daughter. Mildred was raised in an era when discussing sex was not an option. Sex was only meant for having children. In an ambiguous way, she explained to Emily that she could get pregnant by a boy kissing her!

(My grandmother left out saying, if you kiss a boy it could <u>lead</u> to other things and she could get pregnant.)

Panic-stricken, Emily now believed she could be pregnant! She had no idea exactly how to become pregnant and didn't feel she could discuss it further with her mother. Sex was taboo in Mildred's household.

(It was something that Mildred never discussed, but she had to know something about how it worked considering she gave birth to Emily. Not to mention she came from a family of eleven. Surely when brothers and sisters kept popping up and she had to help raise her siblings, she was bound to know something about intercourse.)

The next morning Emily attended school but avoided Stanley. Every morning she would go into the girl's bathroom and look at her stomach in the full-length mirror as the high school cheerleaders gathered for their morning ritual of primping with their makeup and gossiping unmercifully about one another. Emily got to know most of the cheerleaders, whose main objective for attending school were boys. Each girl would have some form of gossip

Wake Up and Die Right

that she just had to share.

"Jenny Michaels is pregnant," said one ruby-lipped teen. The other girls squealed at the news.

Emily saw that this was her chance to ask a question that was weighing on her mind. "How long does it take to have a baby?" she timidly asked.

The ruby-lipped girl giggled and said, "For heaven sakes, Emily, it takes nine months!" as she turned away from the mirror, swishing her ponytail.

"Nine months!" shrieked Emily. Bewildered, her mouth dropped and she turned away as she decided not to discuss it any further with anyone that day.

Nine agonizing months came and went. Emily didn't look or feel any different. "When is it going to get here?" she mumbled to herself. Emily attended school that morning and met with the girls in the usual place.

"Jenny Michaels dropped out of school and moved out of town. I guess she either had an abortion or went to a home for unwed mothers to have her baby," one girl said in a sarcastic tone, tugging on her stockings.

Emily had to ask. "What is an unwed mother's home? In fact, what is an abortion?" The girls giggled as Emily put on an uneasy smile.

"Why are you asking such dumb questions, Emily? Are you pregnant?" said the ruby-lipped girl.

A rather plump girl piped up and said, "That is ridiculous! I doubt she even got to first base, let alone a home run!"

One of the older girls walked over to Emily, put her arm around her and said, "Never mind those bimbos. Is there something on your mind?"

Emily was not sure what she was going to say. She explained to her in private. Emily told her about the newspaper boy and, in addition, of course, what her mother said about the situation.

"Oh my gosh, Emily! Have you been waiting for nine months to see if you are pregnant?" she asked wide-eyed. "Honey, let me tell you some things your mother left out." She grabbed Emily's arm and walked her out of the bathroom toward her locker.

As relieved as she was to know that she was not going to have a baby, she was annoyed with her mother. "Nine months, nine months I waited, scared I'd wake up to a big belly and a craving for pickles and ice cream! I need to get out on my own. I want to go as far away as I can from here, Emily said to herself." Eager as she was to move out on her own, she continued to live with her mother and stepfather off and on for five more years. "*Off and on*" is just that. Emily ran away on a regular basis and then returned home after a few months of bouncing from one girlfriend's house to another.

During one of her run away from her mother's rules, she unwittingly fled from the safety of her home. She met up with some girls who were having a party. There were a lot of boys, drinks and drugs. Emily was not much of a drinker and didn't take drugs. She would nurse a glass of beer all night. What she didn't know, someone had spiked her drink.

The room started to spin and the voices of the people at the party seemed distant and muffled. She didn't remember much after that. Emily woke up in the basement. She was dirty and her clothes were torn. Stumbling to her feet, she felt a dull twinge. She noticed what appeared to be several deflated balloons on the cellar floor. She staggered up the rickety stairs, trying to find her way to the bathroom. A hot shower and clean clothes couldn't take away her sullied feeling. As the morning grew to afternoon, Emily had flashbacks of the night before. "What really happened?" she said to herself. "Who else knows?" Emily didn't mention it to any of her friends. She couldn't bring herself to talk about it. Over the next few days, several bruises appeared on both her wrists and ankles. Some almost looked like hand and fingerprints. By now, the eighteen-year-old knew in her heart that she had been violated. "I'll take this secret to my grave before I tell my mother," she swore to herself.

(That is something I know my mother never told my grandmother. She told me and I could see she still felt the shame of the events of that day so long ago, but she kept it to herself. It was not until my mother passed away that I told my grandmother my mother's secret. It was hard enough on my grandmother that she survived her only child, but she felt remorse that my mother would not come to her after

an ordeal as that.)

When Emily ran out of girlfriends to live with, her mother would mourn every night, not knowing where she was for weeks at a time. When Emily did come home to Mildred and Nigel, she was accepted with open arms every time. They learned not to ask any questions as to her whereabouts.

It was when Emily turned twenty-one years old that she decided she wanted to play house and needed to find a husband. How bad could that be?

Once again, Emily thought she had a pot of gold waiting at the end of the rainbow. To Emily the gold was Dane Phillips. They met at a friend's wedding reception. He was not the best-looking guy she met, but he dazzled her with his wit. He got her attention as a prospect for husband material when he told her he made good money as a truck driver. She got goose bumps thinking he could be the one to take her away from all this.

Dane was a stocky man with beady black eyes, bushy brows and straight dishwater blond hair that he wore slicked back. He smelled of VO5 radiating from his mane and diesel from his clothes. His usual wardrobe consisted of white v-neck T-shirt with a pack of cigarettes rolled up in the sleeves. His jeans were too long, so he cuffed them just above his tattered loafers, exposing his dingy white socks. Phillips puffed on his Marlboro cigarette as Emily swooned at the thought of becoming a bride to this James Dean figure of a man. This is it, a way out of the house, to live on my own, she thought to herself.

Wake Up and Die Right

Emily Fennimore and Dane Phillips moved to Chicago. They were married on a hot sticky day in July of 1952, by a Justice of the Peace. Their first residence was in a high-rise apartment about forty miles from Mildred and Nigel. Starting over was refreshing for Emily and she was going to do her best to be a good wife. Everything started out to be blissful, but it seemed doomed as each day went by. Dane would go on long truck hauls leaving Emily home by herself. He would be gone two to three weeks at a time. Many times, there wasn't any food in the house. Famished, she decided that she had to get a job. Considering she dropped out of school and never had a job before, she was not too persnickety about the type of employment she would get.

There was a little café called Gilligan's down the street within walking distance. She remembered a "help wanted" sign in the window. Before she could ask for a job application, she was hired on the spot. The owner, Gustov Gilligan, liked her smile and saw that all the customers' eyes lit up when she walked into the restaurant.

Emily worked hard. She went home exhausted from being on her feet all day. The money was not much, but it would at least put food on the table.

One day she came home late from work. Dane had just got back into town two hours earlier. He was waiting for her as he sat at the small kitchen table drinking a Bud Light. At first, she was excited to see her new groom; she wrapped her arms around him and began kissing him with a bridal passion. In her excitement to see him, she didn't notice he had a tuft of hair missing from the left side of his head. His nose was swollen and there were small spots of blood on his shirt. "Oh Dane, what happened to you?" she said quickly in a high-pitched voice.

Dane's voice slurred as he told her that he had gotten into a fight with some guy in a bar over the guy's wife that Dane had been seeing. Emily's mouth dropped, but his next words shocked her the most. He told her if she didn't like it, there was the door, as he pointed his dirty, dried bloody finger at her. He said, "You can't change me, so you should just get used to the way things are." Emily's eyes widened and her stomach felt as though it were wedged in her throat. She put her hand over her mouth as she ran to the restroom.

Dane briskly followed, yelling, "You should have been here when I got home! It is your fault that I am seeing other women. My dinner isn't waiting for me on the table and I don't know where in the hell you have been. You aren't ever home when I call or come home from a long haul!" Then he leaned in toward her and sniffed her hair. "You smell like hamburgers."

Emily slowly got up off the floor as she had been kneeling at the commode. She ran the water in the rust-stained sink and rinsed her face, took a deep breath and said, "I got a waitress job. You never left me with any money to buy food and I was starving. Besides, I would be here and have dinner waiting for you, but you never let me know when you are coming home."

Dane looked at her with intense eyes and backhanded her across the face. Emily stumbled as she ran into the bathroom door, hitting her head on the door jam.

"I never told you that you could get a job! No wife of mine is going to work!" he snapped. Dane walked over to the coffee table where she left her purse and keys. He began to rummage through the almost empty small pocketbook. He poured out its contents and threw it onto the tattered green sofa, knocking the crisp white doilies onto the floor. He pulled his hand back as if to strike her again. She flinched as he pretended to hit her. Dane then took what little tip money she made for the day and headed toward the door for the nearest bar.

Emily endured this type of treatment on and off for about two years. There were times when things weren't so bad; Emily focused on those few cherished moments. When they did happen, she thought their marriage might be different if they had a baby. She found the courage to bring up the subject of having a baby and wanted him to go to the doctor with her to see why they hadn't conceived. Dane barked back at her, "It's not my fault we don't have a baby. I know there isn't anything wrong with me! Hell, I have two women pregnant across the state right now, you dumb bitch!" Emily gasped; looking intently at the man, she thought she wanted to be the father of her child. By now, her tolerance for

Dane's cruel remarks had worn thin. She hardheartedly walked toward the hall closet and snatched a dusty, dilapidated suitcase.

"Where do you think you are going?" Dane sputtered, hand reaching out for the couch. He plopped his rear end on the cushions so hard that the leg broke off the couch and skid across the room. Emily started laughing as she watched her again inebriated husband roll onto the floor. He lay there pretending to be examining the condition of the divan so as not to give the impression his performance was uncouth. Loathing Dane at that very instant inspired her to continue her quest to leave him. She meticulously pulled each drawer of her dresser open to gather her personal paraphernalia. After she collected her limited valuables, she walked across the living room with the fortitude to continue out the door and never look back, this time. Holding her head high while biting her bottom lip, Emily felt things couldn't get any worse. They could only get better. She shut the door behind her, standing with her back to the apartment. She closed her eyes for a split second, took a deep breath, continued walking down the dimly lit hallway of her high-rise apartment.

Emily took another position as a server to avoid making contact with Dane at Gilligan's. She moved into the Bridge Port Arms hotel in one of Chicago's suburbs. It was small. There was barely enough room to spit, turn around, and avoid being hit. (*Sounds like a dumb saying, but that is how my mother described it to me.*) She worked hard and didn't have much of a social life until the day she met a tall, dark, wavy-haired Russian named Casmir Chekov. They met in the elevator of her hotel apartment. Cas, as his friends called him, was a hardworking construction worker who fell hopelessly in love with Emily at first sight. Emily, on the other hand, wasn't ready for a relationship, not to mention she was still married to Dane.

Working as a server left her little social time and required long and grueling hours. The pay was inferior to minimum wage and she barely could afford the forty-dollar-a-week rent and food. When a position came open at the Bridge Port Arms, she jumped on the opportunity to work close to home. She started working part time as an elevator operator until there was a job opening for a telephone operator for Illinois Bell.

Cas was so smitten with Emily that he just couldn't keep his eyes off her. He made every endeavor to see her as she worked. Standing next to the elevator call button wearing his gray fedora hat and waist-length leather jacket, he greeted her with his charming smile. With his head slightly bent downward and his hat brim cocked over one eye, he gradually started a conversation in his broken English. Emily beamed as she greeted the handsome Russian. Even though she acted indifferent to his charisma, he was not going to admit defeat. Cas could have any woman he wanted, but this time he met his match. The more she tried to evade him, the more he sought her.

After about two months of continual pursuit, Emily agreed to go out for dinner and dancing. She was fascinated by the bronzed Russian's physique. His piercing blue eyes made her melt as she gazed into them. Their evening was enchanted and Casmir was her Prince Charming. "This is just too good to be true," she said to herself. However, when he said he wanted to introduce her to his father, Vladimir, she knew he was serious about her. Cas didn't say much about his mother, but there seemed to be some tension whenever she mentioned her.

He told her that he came from a family of five children. He was the youngest state side. When Emily talked to Vladimir, he, too, had broken English. He told her of the long trip on a ship and the disheartening story of his travel to the United States to better his family.

Vladimir was a short, stocky, jolly man with rosy cheeks and gentle mannerisms. He kept calling Emily "Marda". Emily began to feel a sense of closeness with him. He felt the same way about her. He slowly began to confide in her the tale of his trip to America in the 1930s. He was dedicated to his family. It was hard for him to come to another country alone to earn money to send to the children and wife that he adored.

One month before he sailed to America, his daughter Natalya was born. Her birth was what made him decide that he had to build a good life for the children in America.

Wake Up and Die Right

Faithfully he sent money home and sent for his children one by one. His wife was the last to arrive. He sent for her and Natalya, but was heartbroken that she came alone, leaving Natalya behind with relatives. Emily could see the hurt in Vladimir's eyes whenever Natalya's name was spoken.

Emily noticed there was an unusual closeness between Casmir and his mother, Marlonnia. Yet he seemed to despise her at the same time. His mother was a strange little woman. Her dark hair with streaks of silver framing her face appeared disarrayed. She was short with broad shoulders and resembled a refrigerator from the rear. Emily recalled that she smelled like cooked cabbage. Marlonnia never spoke English around her and gave Emily the evil eye as though she placed a curse on her whenever Cas was around.

As time evolved, Emily wanted to learn more about Marlonnia. Some of the stories she heard came from Casmir's sister-in-law, Lucia. She had married Algirus Chekov, Casmir's oldest brother. She was about five feet tall, a loud Sicilian woman who reminded me of the late comedian Totie Fields. She said what was on her mind and didn't care who or what anyone thought of her crude remarks.

Lucia was well known as the family gossip. She frequently told Emily that Marlonnia was far from being a stable person. Lucia whispered bits and pieces of scandal about her mother-in-law, who had been in and out of mental institutions while in Russia and America. Vladimir remained devoted to his wife and never spoke a harsh word about her.

Lucia told Emily that she herself was recovering from cancer and had had a mastectomy where her right breast was removed. She was not the shy type. She would frequently go to bars and hustle men, right in front of Algirus.

One time a drunk was commenting on her ample bosom and wanted to touch it. Lucia, who didn't have to be drunk to say or do some of the things that she did, said with a thick Sicilian accent, "Okay, big boy, you close a your eyes." The man eagerly awaited the chance to hold her breast in his hands. Emily watched as Lucia pulled out her prosthetic breast from her bra, placed it in his hand and said, "Enjoy" loudly for everyone in the bar to hear. The drunk snatched his hand back as if he had touched something hot. Lucia laughed as Algirus just had a dumb smile on his face like Stan Laurel of the Laurel and Hardy comedy team.

Uncle Algirus was the big silent Neanderthal type. I always felt sorry for him. Everyone knew he was hen-pecked but had a big heart. He had that gentle giant look, which was sweet, but a big dummy. Lucia and Algirus didn't seem like a compatible couple, but they say opposites attract.

Lucia was not only brash, but also the pipeline to smut and family secrets. She eagerly told Emily about all the skeletons in the Chekov family closet. It was hard to grasp the rumors she told as being reality. When Lucia started to tell the most implausible stories about Casmir and his mother, Emily tried to turn away but couldn't. She hung onto every word Lucia whispered to her.

She said Cas had been sickly as a child in Russia. There was little food, relentless cold weather. His parents' bed was next to an old rusted potbelly stove. The crackle of the cinders was heard in the tiny room. There was a strong smell of the birch wood burning. As he did every morning, Vladimir would leave for one of his two jobs at dawn. He would first wake his young, sickly and then towhead son, Casmir to get into bed with Marlonnia to keep warm. Lucia said Marlonnia had not been in her right mind for years. She began to fantasize about her youngest son as a lover. When he reached his middle teens, Cas became her secret, forbidden lover on a regular basis.

During this stressful mother and son relationship, she found ways to convince Casmir that the love they shared was special and he should not tell anyone because it could cause jealousy amongst his siblings and father. Even though he felt strange about his taboo relationship, he continued because there was no one to say other wise. Besides, what mother wants, mother gets!

There were many cold days and nights, so often Casmir satisfied his mother's needs. It was two and a half years after their illicit romance began that he learned his mother was expecting a child. It was Natalya. The rest of the family dared not speak aloud that it was a rumor; Casmir fathered Natalya and that is why Marlonnia left her behind in Russia.

Casmir was naïve to the fact that his sister could have been his child. It was never anything his mother talked to him about or to anyone else. Vladimir was just as naïve to the situation. He loved Natalya unconditionally as he did all of his children.

As Lucia went on to describe Marlonnia, as anything other than your typical mother-in-law, Emily just couldn't walk away from the scandal. She was mesmerized as Lucia's story continued.

She went on to say that, Marlonnia was not nurturing to her children as most mothers are. The only form of closeness she had physically was when she breastfed them well into their early teens. This was their main source of nourishment due to the lack of food. The sheer size of Marlonnia left no doubt, where what little food they did have, had gone. Her children never went hungry as long as she supplied them with mother's milk.

Marlonnia wasn't much of a chef. She often would cook everything in one big pot. She diligently placed it in the center of the living room floor of their two-room shack. Oddly enough, she never felt the need to wash it out. There weren't any cooking utensils used. Casmir and the other children ate with their hands. They scooped up cooked potatoes served many days prior, only to have fresh food mixed in with the aging potatoes.

Marlonnia had a temper feared by all who knew her. Algirus told Lucia that he remembered when Casmir was about eight years old; he was trying to make repairs on the tin roof while it was raining hard. A bolt of lightning struck close to him, startling Cas and he lost his footing, fell off the roof, he hit his head on a plank of wood. He was scared and dazed. He had a concussion that distorted his vision. His only thought at that time was to hide. Cas knew Marlonnia would be angry because he hadn't fixed the leak. He feared that she would beat him sadistically as she had in the past. Surely, the headache was nothing compared to the thrashing that he would have gotten. Casmir staggered to the railroad yard about 900 feet from his house. He crawled under one of the railroad cars to get out of the rain. He lay there for most of a week, wasting away from the lack of food and water and covering himself up with ink-smudged newspapers.

Weakened from hunger and the head trauma, Casmir reluctantly returned home. He found it odd that his mother acted as though he had never been gone. She never said anything to him but motioned for him to suckle her breast milk. She stroked his now coal-black hair tenderly. Then she cradled him in her arms as he got his strength back.

Emily was dumbfounded by Lucia's account. Not sure if she wanted to continue her relationship with Casmir, she mumbled to herself, "What a squirrelly family!" As she reminisced about what Lucia had told her, she pondered about her own past. Emily felt Cas seemed more attuned to her needs than anyone she had met. Perhaps it was their hard childhoods. After all, you can't pick your relatives. She sympathetically thought about Cas and the decision she was going to make if she should stay with him. "He is so sweet and very handsome. He has never treated me anything like Dane did", she reminded herself.

Emily didn't hesitate when Cas asked her to move into a small apartment with him. She felt giddy, yet she didn't feel comfortable because she and Dane were still married. Casmir smiled as his eyes twinkled and he told Emily that he would pay for her divorce if that were holding her back. She blushed, and then excitedly agreed to move in with him.

Chapter 2
Not Daddy's Girl

Emily and Casmir lived together for four years. After two years of bliss, Cas began to drink excessively. First, it was only on the weekends; then he started to come home a little later than the week before. As the weekend approached, Casmir started drinking on Friday night and continue until late Sunday afternoon. Emily thought that, after all, he worked hard as a construction foreman and they lived comfortably on his paycheck. Emily didn't need to work, there was always food on the table. She reasoned that he deserved to have some form of relaxation.

Over the years, Emily could see the changes in Casmir. Not just the drinking, but also his eyes would change from an ice blue to cobalt blue. She later would say that he was having one of his "spells". When he was in one of his spells, he would become very distant and angry. Sometimes it would last a week or more.

In September of 1956, during one of Casmir's "spells", Emily learned that she was pregnant with her first child. She was so excited. She couldn't wait to tell Casmir. She hoped he would be as happy as she was. Several thoughts flooded her mind as to a loving way to give the good news to him. She fixed a candlelight dinner, put on her best dress, fixed her hair the way he liked it, she put a sign on the front of their apartment door that read, "CONGRATULATIONS, DADDY".

Her happiness was only one-sided at that point. Cas came home, gazed at the sign and tore it off the door. He flung the door open as the doorknob made a thumping sound, making a hole in the drywall. He set his keys and hat on the hall table heavily stained with coffee rings from his leaking thermos.

He blurted out, "What the fuck is this?" Startled by his reaction, she nervously stuttered as she told him she had gone to the doctor that day.

"We are going to have a baby sometime in the spring." Cas froze with a malevolent stare, the same look worn by Marlonnia when she was displeased. Emily looked deep into his piercing dark blue eyes and apprehensively watched his nostrils flaring and could hear his teeth grinding together. Not at all what she expected his reaction to be over the news of becoming a father. Perhaps he was tired; after all, he had worked late, she thought. There was a noticeably strong odor emanating from him.

"That is the last thing we need, Moth-err!" he

Wake Up and Die Right

---

said in a possessed-sounding whisper. He repeatedly chanted the words "Mother, mother!" He reached over the kitchen table as Emily was setting it and grabbed her wrists, clenching his teeth as he whispered in a deep, demonic voice, "I will kill you mother! You ruined everything. Get rid of it!"

Emily struggled to get away, cautiously reassuring him, "I am not your mother; I am not your mother!"

(*Of course, getting rid of her baby was not going to happen as long as Emily had been waiting to have a child. She needed to have this baby for her.*)

"No one will take my baby from me!" she said as she ran out the door and fled to the only place that she could think of at that time—Mildred's house. Tears streaming down her face as her makeup puddle under her chin, from the hours of weeping, she went home to her mother.

Mildred's reaction wasn't what Emily wanted to hear either. Her mother was clearly upset and expressed how ashamed she was of Emily for getting pregnant and not being married.

"Emily, how could you do this to me?" she said, selfishly.

"This is not about you, mom; this is about a baby that I am going to have", she said very firmly. "Casmir was not happy about it came home drunk and I was scared that he might hurt my baby," she cried out.

"What do you expect, Emily, after living with him for four years? This was bound to happen. You are so foolish to think having a child out of wedlock would make things better," Mildred said sarcastically. "You are welcome to stay as long as you want, but dear God, what are you going to do with a baby now?" she continued.

Emily wiped her face. She thought to herself, "What am I going to do?"

It was about two days after the news of a baby that Casmir called Mildred's house and asked for Emily. He told Mildred, "I love Emily and want her to come home", he said with a sincere tone. Emily couldn't resist his beckoning call as she listened on the extension line. She returned home with the insistence of Mildred to get married so as not to embarrass her any further.

"What will people think?" she said repeatedly to Emily. "I don't want the embarrassment of your pregnancy with no husband, she said angrily." Emily didn't respond to her mother as she packed her suitcase once again to go back to Casmir.

As Emily entered their apartment, she saw the room filled with balloons and roses. A card written in broken English said, "Dis baby, I will always be there. Wit Love Cas." Emily began to swoon, forgetting the disturbing things he said. She dared not ask Casmir what triggered him to act the way he did when he heard that they were expecting their first child. Deep down Emily knew it all had something to do with Marlonnia. She never spoke a word about it again to him, but hoped that it would be the last time something like this would happen.

(Note: Today psychologists would say that Emily was suffering from a classic case emotional abuse or as battered wives syndrome. Many times, I have wondered if this is something that is hereditary or programmed into us, or just taught. Do the things that we see and react to as children carry over to adulthood? Cas was going through some long-term abuse trauma himself.)

Every day Mildred called Emily to see how she was feeling and if things were all right between her and Casmir. As a daily ritual, she would impress upon Emily that she should marry Casmir. It would be shameful for her to give her a bastard grandchild.

Mildred didn't waste any time confronting Casmir about doing the right thing. He told her that he loved Emily but was not sure about becoming a father. Mildred was a very shrewd woman when it came to getting what she wanted. She reminded him that no matter what he decided to do, he was still going to become a father. Casmir gave into Mildred's harsh reasoning and decided that he should be a man about the situation and marry Emily and give their unborn child his name.

In October 1956, Emily and Casmir had a small ceremony at the Cook County Court House in Chicago. Emily looked stunning in her pale blue two-piece suit and matching pillbox hat with a tiny veil. She carried a small bouquet of yellow roses and baby's breath. Casmir was just as handsome as Emily was beautiful. He wore a dark navy blue suit with a light blue shirt and yellow tie and yellow rose bud boutonnière.

With some relief that her daughter had tied the knot, Mildred made sure that no one would conclude that Emily was two months pregnant when she married. Therefore, she ordered two copies of their marriage certificate. She kept one copy and altered the year to show that they married in 1955.

Even though Mildred had pressured Cas into marrying her daughter, she noticed the marriage was not as harmonious as Emily had hoped it would be when Casmir started coming home late each night just as Dane had in the past.

(*How is it when a someone gets out of a bad relationship, they find that they attract the same type of person and not notice it until it is too late?*

Many times, he stopped off at the bar and had a few drinks before coming home to his, by then, very pregnant wife. Disgusted by her size and the thought that he was going to be a father, an enormous rage built up within him once again. He was having one of his spells. This time his eyes looked almost black. Just as in the past, he would start yelling at Emily and call her "Mother, Mother, Mother!" Then he would smack her with an open hand as he yelled out "Mother!" Emily kept quiet with each slap. She was good wife waited at home, as he stayed out late at night.

She knew this wasn't the time to confront him about his cheating. She knew by the strong reek of stale perfume on his clothes. It was almost as if the woman was blatant in wanting to make sure Emily

Wake Up and Die Right

knew she was there by the makeup on Casmir's collar. The week prior, while doing his laundry she found lipstick markings in his clothing. This woman was going out of her way to mark her territory. However, Emily would humbly continue to do her laundry and not say a word. Lucia wasn't one to keep a secret. She confirmed Emily's suspicions there was another woman. What Emily didn't know and Lucia was eager to share, it was Cas' sister-in-law Tiffany! She was married to Algirus and Casmir's brother Prancus. Lucia said Casmir was so used to keeping it in the family that she thought for sure Emily would have figured it out by herself.

Cas' eyes would tell her when she had some smooth sailing or rough times ahead. Then she would have her chance to confront him about his improprieties. Of course, he denied everything, but Emily knew better since she had the information from a reliable source, Lucia.

(*Emily said Lucia was better than a fortune-teller was and a private detective rolled up in one. She saw all and knew it all*!)

As for Lucia, she was livid that Emily wasn't handling the situation the way she would have. Her idea of revenge was to castrate Cas and rip every hair out of the head of their sister-in-law. The one thing they both agreed was not to tell Prancus of the affair. He was in bad health. He was only thirty-five years old, but he'd had two heart attacks within the past year.

"This would kill him if he knew the little tramp

was whoring around, let alone with his little brother," said Lucia.

So, Lucia felt it was up to her to have a little tête-à-tête with Tiffany. When Lucia finished cussing out Tiffany, she bluffed by saying she was going to tell Prancus, who would cut her out of his vast fortune of a life insurance policy. Being a gold digger as Lucia suspected, Tiffany called off the affair with Cas. He never knew Lucia was behind it all. It didn't seem to bother him; Tiffany didn't want to see him anymore. Cas just went home to Emily and acted as if nothing had happened. As for Lucia, she felt proud of herself for saving two marriages.

It was her ninth month of pregnancy; Emily was going through the burst of energy that most women feel when their due date is near. She cleaned the house, packed her bags for the big day and finished the laundry. While hanging up the laundry on a beautiful spring day, she watched kids chasing stray cats and throwing rocks at them. The neighborhood was swarming with cats. Emily had walked to the pharmacy earlier that day to pick up her prenatal vitamins, she complained to the about the neighboring cats multiplying. One of the local pharmacists recommended that Emily get saltpeter to put in food and set it out for the strays. He said it would not hurt the cats, just discourage them from doing what cats do best—multiply. Emily tried the remedy and saw how well it worked. It gave her an idea.

"This might just work, putting saltpeter in the

saltshaker in their apartment, she said to herself. Perhaps this will keep Cas close to home." She giggled as Emily found that saltpeter not only worked on stray cats, it worked on husbands that go astray too!

As Emily talked to one of the neighbors, gossiping about the remedies for straying husbands, she continued to hang clothes on the line, when one of the boys threw a rock at a cat and missed, hitting Emily in the stomach. Emily doubled over fearing the worse, the neighbor screamed for Cas to come quickly. Casmir was in the cellar of the apartment complex doing a little maintenance work for the property owner when he heard the neighbor yelling for him. He jumped over ten steps in one leaping bound. In a matter of seconds, he was at Emily's side. When he learned what happened he took off running after the sixteen-year-old assailant who threw the rock. The boy had a one-block head start; but Cas caught the teen by the back of the collar and turned him over to the boy's father.

This was the first time that Casmir took any interest in their child. Concerned that the baby may have been hurt, he picked up Emily in his arms and carried her to the car. He took her to the hospital where her doctor was on call.

An exam revealed that the unborn child was going to be all right. According to the doctor, the baby had already positioned itself to be born. Emily felt confident with her baby in the care of Dr. Orchid. His voice was soothing to the distraught mother-to-be. She smiled at the thin, short, middle-aged doctor with a hollow face and a Hitler-style mustache. He had a little laugh when he told her that the rock only grazed the infant's buttocks.

"Go home and just wait for the arrival of your child," he said in a reassuring voice.

At that moment, Casmir cried with relief that the baby was not hurt. Emily was touched by his tenderness. She hoped that this was an indication he would be a good father. The next morning Emily got up as usual to make Casmir's lunch for work and drank coffee with him as she traditionally did every morning. As she saw him off to work, the contractions began. By that afternoon, she was having strong labor. She rolled herself off the bed and slowly stood up. With a loud "whoosh", her water broke with such a force that the tops of her feet blistered. Emily called to her spunky sister-in-law down the hall to take her to the hospital. Lucia was so excited that she ran around like a chicken with its head cut off. She managed to call Dr. Orchid to tell him that they were on their way to the hospital. She called Algirus at work and told him that the baby was on the way and he should go to Emily's house and wait for Casmir to get off work since there was no way of getting a hold of him on the construction site.

Lucia was at Emily's side in a matter of minutes. Her loud, boisterous Sicilian voice yelled down the hall of their small apartment complex.

"Move outta you way, dumb sons of bitches,

Wake Up and Die Right

pregnant woman, baby on da-way!" She drove Emily to the hospital and got her checked into her room. Lucia didn't have much in the way of people skills. She had little patience when the hospital staff was asking questions about Emily's insurance. She told them where to go!

"What'za matta wit you guys? The frigging baby is coming and you are giving me a song and dance. I'm notta the fa-tha."

After twenty-eight hours of hard labor, Emily introduced to her daughter, Svetlana "Loni" Chekov into the world.

(*This is where I enter the picture.*)

Still groggy from the gas mask used to relax my mother, she still smiled even though exhausted. Surprisingly dad entered the room with a big smile. However, his smile didn't last when he took his first look at me. I had many of my mother's features but was dark, almost black. In mom's twilight haze from the gas, she kept saying, "I'm white, Cas is white". Then as she was looking over at her new bundle of joy, she said, "How come she is black?" Of course, my dad was concerned about the fact that he didn't have a pink faced baby girl. While he wondered if mom had been cheating on him, she began going down his family tree.

She said, "Everyone is white on my side of the family. I don't know anything about your side!"

Dr. Orchid started laughing and said, "Okay, you two, this is not an issue of race. It's Loni's heart valve causing her to turn dark blue. There is nothing to worry about."

The nurses could hear a big sigh of relief from both my parents. Within a few hours, the nurse handed my mother a now pink, rosy-cheeked daughter. Mom said that my dad whispered, "I love you, my little baby" in Russian. After a week in the hospital, they brought me home.

For a new mother, it is stressful enough to have a new baby, but when the baby is allergic to both bottle and breast milk then becomes colic, it can be unnerving. I cried day in and day out. Dad just couldn't take it any longer and began coming home late and drinking again. The more he drank the more he seemed to loathe me. I guess I took up all of my mother's time and he felt left out. My screaming almost brought him to the brink of wanting to smash my head up against the door. Mom's love and patience was what was keeping her strong.

(My mother's soothing voice would calm me down when she would sing and rock me to sleep.)

One night my dad didn't show up for dinner when he got off work. My mother cleared the dishes and put the food away. She tried to keep herself busy so as not to worry about where he was and who he was with that night.

On a good night when I wasn't colicky, mom would proudly display me in the oversized baby buggy that seemed to swallow me up in size comparison. So, we went for a stroll around the block a couple of times. Going for a ride in the cool evenings seemed to be as comforting as my mother's voice.

She carefully placed a mesh screen blanket over the canopy of the buggy. She walked along the sidewalk, waving to neighbors as she passed by their homes. The full moon lit up the neighborhood, as it got dark. There was suddenly a screeching sound of tires from behind when mom saw my father's old decrepit station wagon coming straight for her. She began to walk faster as he got closer. Mom broke out into a panic sweat and started running, pushing the buggy as fast as she could. She knew the buggy was slowing her down, so she stopped running long enough to reach into the buggy and grab me in her arms with one quick, steady motion. Just as she turned away, her next move was to jump over a four-foot fence that was between her and the oncoming car. As my dad got closer, he drove up onto the sidewalk and rammed his car into the baby buggy! Neighbors who saw us pass by their house as she was waving to them just moments earlier, screamed in horror, not knowing that I was no longer in the buggy. They saw it crumpled underneath the weight of the rusted car.

I could feel my mother's heart was still racing as she looked at the furrowed buggy. She watched as dad stumbled out of the station wagon and fell as he tried to look under the car at the mangled metal. He never said a word.

(*Mind you, this was a time and era when most people didn't get involved in other people's domestic problems.*)

No one bothered to call the police. The look on my mother's face was dismay and disgust. Her sweat rolled down her face as it fell onto my cheek. She held onto me tightly, almost suffocating.

(*Not making a sound, somehow I knew it was going to be all right and this was something that imprinted on me at my young age.*)

The days and years came and went. Things never really changed between my parents. Dad would go in and out of his spells weekly. He never held or played with me. It was obvious that his affection toward me never changed, either.

My father pretty much stayed away from my mother as long as she kept saltpeter in stock. Apparently, she didn't use it enough because seven months after I was born, mom got pregnant again. Once again, dad was not happy with another mouth to feed, but he seemed to accept the idea better than he did with me.

My sister Deidra was born on a cold, snowy winter morning. She looked more like my father than I ever did. She weighed less than six pounds. At almost one and a half years old, I loved my baby sister and kissed her, as any child would do to a baby doll. I could feel the negative feelings my father had toward me in comparison to how he fussed over Deidra. I don't think I was missing much. His affections for her were not your typical father-daughter bonding either. He just seemed to accept that she was there. Mom glowed with Deidra, just as she did with me. My mother always made sure she had plenty of love and kisses to go around for both of us.

The fall of 1961, the Chekov family moved to a small town about a hundred miles away from Chicago. A small suburb of Loves Park would be a great place to raise a family. I know that it was mom's idea to move. Dad just thought about work and that it was more plentiful in the outskirts of a big city.

In the summer of 1962, my mother gave birth to her third and last child. It was my brother, Nikhail. He was an ugly cuss. Wrinkled face and huge! There was no mistaking him for a girl. He had large hands and feet and almost looked like a six-month-old baby at birth. Now, he was someone my dad was proud to call his child. A son, he would pass the name along to his heirs.

(*Probably the same disoriented genes, too!*) Nikhail was a strong-willed child and had so many characteristics of dad. It was scary for my mother to have almost a clone of my father. Nevertheless, he was just as much her pride and joy as her two daughters were. He was just one more child to love as far as she was concerned. He was a real pain in the butt for his sisters. No matter how much Deidra and I told our mother to take him back to the hospital, she would not do it.

The birth of a son didn't change anything with dad. He still had his usual spells, alcohol and a love for the women. My mother would just try to wrap herself into being a good mother and wife.

(This was an era where the women stayed home and took care of the kids and the men brought home the paycheck.)

As we grew, Deidra and I began to see more of the torture that mom endured by staying with our father. She had no trade and never graduated from school. She would just have to accept the decisions that she made and protect her children the best she could. Even that would be hard for her to do.

Many times dad would get drunk and start beating on my mother. Through the years, she had her hands broken or her teeth knocked out because dinner was cold when he came home late from the bars. (*It was déjà vu with Dane all over again.*) Long before microwaves and after caring for three young children all day, plus cooking and cleaning, it was hard to stay up until your drunken husband came home from the bar at two in the morning and have a hot meal waiting for him. That is just what he expected. When it was not there, she would have to pay the price.

Around the time my brother turned a year old, my father started to stay home at night but would drink until midnight. He made a little sanctuary for himself in the basement. My father was good with his hands and built a bar downstairs. He was talented and the type of person who could put anything together and make it work. Every six months when people would clean house and throw out large household items, dad would go around the neighborhood and pick up televisions that were thrown out on the curb. He would repair and sell them.

As he built his little television repair shop in the basement, he began to spend most of his time down there. Eventually he started sleeping down there after putting a queen-sized bed in the corner area of the basement and then closed it off as a bedroom. He spent many hours working on the televisions when he was not working or sleeping. Often, he would yell for me to bring him a beer from the old refrigerator in the garage where he kept cases of beer and pop. Mind you, he never called me by my name. I was not sure if he even knew what my name was. He just referred to me as "Hey you, the oldest one." After he had a few drinks in him, he would become more talkative. I felt comfortable and thought he was taking some type of interest in me or even acknowledging my existence.

I remember him asking about kindergarten. I was thrilled that he inquired about me. I still remember when I brought home some kindergarten creation with a half peach for a body, apricot head and raisin eyes and toothpick limbs. Oh, I wanted him to love me, but I would settle for him just to like me. I know that it was too much to ask that he act like a father to me. It would be nice if he gave me a hug or said he was proud of my drawings.

It felt unsettling one day, the way he looked at me. The way he would talk ask me about how was my day at school, scared me. I felt like I was trying to sweet talk a grizzly bear. Then he leaned over and gave me a kiss. He praised me for being his good little girl. It was a strange type of kiss. I started to feel sick when he put his tongue in my mouth. The smell and taste of the beer made me vomit all over him.

This set him off in a rage. He grabbed me by the hair, yanking me to the ground, telling me to clean it up. I tried calling out to my mother in a five-year-olds' squeaky, quivery voice. When she came downstairs, she saw me trying to clean up the puke, only to heave again. She told me to go upstairs to bed and that she would clean it up. My dad was cussing under his breath and calling me a dumb kid. He was loud enough that I could hear. Loud enough for me to remember how his words cut into my heart.

"That damn kid can't do a simple thing like bring me a beer without making a mess. Little bitch!" as he spit with every cruel word when he spoke.

I went up to my room, only to run in the bathroom to throw up for a third time. Deidra walked into the bathroom when she heard me heaving. She started vomiting too. Poor mom, she had her hands full cleaning up the mess upstairs as well.

I never said anything about what happened with dad other than I didn't like to kiss him. No one questioned why, so nothing else said.

The following week my dad's sister, Aunt Noelle, called. She said that she and her husband, Antonio, were celebrating their anniversary and wanted our family to join them for the weekend at their home in Chicago.

The bags were packed and loaded onto the rack of the old station wagon. We left for Chicago on Friday night after dad came home from work. I watched as my mother carefully put blankets and pillows in the back of the wood-paneled station wagon so we could lie down and take a nap during the trip. It was exciting for Deidra and me to take a trip and visit relatives. Nikhail was too young to care what was going on around him. As long as that pacifier didn't fall out of his mouth, it would be a quiet trip. He had been cutting teeth all week, running a fever and had a mild cold.

We arrived at Aunt Noelle and Uncle Antonio's house late that night. It was not a big house but big enough for them and their four kids. Everyone shared a bed together so that five more people could fit comfortably for sleeping arrangements. My mother decided to sleep in one room with Deidra and Nikhail since they were too small to be left alone. Aunt Noelle said that the bed in the other room was big enough for dad and me. So, that was the sleeping arrangement.

Mom tucked all of us kids in bed, gave each a kiss on the forehead and sang a lullaby. Once we were all asleep, the adults had Aunt Lucia and Uncle Algirus come over to join an adult gathering by playing cards and having a few beers. As the card game went on into the wee hours of the morning, the empty beer bottles filled the cases. Mom and

Aunt Noelle nursed only one beer because they knew they would have to get up with the kids. They called it a night around two-thirty in the morning. Dad and uncles Algirus and Antonio drank for about another hour before going to bed.

Dad stumbled around, in the barely lit room where I slept. He took his clothes off, leaving his underwear on. It took only a few minutes before he started snoring. He twitched and flailed in the bed. The snoring didn't fully annoy me until I was awakened by my father's big, calloused hand easing onto my panties. I cried in silence in fear that I would wake him. I wanted to yell out for my mother but knew that she probably would not hear me at the other end of the house. The more I tried to pull away the more he would draw me closer to him. My mind was busy trying to think of anything else or be anywhere else than in Chicago.

I studied the pattern of the wallpaper on the wall by the faint night-light. Every minute that went by, I hated him more than a small child could ever imagine! The night seemed to go on forever as I lay waiting for the room to light up from the morning sun. As he rolled over, it was a chance to get away. I had peed on myself from fear. I knew somehow that something was wrong. How does a five-and-a-half-year-old tell her mother what daddy did to her when she did not know what happened?

What was I going to say to my mother? I could hear her in the kitchen with Aunt Noelle and Aunt Lucia making breakfast and drinking coffee. I

Wake Up and Die Right

peeked around the corner of the doorway and saw her taking a bottle of milk out of a pan of water. Watching her carry Nikhail into the kitchen and feed him, I waited for her to set him down in the playpen before coming out into the kitchen. As I crept down the short hallway from the bedroom to where my mother and aunts were, I waddled as I walked.

"Good morning, Loni", she said. "What is wrong? Why are you walking so funny? Did you wet yourself last night?" I couldn't speak. I looked at the floor and shrugged my shoulders. "Svetlana, what is wrong?" she called out to me. Mom noticed my face was wet. I could taste the salty tears as they ran down my chin and neck. The collar of my nightgown was soaking wet from my silent cry throughout the night. She put her arms out to embrace me as she always did and I ran to her, holding onto her as if I had seen a ghost. "Baby, talk to me", she said to me in a calming voice.

She took me into the bathroom and washed my face with cool water. Again asked me, what is the matter? I didn't know how to explain what happen other than "Daddy hurt me. I hurt, daddy hurt me", pointing downward to my urine soaked panties. My mother grabbed and held me to her bosom and kissed me. She said that everything would be okay and tried to comfort me with cool compresses on my neck after she cleaned me up, she then put me in the bed with Deidra, who was still sleeping.

She briskly walked into the kitchen and sat

down; trying to think what she was going to do about the situation. Aunt Noelle and Lucia could tell that something was very upsetting and tried to console her.

She told them what I had said. Aunt Noelle looked at mom and said, "Emily, Cas used to do that to me when we were young. I wondered if he would ever do that to any of the kids."

Before my mother could respond, dad got up and came into the kitchen for a cup of coffee. He didn't show any emotions one way or the other. Just as he poured a cup of coffee, my mother grabbed the frying pan sitting on the stove that she had used to fix eggs and bacon that morning. She gripped it in both hands, BAM! She walloped him upside of the head. I never heard my mom cuss like a sailor before. She didn't give dad much of a chance to defend himself. She rattled off with each strike of the frying pan, "This is for what you did to my little girl!" BAM! "That is for any future plans you might have with my little girl!" BAM! BAM! "Hell, this is for the hell of it." BAM! Dad was dazed, his eyes crossing and blood running down his face. Uncles Antonio and Algirus stepped in and grabbed the frying pan from mom before she killed him.

Dad swore that he didn't know what she was talking about, as she screamed at him. "Where did you get a crazy idea like that?" he said as he dodged mom's fists. She told him what I had said to her, with my aunts and uncles present.

(I really think he was more embarrassed about

Wake Up and Die Right

the family knowing what happened than concerned that this was something that could be detrimental in my life.)

"I had to be dreaming, thinking I was in bed with you," he replied with a bewildered look on his face. It took both my uncles to keep my mother away from my father. She showed such strength and anger that it scared my dad. She was out for blood! His blood!

I don't remember much after that. I seem to have a memory lapse when it comes down to when and where and how we got home. I spent a lot of time at my grandmother Mildred's house. I suppose it was my safe haven. Sometimes it seemed like I lived there. Deidra thought my grandparents played favorites when it came to me; perhaps I thought the same thing too.

I know there were many times I wanted to go home to my mother, but she would tell me I couldn't because my dad was either drinking or having one of his spells.

Dad seemed to have this thing about me. He hated me but wanted to love me, then would do mean little things and go out of his way to hurt my feelings. I remember that I had a beautiful collection of dolls my grandfather brought from England. Several of them wore beautiful satin gowns and bridal dresses; there were porcelain Asian and angel dolls that had hair that looked like strands of fine spider web. I watched as my father packed all of the dolls into the dilapidated suitcase my mother used when she left Dane Phillips. He stored them in the false ceiling in the basement. I used to beg for my beautiful dolls, but my father said they just disappeared. No matter how much I asked him for them, he gave me a smirk and said he didn't know what I was talking about, which frustrated me. After a while, I gave up and decided never to mention them to him again. I didn't want him to see the hurt in my eyes. Somehow, I felt this was his way of holding my dolls prisoner for my silence for the things he had done to me. Even at my age, I knew something was wrong with our relationship. So many times, I wondered if he had the same hate for my sister as he did me. Did he ever abuse her, or did he like to torment her as he did me?

As far as we all know, he never bothered Deidra. Well, at least she does not remember anything. She is blessed not to remember some things if it ever happened to her.

As for me, I never forgot. Even now, I can envision the ugly feather design on the wallpaper at my Aunt Noelle's house. There was the smell of sweat and sour after-shave on my father's clothes and his callous hands touching me are memories that stayed with me.

By the time I was twelve years old, I stood six feet tall and weighed one hundred thirty-five pounds. I was physically mature for my age and proud that my first bra was a 36B. I totally bypassed the training bra phase, unlike Deidra. I was shy and didn't communicate well with others. Most of the

Wake Up and Die Right

---

time I would stay in my room, drawing or listen to the radio.

Deidra, on the other hand, was just the opposite. She was always smiling and was a real people person as she is today. Her laugh was contagious.

She was a lot shorter than I was, no one could ever imagine we were sisters. Besides, there is the fact that we never looked or acted anything alike. We fought like most siblings; jealousy was a routine part of our squabbles. Now that we are adults, we had a chance to talk over our differences and I found that she was just as jealous of me as I was of her. Of course, growing up we never would have admitted that to anyone, let alone to each other.

While Deirdre was a social butterfly, she was also very attractive with her long, naturally curly brown waist-length hair swaying as she walked. She was popular with the boys and had just many girlfriends. She was good in all school subjects, while I, on the other hand, seemed to have trouble with everything I tried with the exception of art. Boys were not anything I was good with, either. I didn't think I would ever get my first kiss, let alone get a boy to notice me. My imagination led me to be fearful I would die a spinster if a boy didn't kiss me before I got out of high school. So when I was around twelve-years-old, I found a unique source of talent to get attention—it sure was not my witty personality, but barking like a dog. Not just a dog, but I could imitate various breeds of dogs. Bulldogs, hound dog, big dogs and little dogs.

(*Hey, at that point in my life, that seemed to be my only talent.*)

However, instead of getting positive recognition it became a major factor for cruel jokes. I couldn't compete with Marcia, a Honduran girl who could imitate a monkey. She was good. She was taller than I was and weighed about the same. Her short jet-black hair and dark skin accented her huge white teeth. That resembled much like a horse's mouth. I am not sure how she did it, but she won people over with her talent. Well, that was middle school. Surely, things would start out fresh when we prepared for high school.

Because I looked older for my age, it was even harder to fit into any form of middle school, let alone when we got to high school. On the other hand, my sister was always up to date with fashion. She wore the latest style in matching hot pants and go-go boots. She and her friend LuAnn wore florescent pink bikinis with navy blue polka dots almost every weekend when going to the public pool down the street from our house.

I was not allowed to wear a two-piece swimsuit to the public pool. My mother and grandmother said I had to wear an oversize shirt or sweater to cover me up when coming or going in public. Heaven forbid I'd wear shorts or teen apparel because they thought I might entice my father. I was very self-conscious about my body. I started to slouch to hide my height, then I dressed very off the wall.

Whenever my father came home from work, for

Wake Up and Die Right

some reason I still felt the need to try to win him over. I would greet him when he pulled up in the driveway and carry his still leaking thermos into the house. My mother and grandma were careful not to allow me to dress seductively.

(*Like a twelve-year-old could become seductive. I didn't even know what the word meant.*)

I do not know why mom put up with the things she did. When dinnertime came around, mom would have to make two different meals. Dad wanted to eat hamburgers with mayonnaise. Occasionally, he would indulge in hot dogs and mayonnaise. She'd make a well-balanced meal for us kids. There was this one particular time mom asked me to take dad's dinner to him while she was trying to feed Niki.

I crept down the creaking stairs, almost tiptoed to where my father was attentively working on his television sets. Dad actually started to talk to me, asking about school and my hobbies. That was the most he had talked to me in a while and I did have a little anticipation that he was trying to bond with me. Then I glanced over the bar and noticed he had several empty beers cans lined up and he had started making a pyramid with the cans. That was when I decided it was not worth the effort to have a conversation with him. As I turned away to leave, he grabbed my arm and began rubbing it.

Before I could pull away, he French-kissed me again and then said, "Don't tell your mother!" I told him that I would not and ran up the stairs having dry heaves. Mom was the first place I ran to, but I just couldn't say anything to her about it. I didn't know if I was afraid of my dad because I knew that mom would confront him. I saw what he had done to her in the past—breaking her hand, throwing her wedding rings in the field out behind our house.

Sure, there were times that mom called the police when he was beating her, smashing the televisions and knocking her teeth out. The police would come to the house and arrest dad. As a child, I had a strong feeling of pity for him. I would cling onto his leg and beg the police not to take my daddy to jail. Mom and I never told the police what he had done to me; it was our secret.

When dad would go to jail, it was usually for domestic disputes and his drinking. Mom would press charges and the next day she would scrounge up cash to bail him out. Even as a child, I didn't think this was the smartest thing to do. After all, he was our only source of income. I can see now why my mother put up with the physical abuse. She was not being dumb about it; she was making sure the state would take all of us away if we had no income. So, jail was just a time for him to cool off after one of his drunken sprees.

Most of the time dad knew it was for his own good and never took it out on mom when he came home. Well, as long as he didn't miss any work over the incident. Luckily, for him, most of his violent spells were on weekends. He never saw himself as the problem. Mom was his problem, for calling

Wake Up and Die Right

the police and he reminded her of this every day.

It was scary going to the jailhouse. It was an old, mildewed smelling redbrick building, six stories high. The only parking was several blocks away. It was usually around the holidays when dad was at his worst. Mom would bundle us up in our tiny snowsuits, carrying Niki in one arm and Deidra in the other. I would hang on to my mother's coattail as we walked in the winter cold to bail out my father.

Christmases were not my fondest memories as a child when dad went to jail. Virginia got a letter from an editor that said, "Yes, Virginia, there is a Santa." I learned that an early age there was no such thing as Santa, at least in our household. My father told me, Santa put me on his naughty list. I believed it. That had to be why my father hated me and my mother was subjected to so much turmoil because I unwittingly made my father do things.

Dad was typically humble after mom bailed him out of jail. He didn't say much to us. I could see that he was inept or too proud to say he was sorry. Mom forgave him as usual, at least until the next time.

(At first, I thought my mother fell for it. However, as I look back, I know that it was just something she had to do for us.)

My mother allowed my father to beat her if it kept us kids safe from his wrath. I felt that I was in my own little world, angry and hated everyone because I couldn't talk to anyone. Dealing with the fear of my mother finding out my father and my little secret, worrying that she would kill dad or worse, her being killed by dad. Then it would be entirely my fault if it happened. That was a lot of responsibility to deal with for a child.

My grandparents were very loving toward me. Grandma was not someone I could tell my deepest, darkest secrets. Any time I tried to talk to her, she would sternly say, "Hush!" In addition, she would remind me not to talk about family things to outsiders. *(Outsiders? I thought I was trying to talk to family.)* I can hear her now: "What would people think?"

My grandmother couldn't handle a crisis within the family that may be any part of a sexual nature. I was an adult before she and I could even discuss what had happened to me as a child. I learned she knew about it, but kept it as a family secret and never mentioned it. Her motto was, "If you don't talk about it, it will go away."

Grandma lived by that motto long before I was born. She told me about a young girl who confided in her. The girl was about fourteen and Mildred was in her late twenties. The girl told her that she was being sexually and physically abused and needed help. Mildred said seventy years later, she pondered over her decision not to say anything to anyone because it was an inconvenience since she had a bus ticket to leave the state and did not want to tie up her time with police and court procedures.

The fear she would discard me in the same way as she did that young girl from her past. It weighed heavy on me. I hungered for her love; but even though my grandparents loved me., I was not going to do anything to lose or disrespect it. I kept it to myself.

Like most kids in my situation, I was depressed and wished I were dead. Well, I thought of death, but I knew that I really didn't want to die. I just imagined what turmoil those around me would feel if I did kill myself. Secretly, I wanted to fake my death and sit back to watch everyone around me.

(*I do not think there is a kid that has not thought about death in that way.*)

I did go as far as tying a belt around my neck, then to the doorknob. I would slam the door and try to fall forward. When it didn't work the first two times, I would continue to slam the door until I could get it right. This only brought my mother into the room yelling for me to stop slamming the door.

When my mother asked me about the belt around my neck, I came up with some lame excuse and she seemed to accept it.

Actually, my mother handled the situation pretty well. She didn't act as though it upset her, but she didn't act as though she didn't care. She said something to the effect of, "Honey, if there is something that you are trying to tell me, then tell me. Otherwise, stop slamming the door and giving me a headache." Yep, she knew what was going through my mind. She went through it herself as a child.

I was as depressed as a child could be at that age. When my grades dropped and my attention span became about as long as a short rope, the school decided it would be in my best interest to talk to a professional.

My mother agreed with the school since she had concerns about my depression and the strange thing I was doing with the belt. My father would never pay for any counseling, so my grandparents would have to pay for it in order to keep the peace in the house as my mother did.

My counselor was Marcello Hitchcock. I saw her twice a week for three and a half years. She was a well-dressed, heavyset, unyielding-looking black woman; one of her front teeth was considerably longer. She had an overbite and that one tooth would protrude below her top lip. She scared me at first; perhaps it was because she was my first encounter talking to a black person.

Mrs. Hitchcock and I talked about me and I learned things I really didn't want to know about myself. She called me a "manipulator". She didn't mean it in a negative sense, but as one who could manipulate bad things to my way of tolerating them. She also knew that there were things that I held back and suspected it was my father since he was not my best topic of conversation. Even talking to her, I knew that she might tell the authorities something I might say, so I was very hesitant to discuss my family life.

All of this was going on about the same time my mother was diagnosed with diabetes, high blood pressure and several other medical problems, including her heart. I knew she couldn't go to work. No one could take care of her if I said anything about home.

Once a week we had group sessions. I hated those sessions. I was not the center of attention as I was with one on one. Some of those people really did have some head problems. Nevertheless, they did give me ideas as to how I was going to leave home. I couldn't run away, as I had nowhere to go. I had no money, food, no place to sleep. Especially after hearing the tales of the stuff, they went through. My mother was not going to allow me to live with my grandparents. I am not sure they really wanted to have a teenager living with them. Either way, my grandparents never asked me to stay with them.

I overheard my grandmother talking about my mother living in an orphanage. Surely, kids in school would feel sorry for me and treat me better than they did now. It would be a vacation away from worrying what my father was going to do next.

I discussed the matter with Mrs. Hitchcock. Not knowing the real reasons I felt I had to get away, she frowned and was against the idea. I set out to appear to be an incorrigible child, where they had to get rid of me. Then mom might not have to get the beatings because of me or have to leave dad. When you eliminate the problem, there is your solution. So I thought.

I was good at mimicking others. I watched those popping drugs at school and looked at the color of the pills and size. I had no plans to take drugs.

(Not to mention I had now idea where to go to get any.)

I would go through our medicine cabinet and kitchen cupboards looking for capsules. I would take the medicine out of them and fill them with flour. The only time I took the pills was when other kids were around to see me take them. Then I would go into my act.

(I was good if I do say so myself. I would have made a great actress.)

This normally shy kid acted different because I felt as though I were a different person. I felt like I had a mask on and no one knew me and could act any way I wanted. I was not too extroverted when it came to performing in class, but enough for kids to talk and spread the word. They did just that.

The school counselor called my mother and told her what was going on at school. My mother was worried, so she set up an appointment for me to see Mrs. Hitchcock. Before we would go to the clinic, she and my grandmother would have these long talks about me. They asked me how they could help. That is when I told them that I wanted to leave the house. I didn't want to live there and they knew why. Mom talked to Mrs. Hitchcock several times. I am still not sure if she ever told her what was really happening at home. As far as I knew everything was still taboo.

A couple of weeks later we had to go to court. At age fifteen and a half, my parents gave up custody of me and I was now the ward of the state of Illinois. I was placed in a children's home, then in a sister group home called Mulligan's Group Home in Rock Island, Illinois. Not only was this a new home to live in, I would have to go to a new school. I was starting all over.

My father never said anything to me. He looked away and mom whimpered during the proceedings. I remember turning around to look at my parents as I was being pushed out the courtroom door by one of the bailiffs. It was strange that I would have such a feeling of guilt, sadness, yet relief.

Chapter 3

The Children's Home

I was sitting in a county car when a caseworker met me at the courthouse. She was young looking, yet dressed like an old-fashioned school matron. She wore a black jacket and matching skirt that came to the center of her shins. She had a crisp white blouse and a pendant on the collar. Her hair was up in a bun, somewhat unkempt from the wind blowing. Her shoes were not stylish, but more like sensible shoes, I think best described as orthopedic granny shoes. She didn't say much but had a sweet smile and a fresh, soft smell of Ivory soap. I looked downward as I mimicked being shy. I tried think of anything but being in the car with this stranger.

As I looked down at her sensible shoes, I glanced at the long hairs in her stockings as some curled from the impression of the support hose and others stuck straight out. She wore old-fashion nylons and I could see the impressions of the large

Wake Up and Die Right

---

garter clips through her skirt.

My first day at the main children's home I met the headmistress. I started to feel the fear of God deep inside me. What had I done? Where in Hell did she come from? There is no other way than to describe her as one of Satan's minions.

She was barely five feet tall with high heels, the blue-tinted hair piled on top of her head looked like spun cotton candy. Her office was covered with ashes from her cigarettes that dangled from parched, cracked lips smudged with remnants of her faded lipstick. Her gnarly, arthritic fingers were stained yellow as she held a cigarette tightly in her brightly painted red nails. Her voice was gravelly. She slurred somewhat as her dentures clattered. Her words were as sharp as her name—Cutting, Mrs. Elverna Cutting.

Even though I towered over this imp-like woman, I was too scared to run, let alone speak. She told me to go out into the waiting room while she made arrangements for me. She then told one of the other girls to show me around the home before I transferred to the Mulligan Home.

I met Cami. She was short, very shapely, wearing unseasonably flimsy clothing and a waist-length white rabbit fur coat. Her hair was bleached shoulder length and frizzy. She said that she was almost eighteen, but looked worn and aged for someone who was a teenager. She said she had lived in the Mulligan Home and it was better than being here. While we waited for Mrs. Cutting, she showed me the compound.

There were about six three-story buildings. Inside each building was something like a mass bedroom holding about thirty kids. It looked like military barracks from movies I had seen. Cami said she used to live there but said she was one of the lucky ones to get away.

She said, "My grandmother and mother were drug addict, prostitutes. They gradually had me trained for the family business when I was about ten years old. That was before the state took me away and put me here before going to the Mulligan Home."

Cami said, "The hardest part about living in the Mulligan Home is every two weeks we have to check in with Mrs. Cutting. It is a hard and long walk from the bus stop. It is almost two to three miles in the snow or heat. We usually don't stay very long, but then just as I warm up in the winter or cool off during the summer, I had to turn around to go back to the bus stop."

(Some how, this sounds familiar a generation ago.)

I could hear a loudspeaker with that familiar gravelly voice announce, "Svetlana Chekov, return to the Main Home receptionist desk, ASAP." Cami escorted me back to the front lobby and Mrs. Cutting was standing there tapping her tiny shoe on the worn linoleum floor as the long ash fell from her cigarette.

"Come on, you two. I am taking you back to

Wake Up and Die Right

your houseparent. Get in my car," she snarled. Her car was not much bigger than she was. I got in the backseat in hopes of having a little more legroom while Cami sat in the front. There were ashes throughout the car and it was hard to breathe as Mrs. Cutting puffed on her favorite brand of cigarette, Camels.

The ride to my new home was peaceful, so I let my imagination run wild thinking about Mrs. Cutting. My eyes seemed to burn a hole in the back of her head. I just couldn't fathom this sawed-off version of humanity actually married to a human man.

Her first name had to be Mrs., thus her last name being Cutting. Since she never spoke of having her own kids, I wondered if the homeless rejects were the only way she could have children. On the other hand, maybe she hated her kids as much as she did those in the Children Home.

Before any more thoughts of Mrs. Cutting could amble through my head, we reached the Mulligan Home. We drove up a winding road as we approached a nice-looking green split-level house on a knoll. The snow at that time of year prevented us from parking on the steep driveway. We got out of the car and clambered up the snowdrifts, stepping in the small pathway of stone steps in the snow. When we got to the door, the housemother was standing in the doorway. At first glance, she looked like Morticia Addams or even Lilly Munster.

The living room had a large picture window that looked out toward a nearby wooded park. I could see the top of the trees sway in the cold breeze, ice and snow were on their branches. As I turned around, I saw an eating area with a big oval table that sat eight people. There was a small kitchen just off the dining room. As I looked down the hallway, I saw three bedrooms, one bathroom. In each bedroom, there was a bunk bed. Two girls would share that space. Cami showed me her room and the area that I am temporarily assign. She said that Della sometimes rotated the girls around so we could get to know one another. Other times she just put us together based on our ages. It depended on her mood.

I was going to be sharing a room with Sheri. According to Cami, she was a little younger than I was and not too clean. Besides that, she was okay to bunk with. I put what little belongings I had in the dressers assigned to me. Cami then showed me the rest of the house. We went back down to the bottom landing and then went down about six more steps to the basement. To my right was a door. Cami said that was Della's apartment and we were not allowed inside. I looked around the basement and it was more like a family room with a television, a couch and a sewing area. I thought to myself, "So far it is not bad."

The door slammed closed upstairs. It was Sheri and the other girls, Sally, Barbie and Gina, who also lived at the Mulligan Home. Cami said, "Come on, I will introduce you to the girls." We climbed upstairs and went down the hallway to the first room. Cami introduced me to Sheri. "This is going to be

Wake Up and Die Right

your roommate for a while," Cami said to Sheri. Sheri had a cherub baby face and crooked teeth. Her nose was long and slender; it looked like she had pinched it with a clothespin.

Sheri said, "Hello, So why are you here?" I told her there were problems at home and this was probably better for me. Sheri looked at me and said, "Yeah, right...that is what they all say." Then she went on to say, "Well, my family just didn't want me or my brothers. I don't really care. This place beats sleeping in a broken-down car with no food or bathroom."

Sally came into the room where we were talking. She was tall, not quite as tall as I was. She had big green eyes and the thickest eyebrows I have ever seen. They looked like just one solid eyebrow. Her nose looked like it had been broken once or twice. Even though she was thin, she had a potbelly. She said, "Hi, I'm Sally. I am here because I had a baby and my family didn't want me when I told them who the father was." Then she walked away. Cami whispered into my ear, "What she didn't tell you was her baby was by her grandfather!" She snickered.

Barbie came into the room next. She had fair skin with a mass of freckles and a dark pageboy hairstyle. She looked very intellectual. Barbie and Cami were pretty close in age and shared their room together. Barbie greeted me with a nod of the head and said, "Hi Svetlana. Before you ask, I am here because my mother is dying of cancer and my father left us several years ago. There are seven kids in my family and my mother just couldn't take care of all of us and fight cancer."

I was stunned and just said, "Call me Loni; it is nice to meet you". As we were all talking, Gina came into the room. "What the fuck, we got another one," she said in a half kidding tone.

"My name is Gina and I am a bitch. Don't borrow my shit and I will leave your shit alone. Don't mess with my man and I might let you keep yours. Got it?"

I just answered, "Got it!"

She looked me up and down and said, "So, do you have a name?"

Barbie chimed in and said, "This is Svetlana."

"What in the hell kind of name is that?" she said, curling her lip and crinkling her nose. "It's Russian; she likes to be called Loni", Sheri said in a perky voice. Gina rolled her eyes and said, "Whatever", then walked away. Sheri leaned next to me and whispered in my ear, "Gina is a bit sensitive and has a bad attitude. She's an Injun—Apache."

Gina had a round face and intense black eyes accented by her makeup. She had some type of genetic disorder that made her long raven-colored hair paper-thin. At sixteen years old, Gina was balding. She spent most of her time sitting in the rocking chair, just rocking back and forth, as the wisps of her fine hair stroked her face every time she rocked forward. When something bothered her the faster, she would rock.

Della came upstairs and joined our conversation

by reminding us that the chore list was on the refrigerator and she adds my name. I was nervous when the list showed that it was my turn to make dinner. Della wrote out what I was going to be making that evening. She made out the menu a week in advance. I had never cooked before and there were so many people to feed in the house. Once I got the knack of it, I did pretty well.

(To this day, I still cook enough for nine to ten people when there are only two of us.)

It took me awhile to get used to sleeping in a strange bed and having strange roommates. Even though Sheri was younger than I was, she knew more about sex than I did. In fact, all the girls knew more about it than I ever imagined.

Gina was usually the one who got up, long before the rest of us. She would take her daily shower and douche every week leaving the disposable bottles in the bathroom trash can. One morning I awoke to the bunk bed rocking. I hung my head over the top bunk bed and saw that Sheri was masturbating with the used Massengill douche bottle. Then I noticed that she had a turkey baster in the bed with her.

"What the hell are you doing?" I said in a grossed out way. I jumped out of the bed and ran to the hallway cringing. I envisioned her using the turkey baster and wondered how many times she played with it before it one of us used it for cooking.

Cami and Gina heard the commotion in our room and saw Sheri in all her glory, then ran downstairs to tell Della. Of course, Della was having the same thoughts going through her head as the rest of us about the baster. She told Cami to throw out anything in the utensil drawer that could be used for sexual pleasure by a preteen.

Della set up a doctor's appointment for Sheri. No telling how long she had been using household utensils to masturbate. For that day, Sheri was the talk of the house, especially, when she came home from being treated by the doctor. She had a sexually transmitted disease. Well, of course, it came back to the person laughing the loudest about Sheri's impulsiveness. After all, Sheri was using Gina's douche bottle. Della took Gina to the doctor as well. She coincidently tested positive for the same sexually transmitted disease. Now this came down to the fact that Gina had been having sex with some guy and Della was determined to find out who it was that was spreading a dangerous disease to one of her "underage" girls.

It was not until later in the week, Della learned that when she retired for the evening, Gina changed the front porch lights with red bulbs. This could only mean one thing to me, a house of ill repute, or commonly known as a cathouse.

Gina would turn the lights on and look out the picture window, waiting for someone to approach the house. She turned the lights off before sneaking out and making a few dollars.

Della turn a blind eye to the red light that Gina put outside the Mulligan Home door. While men started coming to the house with lots of cash, Della pocketed it.

I was feeling like I was in the Twilight Zone or some soap opera. The plot started to thicken with one story line ended and another begins. What was next?

Sally started going to church on a regular basis and began preaching to everyone in the house about our sinful ways. She could make us feel guilty even when we didn't do anything wrong. Sally's angelic manner turned to "The devil made me do it", as she would later say. It seems she met a young man at her church and to make a long story short, she got pregnant. Being a ward of the state and having another child at sixteen and a half, it was certain the child would be a ward of the state too!

The father of the baby was eighteen years old, had a job and wanted to do the right thing by Sally. I think he really loved her. She wanted desperately to be needed. Their pastor and his wife talked to Della and asked the courts to allow Sally and her beau to live with them so they could marry and raise their child. It was only five more months before she would become of age and the courts allowed them to marry.

Cami said, "One down, five to go for a happy ending". Sally finally was free. Cami said she never saw Sally so happy in all the time they lived in the Children's Home. The only thing keeping Cami there was that she had a few more classes to get her GED as the court ordered before she could leave the Mulligan Home. She was charge with petty theft as a juvenile and part of a probation agreement was to get a high school diploma. Home would allow Cami to live there for one month after her eighteenth birthday. By that time, she must have completed her GED or she wouldn't be in violation of her probation.

Barbie's goal was to graduate and get a job so she could have her family all together again. She appeared to be the most promising of all of us to succeed with their goal.

As for me, I just didn't see much in store for me in the future. I started a new school and met new friends, one of whom had a bodacious body, fair-haired, blue eyes and perfect teeth and chiseled nose. He was in Army ROTC. My heart would skip a beat every time I saw him. His name was Mason and his sister's name was Angela; she was my first friend in my new school.

Angela and I were good friends and she really understood what I was going through. It seems that she had her own turmoil going on at her home. She had two younger sisters and I later found out my heartthrob Mason was her brother and the oldest of the four children in the Templeton family. Angela told me about her father, who sounded very similar to my father with the exception that he didn't have to drink to be abuse anyone. He was just plain ole mean! She said that he was very hard on Mason and would physically abuse him, at least until Mason started to fight back. They all walked on eggshells when it came to their father.

Wake Up and Die Right

Mason was a year ahead of me and was so handsome that the school photographers used his senior year photo to advertise their photography. On the way to school, I could see a 24x24 photograph of him in the window of Milner Photography.

I met Angela and her brother at the city bus stop where we would catch the bus to go to school. He didn't say much to me but I would catch him looking at me out of the corner of my eye. When I found out he was in ROTC, I had to join up. I was a sergeant and he was a lieutenant. I spent every minute I could to just have him in my sight. I had butterflies and hot flashes at the same time. I knew that there was no way he would be interested in a court-ordered orphan, but he was interested. A simple smile gave me such hope for our relationship to blossom.

Angela and I became so close that she invited me to her house on many occasions.

(Our friendship started because we realized we both had a dysfunctional family life.)

It felt good to have somewhat a family type of surrounding, even if it was temporary. Her mother, Bonnie, was one of the top nurses in the in the hospital where she worked. She was also very much a "Suzy Homemaker" at home. Bonnie wasn't a beautiful woman, but her personality gave her an inner beauty that anyone would envy. She was rather stocky with a worn-out look, probably from the stress of her husband's cruel behavior and having to keep the family together as did my mother. I could tell she was a very loving mother by the way she tried to teach her children to be self-sufficient. Frequently she would take us out to pick berries at various orchids and she taught us how to can fruit and make jellies. Her family asked me come over during the holidays and really made me feel special. That was until they learned that Mason and I had feelings for one another.

Mr. Templeton was a strange little man. His ideas and thoughts about others were very much like Archie Bunker. Chas Templeton was a spindly man. When he would look at me, I felt intimidated, as his lazy eye would involuntarily jerk up, then down and slowly go back into a center position. His lips were clenched tightly together, as though he were wearing a muzzle. I didn't know exactly what it was at the time, but I felt there was more to Mr. Templeton. Angela and Mason never came right out and told me, but it was obvious that their father without a doubt intimidated them.

For example, Angela and Mason found a ring while walking through the park on their way home from school. It was a simple little ring. It didn't look like much but could have been a band from an old wedding ring set. The ring looked like it had been buried in the dirt over time. It didn't seem like a big deal at first, but both Mason and Angela came to me the next week and asked that I tell their father that it was mine. Their father saw the ring on Angela's dresser and became very angry. It was later that I learned how angry he became. Mr. Templeton was aggressive with Mason and they got into fisticuffs.

Mr. Templeton apparently made it a habit of taking it out on Bonnie when he was mad at their kids. When Mason stepped into the physical encounter to defend his mother, his father closed his fist and struck Mason for interfering with what Bonnie had coming to her. He hit Mason in the jaw, knocking him to the ground. Mason quietly got up on his feet and with one punch, KO'd his dad.

This altercation was just because of that damn ring. So, Angela and Mason told their parents the ring was mine. The following week I came over to do some homework with Angela. The elder Templeton confronted me about the ring. I responded in an excitable manner, "I am so glad you found my ring. It belonged to my grandmother. I didn't have a chance to get it sized before it fell off my finger!" Mr. Templeton looked at me with a questionable look. I was not sure which eye to look into for the moment. The air was so thick with tension; I started hyperventilating as I tried to leave. Angela and Mason said they would walk me to the door.

"Oh my God, you were good! I started to believe that it really was your grandmother's ring. You will have to wear it a few times if you come back over to our house. Just so he won't get suspicious!" said Angela.

I asked, "What is the big deal about the ring? You really did find it in Twisted Sister Park, didn't you?"

"That is about the only thing that is the truth about this stupid ring," said Mason. "I just don't want to talk about it anymore. Besides, it won't be long before I graduate and I am out of here!" he said with determination.

Our high school ROTC was having their military ball and senior prom on the same night and he asked me to be his date. I was breathless that he wanted to take me, but I had to get approval from Della to be able to attend. After a week of sniveling, I got permission, but the problem was the gown.

Each of the girls in the Mulligan Home was entitled to twenty-five dollars a month for a clothing allowance. I knew that I would not be able to get a formal dress with the meager allowance. I felt the only way that I could have a beautiful gown to go to this soiree, was to make it.

For years, I watched my grandmother sew. She had a way of making it look so easy. I went to the fabric store and bought a pattern and some beautiful teal satin. The pattern was a two-piece outfit with a six-panel long skirt and high waist.

I carefully cut out the material. I didn't have a sewing machine to make the gown so I had to make it by hand. I had no idea where to begin. I think I had a few parts left over. I feared that it would fall apart while I was wearing it, so I would hand stitch in one direction and then the other. Cami and I would talk as I sewed my lovely gown with its high collar and full sleeves and French cuffs. Not know-

Wake Up and Die Right

ing how to make buttonholes, I used snaps and then sewed on buttons to give it an elegant look.

The day came and I was ready for my Prince Charming. I waited for him to pick me up as I strutted in front of the full-length mirror in the hallway, in my first sewing project.

Eight o'clock came and went. There was no handsome prince to pick me up for the ball. Soon it became nine o'clock and then ten o'clock. My stomach dropped. No phone calls, no note, nothing.

A couple of days after the ball and prom, I saw Angela. She sheepishly walked over to me and apologized for her brother standing me up for the military ball and senior prom. She told me her father wouldn't let him take me. He told Mason to take Gabby, the head of the school newspaper, not to mention his boss's daughter.

I asked Angela why her father would do something like that to me. What did I do so wrong? She mentioned that her dad said I had to have done something bad for my parents to give me up and put me in an orphanage. He didn't want his son to be seen with me. Mr. Templeton never asked me why my parents gave me up to the state. I knew that it wouldn't make a difference if he knew why I was in the Mulligan Home.

It is amazing what a fifteen-year-old thinks is important in life. There is the fear of acne, one's first kiss, being too tall, too short, or fat. I was no different from any other fifteen-year-old. The fact that my parents gave up custody of me was weighing heavily on my mind. The things that happened while I still lived at home were always my beginning and ending thought for the day. Nevertheless, Della had a way to make me feel even more insignificant. She and Mrs. Cutting told me how my parents hated me and didn't want me because I was worthless. Many times, I wondered if she was prepping me for my life or plans of her own. I wanted to get out of that home. I had to find a way out and to be on my own!

(That sounds familiar. It was just a generation ago; my mother was saying the exact same thing.)

I ransacked the cupboards under the sink for a quick way out. There wasn't a secret passageway, but there was a way out of living my life. The first bottle pulled out of the cupboard was Drano. The label said that it contained lye, also known as caustic soda and some other names I can't pronounce. Its chemical action eats away materials (*including skin tissue*). The warning label said that any contact with skin or mucous membranes causes burns and frequently deep ulcerations with scarring.

I envisioned myself lying in a coffin with my face eaten away from the chemical in the drain cleaner. Frothing at the mouth was not a pretty picture. I went to the laundry room and grabbed the bleach. With one hurried motion, I grabbed the quarter-full gallon jug. I placed it to my lips...and began to swallow one swallow right after another! I have no idea how many swallows I had before I started to feel sick and nausea. Somehow, I managed not to hurl. I felt dizzy but didn't pass out. Cami was walking down the hallway and saw me in the laundry room with the bleach jug in my hands. She said she could smell the bleach on my breath and noticed that I had dribbled the bleach down my face and it left fade spots on my clothes.

"What have you done, Loni?" she yelled. Grabbing the almost emptied bleach bottle, she ran downstairs to Della's apartment. When she returned, I was in the fetal position on the floor. Della looked at me with disgust. She kicked me in the rib with her pointed boots. She said, "I am finishing my dinner; you can just wait until I am done, before I take you to the hospital".

Cami called the poison control center and they told her to give me milk and try to keep me from getting sick. Della came back upstairs and just glared at me as she flicked her long locks over her shoulder. Almost thirty minutes passed when we went for medical treatment.

My stomach was pump and I had to drink several things that tasted nastier than the bleach itself. I wasn't able to talk for a while because I burnt my vocal cords. It was just as well, because I didn't have anything to say. With my eyes fixed on a fly walking on the wall, I wondered if this call for help would get me out of the Children's Home and back to my family.

Unfortunately, I learned this was the wrong avenue to take, as I shortly thereafter found out. Since I was a ward of the State of Illinois, I had a legal guardian.

(Fancy that, I had a guardian and didn't even know it. I never met or knew his name. He never came to the hospital to talk to me to see what the problem was.)

Bob Crookshank was his name. He signed papers to have me placed in the Sanford Center. This was a mental institution, not a placement for emotionally upset children, but for full-blown raving maniacs.

The next day I sat in the atrium and watched the daily activities. Out of the corner of my eye, I noticed a frail girl weighing about eighty pounds with long dark hair in the middle of the room. Her hair was covering her face as she steadily looked at the chipped tiles on the floor. She sat in the chair with her knees bent up to her chin and her arms wrapped around her legs. As one of the staff called out her name, Lauren, she looked up and I could see that the left side of her face looked like pulverized.

The white of her eye were a bloody red. It was impossible to see where her dark brown irises were; in the pulp-like mess on her face. Her cheekbone were only fragments of chipped bones the size of chopped nuts.

Lauren and I were assigned to share a room. As my throat and vocal cords started to heal, we had enjoyable conversation. She said that she was in the institution because she had an eating disorder. Since she has been locked up, a deranged patient broke loose from the medical staff and went after her.

Wake Up and Die Right

Lauren said it was only a matter of minutes; where the two-hundred-pound portly patient grabbed her by her long tresses and beat her head on the cracked tiles. She said that she didn't remember much when it happened, but when she woke up two weeks later, she had a hellacious headache.

She took me around to meet some of the other tenants. The first room we went into was Zelda's room. Zelda was about my age. She was tall and had short curly hair. . She wore thick glasses and had huge pustule sores going down her neck to her chest and back. I noticed there were several chunks of her hair missing.

Lauren whispered", Zelda twists her hair around her fingers and pull it out at the roots. She also tried to commit suicide by drowning herself in the toilet. Not very creative but she came close the last time she tried."

A couple of doors down, I met Randy. He was a scrawny guy with a big, uneasy smile. He wore his strawberry blond hair in a Mohawk. He was in Sanford Center because he was painfully shy. Many times the other patients would tease him. Lately, Zelda was teasing him. She cornered him in the break room and threatened to beat him silly because he kept smiling at her. Randy couldn't help but smile when he was nervous. Zelda didn't care to hear why he kept smiling or even why he would giggle at times. I don't know why I did it, but I jumped in and yelled at her to quit giving Randy a hard time. However, my voice sounded so deep because the bleach had burned my vocal cords it scared me! I towered over her and put on my most fierce face. It was then Zelda backed away from Randy and went into her room.

Randy was so relieved and thanked me for helping him. He stuck to me as if I were his bodyguard after that incident with Zelda. The last person I met was a juvenile delinquent named Baumgartner. "The Baum", as he liked to be called, was very short and corpulent. Most of his teeth were rotten or missing. His breath was unexplainable.

During the month and a half that I was in Sanford Center, no staff member ever talked to me. I didn't saw a shrink. I watched as each of the other patients received medication and had both group and private meetings with the doctors. I started to feel a lot better but I didn't have my appetite because everything I ate or drank tasted like soap.

The first week at Sanford Center, my father came to see me. He had just gotten off work and drove straight over to the institution. He looked tired and had dried mortar on his shoes, clothes and hands. I could see that his eyes were red. Dad, cry? I couldn't imagine him doing that, yet even though he had dried mortar dust all over his face, there were wet streaks. Of course, he would not admit to any emotions for anyone, but I sensed that he was very upset with me being in the Sanford Center.

I remembered mom telling me about his mother being in a mental institution several times and I wondered if it brought back memories to him.

That was the first time he said, "I'm sorry, Svetlana." His words stunned me—he knew my name!

"Why are you sorry?" I asked.

He had his head lowered, fumbling with his keys, he said, "I know that it is all because of me and my drinking that you are in this place."

I naively told him, "You didn't make me drink the bleach!"

As he slowly looked up at me, I could see the hurt in his eyes and almost feel the pain he was feeling at that moment.

"I promise not to drink ever again," he said in a very determined and believable voice. "My drinking was my way of escaping my past, just as you drank bleach to attempt to escape your present situation."

Somehow, after meeting with my father that day, I had a feeling that everything was going to be all right between him and me.

(He kept his promise and didn't drink again. A few years later, my father had a heart attack and was revived twice. He said that he saw the light and was not afraid to die. Dad told me he had been given a second chance to make things right. Just before he had a massive second heart attack, my father asked me to forgive him for the things that he had done. I forgave him but deep down I knew I couldn't forget. These things were embossed in my mind's memoirs. They would be a challenge for the rest of my life.)

As the weeks passed, I saw my first psychiatrist who evaluated me. He was a balding man who smelled of pipe tobacco. Lounging in his high-back leather chair, tapping his pencil to his lips, he just looked at me over his thick spectacles for the first five minutes that I was in his office.

"I don't know what to think of you, Svetlana. You, unlike the other patients, you are not mentally disturbed. Nevertheless, you do know how to manipulate the system. This time you just went backward instead of forward to reach your goal. So what is your goal?" he said.

I flinched back in my chair. I felt uneasy as I squirmed in my seat. "My goal is to get out of here and then get out on my own." He smiled and said that nothing wrong with me except that I was too smart for my own good. He was recommending that I return to the Mulligan Home with no further counseling required.

He said, "If you want to be out on your own, you know what you have to do." I watched him as he filled out my discharge paperwork and told me to go and pack. I had twenty minutes to pack up my stuff and say good-bye to my new friends before Della came to picked me up. She seemed to be annoyed with me and that they didn't keep me longer. I often thought she might need a vacation in the Sanford Center herself. Perhaps they could help her with her disassociated behavior with others.

There was not much of a homecoming. Cami welcomed me back and told me that she had completed her GED and was moving out over the weekend. She was excited and said she is going to share an apartment with her cousin. Cami gave me a hug and wished me all the luck. I hated to see her go.

I knew I had to get a job to be out on my own. I only had one year of school left and I didn't want to spend it in an orphanage. So I decided to quit school and get a full time job as soon as I was able to leave the home. If Cami could get a GED, I was sure I could do the same after I found employment.

Angela and Mason both worked part-time after school at a nearby hospital. I asked Angela if she could put in a good word for me with her boss.

I turned seventeen in four months and legal age as an adult in the state of Illinois. I was able to leave the Children's Home. A few weeks later, I got a call from Mrs. Baker in the personnel office of the Jewish–American Hospital on a Friday afternoon. She asked me if I could start Monday. I replied that I could. She told me to report to the third floor, Geriatrics Unit. I said, "Ye-s-s-s, I will be there early Monday morning!"

Chapter 4

The Day I Misplaced The Corpse

The first few days I was in orientation, I didn't get a chance to see much of Angela or Mason, except in passing. When I started my new duties, I would often visit Angela at lunchtime on the seventh-floor cardiac unit but tried to avoid Mason because I was still upset about him standing me up. I felt he could have at least called me so I wouldn't look and feel so foolish. I bit my lip every time I did see Mason in his hospital uniform He looked so handsome in his white pants and bright red shirt. I could see why Milner Photography used his senior picture to advertise their photos.

(The huge portrait of him was still in the downtown window long after his graduation.)

It had been over a year since the military ball and senior prom. One day, I didn't dodge Mason fast enough and he cornered me in the nurses' break room and said he needed to talk to me. He told me

Wake Up and Die Right

he didn't have any choice when it came to his father interfering with his love life. He sounded so heartfelt when he said he was so sorry about standing me up on our date. Everything he said was exactly what Angela said about the matter. He tried arguing with his father but it was a losing battle and he only hoped that I could understand.

After meeting with Mr. Templeton as I had, I couldn't hold it against Mason, not really. Mr. Templeton told Mason he had other plans for him and told him that he would take Gabriela "Gabby" Conley, the school newspaper editor, instead of some rag-tailed Russian orphan. I felt like I took a big dip on a roller coaster. I knew his father wouldn't have approved if he knew my feelings for Mason. I wondered if Angela had any idea how I felt about him. In fact, I don't think Mason really knew how I couldn't stop thinking about him until just before he left for the Army.

Mason signed up for the delayed entry program for the Army after graduation. He was only working at the hospital until he was to leave for boot camp.

Mason said, "I am leaving in two days. Will you wait for me?"

I was surprised but managed to mutter, "You're leaving in two days? Yes, I will wait for you.

Just as I whispered those words, he said, "But it has to be our secret. I don't want my parents to interfere."

(Another secret in my life, but this one I was willing to keep, for now.)

It was hard not to tell his mother, who was now the head nurse on the surgical ward. I wanted to burst when I saw her and tell her that her son asked me to wait for him. I was afraid that if she had an inkling of our arrangement she would not have helped get me hired on at the hospital as a unit aide.

I kept my promise and waited for Mason to complete boot camp and his Military Police training. We wrote to each other almost daily; somehow, we always had something to write. I saved every letter he wrote me and read them repeatedly. I thought I was going to pop a cork keeping it a secret from Angela. I knew that I had to keep myself busy so I would not dwell on missing Mason.

It was the fall of 1974, my first job and my first day after a month long training at the Jewish-American hospital. I still remember making the whopping sum of one dollar and twenty-five cents an hour. It sure did seem like a lot of money back then. I rented a room at a rooming house two blocks from the hospital for eighty dollars a month. It was within walking distance to work, so I frequented the hospital cafeteria and I started to be acclimated to hospital food.

The cook was a pudgy, frumpy old woman with white roots and wore a black hair net with metallic specks of silver weaved through the netting. She had an infectious smile. It was not so much her smile that caused everyone to react but the bright red lipstick she painted on her lips that made everyone smile. I really enjoyed the smell of the spices in

Wake Up and Die Right

her chili. I ate it almost every day. The food was good, but nothing like mom used to make.

I started missing my mother. I didn't go home much when I was out on my own. I tried to visit once a month on a day off. Mom and I talked on the phone during the week. There were many times that all I could talk about was Mason. I would tell her about the latest letter he wrote and I asked her the proper way to respond to him without sounding too anxious. We would laugh and cry together. It was as if we were best friends. Then mom talked about dad. She told me how he had mellowed out over the years. Occasionally I would talk to him when he answered the phone.

I wrote to Mason that my father and I were on better terms. One day Mason surprised me when I was visiting my parents. He called just prior to my getting there and talked to my mother. He told her that he wanted to ask me to marry him and wanted to know if she thought I would accept. Mom was acting like a giddy schoolgirl when I arrived at her house.

She said, "You just missed Mason's call. He said that he would call back in about ten minutes and had to discuss something very important." When he called back, we talked about the usual things, and then he asked that my father pick up the other line. He courageously asked my father for my hand in marriage. My father starting laughing and said ever so wittingly, "Why not, she's not a tax deduction for me anymore, so she might as well be yours!"

My heart seemed to pound so loudly that I couldn't hear what Mason was saying to me. At that instant, I imagined myself in a beautiful white wedding gown and him in his dress uniform walking down the aisle under an archway of gleaming sabers. My daydream was interrupted by the sound of Mason's voice calling my name.

"Loni? Loni? Svetlana, are you still there?" he said in a panicked tone.

"Yes, Mason, I am here", I said in a sighing breath.

"Does that mean you will marry me?" he asked.

"Oh my gosh, yes, yes, yes, yes, I will marry you!" I stuttered.

We talked for about a half an hour longer, then made plans for me to fly to his next duty station in California, when he finished his military police training in Kansas. We will make it official by getting my engagement ring. Within a week, I was on a plane going to California. The butterflies were nothing compared to the goose bumps on my arms when I first laid eyes on him in the airport.

He looked awesome. Mason was buffed out from boot camp and all the military training and exercises. His jeans were tight in the thighs and his shirtsleeves barely went around his biceps. His skin was tan and his hair was bleached from the sun.

We had a fabulous week together and I met his friends. The second day after arriving, we went to the PX to pick up my engagement ring. It had alternating white and yellow gold-brushed bands to form

Wake Up and Die Right

one wide band with a diamond mounted in the center. He couldn't wait to leave the PX to place the ring on my finger. As we walked outside, the sun blinded me as it hit the gold and diamond. The diamond was not a large stone, but it was as big as the state of Texas as far as I was concerned.

Three times Mason asked me to elope while I was there. As tempted, as I was to become Mrs. Mason Templeton, I told him I wanted what every girl dreams of—to have a beautiful wedding and wear a white gown. All of our friends and family were back in Illinois and I had just been hired at the hospital. I needed the job to pay for things we needed for the wedding. We agreed to wait until he came home on leave. So I returned to Illinois and kept our secret a little longer.

(My job at the hospital was not hard, but the first few months were unforgettable. My duties were simple and consisted of running to various floors for supplies, picking up medication from the pharmacy, filling patient water pitchers and taking dead bodies to the morgue.)

The day began by collecting the water pitchers from the rooms on the third floor geriatrics unit, placing them on a wobbly silver cart. It was in room 334 I noticed a peculiar water pitcher bent at a forty-five-degree angle. I placed it on the cart with the other containers. Then I went to the utility room and filled the pitchers with ice water from the ice machine. There was a feeling of awkwardness as I diligently tried to cram ice in the small opening of

Kerrigan Rhea

the bent water pitcher. The head nurse, Ms. Ardouser, could hear the student nurses giggling in the break room as they watched me performing my duties. She had a stern look about her when she pulled me aside. There was a faint smile behind her wrinkled, bulldog face as she told me that the strange water pitcher was actually a patient's urinal bottle.

My tall frame felt as though it had shriveled to the height of a three-year-old child. My shirt collar seemed to tighten with every embarrassing moment. I couldn't speak. It was as if peanut butter was stuck in the back of my throat. I spotted the head nurse out of the corner of my eye. She had a sneer behind her grin, and then winked at me. I took a deep breath and sighed with relief. I was sure the student nurses in the break room could hear it.

Over the loudspeaker came, "Code blue, code blue, room 334". The medical staff scurried through the halls like busy ants. I tried to stay out of everyone's way, filling the remaining water pitchers and returning them to the patients.

When I got to room 334, the doctors pulled the sheet over an elderly man's face. All the life support systems were disconnected. The staff seemed saddened that someone's grandfather had passed away. Chills went up my spine, yet I was relieved to know that the patient in room 334 would not need the iced down urinal bottle that I had almost served him.

My next thought was to get out of there in a hurry. While attempting to leave the room, I was detain, when the shift supervisor brought it to my attention that part of my duties were to strip the deceased and take him down to the morgue. It sounded simple enough, but somehow I knew it would not be so easy. Not only was this my first encounter with the male anatomy, but I was scared stiff. Here I was in a hospital room with a burly, bearded, longhaired male orderly named Brewster, stripping the faded hospital gown with tattered tie strings from the body of a small, frail, elderly man. I held my breath as I neared the body.

(*Recalling as a child when my sister and I were in the backseat of our parents' car, we would hold our breath when passing a cemetery, believing that it would protect us from catching the dead man's germs.*)

I squeezed my eyes tightly together, not closed, but a squint, so as to sneak a peek through the small openings. For some reason, I felt inconspicuous having my vision obscured by the thick mascara on my lashes. I tried not to see anything that was not familiar to me, but I was somewhat curious.

Since we were being so personal with the patient in room 334, I asked the pony-tailed orderly, "What was the patient's name?"

"Jeremy Preston," he replied.

"How did he die?" I asked.

"Brain cancer," he grunted as he pulled the morgue cart up against the hospital bed. I felt depressed as I looked at Jeremy's sunken face. I overheard the nurses talking outside his room. He had no family. There wasn't anyone to grieve over his passing. I felt my eyes well. Just before I could say anything to Brewster...I saw IT! The one thing that I was trying not to look at wasn't dormant.

Just as my eyes were upon IT, Brewster asked me which end did I want, heads or tails. I gasped. "What are you talking about?"

He said, "Do you want to grab Jeremy's head or his feet so we can put him on the morgue cart?" It was not an easy decision for me because IT was in the middle. When I didn't answer right away, Brewster chuckled and asked if this was my first corpse. The only thing that came out of my mouth was "Huh, huh." Then he said, "Haven't you ever seen a naked man before?"

"Nope!" I squeaked back.

"You don't have to feel sorry for the old guy," he said. "He died happy."

"How can you tell?" I naively asked. He almost choked on his chewing gum, laughing as we flung Jeremy onto the morgue cart.

"You're looking at IT kid, that's how I know. Just before he died, a student nurse came in and gave him a bath."

(Back then, being young, I didn't know much about life. I didn't know what he meant. It was not until twenty years later when I started to think about writing a book that I understood the meaning behind what Brewster was hinting about sex.)

Jeremy had been strip and placed on the morgue cart. My journey to the hospital morgue began.

Lizzie, another unit aide in training, was going to accompany Jeremy and me. Brewster gave us general directions to the mortuary and said we were on our own. He had to get back to emptying bedpans before things piled up.

Lizzie was a quiet, middle-aged black woman from the bayou of Louisiana. She was tall, thin, gangly, but had beautiful big eyes. Lizzie had a little stutter when she talked; said a root doctor put a hex on her when she was a kid. He caught her stealing chicken eggs from his henhouse. Since he scared her so bad, she had been short of breath, wheezing and stuttering, ever since that night. Her family nicknamed her "Wheezer".

We took the body down the back elevators, through the long, dark, maze-like corridors. The hospital was doing remodeling in the basement of the hospital. The construction workers left various electrical cords lying on the floor of the passageway. The cart hit the cords. It jumped and so did I when the corpse let out a groan from the oxygen that was still in his lungs.

Not only did Jeremy let out an eerie moan, his arm swung out of the morgue cart and hit Lizzie in the leg. Lizzie and I just looked at each other. Her eyes were big as saucers. I felt my heart drop. My toes curled, my palms sweat and my butt puckered. Lizzie screamed, "Au-sh-h-h, sh-h-h!" I am not sure if Lizzie's butt puckered when mine did, but she was trying to tell me something. She looked pale and started walking with her knees close together, as if she had to go to the bathroom.

I pushed the cart at a fast and steady pace to the entrance of the mortuary double doors. As I pushed the doors, the hinges gave forth a squeak straight out of a Steven Spielberg creation. There were numerous empty morgue carts parked in the refrigerated room with the stench of death and formaldehyde. I looked over my shoulder for Lizzie, but she was nowhere to be found. The mortician attendant told me to push the cart inside the room and register the patient in the "Guest Book"

After I had Jeremy, all checked into his new accommodations, I swiftly traced my steps back to the third floor. There I found Lizzie mumbling something and shaking her head. About forty-five minutes later, the morgue called the nurses' station and said that Jeremy was missing. Everyone looked at Lizzie and me for some answers. I thought there was an elderly, naked man who died happy, wandering the hospital corridors. Lizzie kept saying, "He's a z-zombie, he ain't dead!" Luckily, for Jeremy and us, a resident physician found him about thirty minutes later.

It seems that shortly after I left the morgue someone else placed an empty morgue cart in the room. The occupied cart was set aside from the others. It had been mix in with the empty ones.

(*Morgue carts are specially made with a false top that makes the cart appear to be an empty gurney to a layman.*)

I never would have imagined my first job to be

so exasperating. It was an adventure and a learning experience. As a result, after doing this for a living, I decided not to pursue a career in the medical field.

I hadn't seen Lizzie since that first day at the hospital. Last, I heard, she was having nightmares and had checked herself into the hospital's fourth floor psychiatric unit. She was sure zombies where going to get her.

Mason's letters started to dwindle in the next few months. He was never available when I would call him at his barracks. Then one day I heard from him. He called me at the hospital and said he told his parents we were engaged to be married. His parents were angry and demanded that I give the engagement ring to his mother.

"Your mother?" I squealed. "If you want the ring then you have to come and get it," I said as I felt as though I was going to faint. "We can't break up just to pacify your parents! My grandmother has already made my wedding dress. I put a lot of time and money into making our wedding beautiful and memorable."

He told me he was only saying this to throw his parents off track about our relationship. "I know better than that!" I told him, "You are a momma's boy and can't make decisions on your own. I will give back the ring, but you have to get it personally and look me in the face and tell me why you are doing this." The phone went silent and I hung up.

Every day I would see either Mrs. Templeton or Angela. Neither would talk to me. I had to corner

Angela after months had gone by and ask her why she was so distant to me and why she didn't approve of Mason and my plans to be married.

"Loni, I don't object to you and my brother getting married. My father objects to it," she said in a solemn voice.

I asked, "Are you so afraid of your father that you would turn your back on a friend?" Angela started to turn away and said, "Yes, Svetlana, I am!"

It wasn't until Mason came home on leave two months later and visited all of his former hospital co-workers that it finally sunk in—it was truly over between us. He avoided me when people were around. However, he pulled me aside and said that he wanted to spend time with me. We made plans to be together at his friend Rusty's house. Once again, he stood me up and left me heartbroken with his best friend trying to pick up the pieces.

Rusty worked at the hospital as a pharmacist technician assistant. He was still going through pharmacy training. Mason and Rusty were friends all through high school. He said that he couldn't understand why Mason was not brave enough to confront me now that he was out of his father's home. When I asked him if he knew what kind of a hold Mason's father had on him and Angela, he said, "It is better left unsaid."

When Mason's leave was up, he went to his duty station. I knew that I couldn't stay working at the hospital, seeing his mother and sister every day, without thinking of him. I wanted to get away and leave town. I just didn't know how I was going to do that I was only making one dollar and twenty-five cents an hour.

I kept to myself most of the time. Then one day I decided that I would join the military. That would be a way to leave town and see the world. I didn't think the Army was big enough for Mason and me. Therefore, I chose the Navy; I always loved the crackerjack uniforms.

Chapter 5

To Serve My Country

It was nearing the end of the Vietnam War when I went downtown to the Naval Recruiting office. I was still seventeen at the time, but felt much older. As I cautiously went inside the office, I saw the American flag in the corner. A female second-class petty officer looked up and acknowledged seeing me. She was sitting at a small desk; there was a Naval Seal on the front of it. She welcomed me inside and said she would be right with me. I watched her escort a potential male recruit to the video room to watch a boot camp tape and job selections. While waiting for her to return, I saw two other rooms with larger desks with the same seal. I read the nameplates on the desks, one Senior Chief Robert Varney and the other Chief Keith Levinsky.

The petty officer returned to the front office and greeted me again. She said that she was Yeoman Second Class Landon, but I could call her Debbie. I

Wake Up and Die Right

was in awe when I looked at her in her navy blue wool suit and tie. Her bright red stripes showing her rank stood out on her uniform. I told her that I wanted to join the Navy and see the world. I knew that there would be no other way for me to leave the town where I grew up. I did confide in her that I had a broken heart. She nodded her head as if she understood and said that many people came there to do the same thing. As she explained the procedures to enter the Navy, she said that I needed to take a test to see where I might qualify for training.

When done taking the test, she told me that I could choose from a good selection of jobs openings. After viewing the videotape, I told her that I didn't want to be stuck in the job like a mess cook or scraping barnacles off the bottom of a ship.

I spent most of the day at the recruiting office. Around lunchtime, Senior Chief Varney and Chief Levinsky came into the office after taking some recruits to AFEES in Chicago for their physical. Senior Chief was balding, wore wire frame glasses and was a little plump for a ranking military man. He had red chevrons and five hash marks on his sleeve. Chief Levinsky was sharply dressed in his dress uniform. He wore so many gold hash marks on his sleeve that they appeared to run together as one. Both chiefs greeted me and invited me to join them and Debbie for lunch so they could get to know me better and see what it was that I wanted to do with my career.

Chief Levinsky was very charming, though

Senior Chief Varney was a bit brash. Debbie told them what my scores were from the ASVAB. Levinsky said that I would need to get a higher score to ensure that I was not locked into any one particular job code. He said that he was willing to help me study for the test and take it again in six months. This way I would be prepared for the testing and surely have a much higher score and pick any job I was interested in going to school. "You did pretty well for a dry run, Loni," he said encouragingly.

I went to the Recruiting Office about once a week and they gave me a test that they made up to help me prepare. I never wanted something so badly as this. The recruiters could see my determination. I wanted to join the Navy and get to travel away from Illinois. Many times, I talked to my parents about joining. They were supportive. They thought this would be a way to start things out fresh by getting away from my past, our past.

My father said there had never been a female on either side of the family ever enlisted in the military and he was very proud of me. My grandparents showed their enthusiasm and support.

In December 1975, I took the ASVAB test again. I scored considerably higher than I did the first time. Chief Levinsky told me that he knew I could do it! I felt so good about myself. I signed my enlistment papers. I was scheduled to leave in January. I had one more Christmas at home before embarking on something new.

Wake Up and Die Right

Boy, did we have a great Christmas. A month earlier, my very first car that I bought was demolished when someone hit it during a flash flood. I collected on the insurance, so I had some spending money after the car was paid off. The insurance company wrote out a check for eight hundred dollars to me. It was a Christmas I had only dreamt of having. My parents, grandparents, sister and brother were all there for me. Setting aside any animosities from the past, we ate all day, laughed and reminisced about what little but good memories they still held.

Dad and grandpa would tell me about their military stories and some of the things that I would probably have to do in boot camp. It was probably one of the best holidays that I could ever remember with all my family. There was no fighting, no drinking, just love and everyone happy.

January came around very quickly. That last night I spent at my parents' house I was waiting for Chief Levinsky to pick me up so I could take my physical and sworn into the Navy in Chicago. Later that month I got orders to ship out for boot camp in Orlando, Florida on January 29, 1976.

My mother crept into my room at five o'clock in the next morning. She gently kissed me on the head and brushed back my hair from my face. She told me it was time for me to get up and serve my country. I woke up to a smile radiating from my mother. She looked as though she had not been to bed yet. She said that my father and she talked all night long about me. It was probably the first time in my life they talked about me. My mother said the only tears they had were from being proud and they were going to miss me. She said my dad couldn't sleep either. I asked her where dad was, she said he was in the kitchen drinking a second pot of coffee. Mom told me to hurry up and get ready so they could take me out for breakfast and drive me to catch my bus leaving for the O'Hare airport.

I cleaned up and got dressed. Still wiping the sleep from my eyes, I saw dad in heavy thought looking out the kitchen window at the newly fallen snow. He looked up at me and beamed.

"A lot has happened to you in your young lifetime," he said, looking out the frosted windows. "You are stronger than I have ever been. You have a will that does not give up even when all around you feels defeated. Svetlana, I really do love you. I just have trouble showing it." I didn't know what to say other than I loved him too.

Just then, my mother walked into the kitchen and hugged me. She had just come from my sister and brother's room to wake them so they could say good-bye. My sister was stretching and yawning as I remember her in her little baby doll pajamas. Her hair was tangled in the small button in the back of her nightwear. She shuffled toward us, gave me a hug and said good-bye, that she loves me and will miss me. My brother, already towering over me even as he was five years younger, looked like he was walking in his sleep. He gave me a hug and told

Wake Up and Die Right

me that I was "nuts for going into the military", but it was "cool".

We said our good-byes. Mom and dad took me to the International House of Pancakes (IHOP) across the street from the bus station. My stomach was in knots with excitement and fear of the unknown. I watched dad play with his food on his plate, not eating a bite. Mom only took a couple of bites out of her buttered toast.

I said in a perky voice, "You would think someone died the way you guys are acting. It is a job. I will be back!" Dad smiled and mom let out a big sigh.

"If you are done eating, I will get the check and we can walk across the street and wait for the bus to come," Dad said in his broken English. Mom whispered in my ear and said, "Remember, when things get tough, wake up and die right. Things will work out for you." Her words stuck in my head.

Chief Levinsky was at the bus station waiting to greet my parents and me and give me my orders. Ten minutes later the bus pulled into the bus station. I sat in a window seat so I could take one last look at my parents before I left for a new chapter in my life. They waved to me as the bus pulled away. I waved back until I could no longer see their hands. As they slowly faded from my sight, my mother put her head on my father's shoulder and he put his arm around her walking to their car.

The bus ride was about an hour to the airport. The plane was due to arrive in Chicago in another hour and a half. I spent my time trying to find some reading material for the four-hour flight to Florida. I couldn't help but call home when I got to the airport and talk to my parents one last time. They both had been sitting at the kitchen table drinking coffee, hoping that I would call. I must have talked to my parents the whole time I was waiting for my plane. I heard the flight announcement that my plane was boarding in ten minutes. I hurried my last few words to my mother and told her I loved her but had to go. I could hear her crying as she said she loved me and would write.

When the plane landed in Orlando, a Petty Officer First Class met me. He was wearing a red braided aiguillette and bellowing out orders for recruits to get on the military bus as he called our names. We were on that bus for about twenty minutes before entering the Recruit Training Center (RTC) Orlando, Florida. The same petty officer shouted for us to line up on the yellow painted footprints on the pavement. Once again, our names were called out. We marched to the appropriate barracks.

My new company was 3040D, the third floor of building five. When we entered the barracks, it was cold and had an antiseptic smell. There were two rows of thirty bunks. The floors shined like polished glass. *(Very similar to the children's home.)*

My company commander was Petty Officer Second Class Murdock. Her assistant was a recently graduated recruit, Airman Benson. Benson assigned us our bunks and ordered all thirty of us to stand at attention in front of the assigned bed. We had instructions to take all of our personal belongings, with the exception of the clothes on our backs; we boxed them up to be shipped home.

Murdock was an air control man who spent eight years in the Navy and two of those years as a company commander. She appeared to be an intense career woman. She had salt-and-pepper-colored hair cropped extremely short. She had what appeared to be as a dark five o'clock shadow above her upper lip and long dark fuzz on her arms. She didn't look very feminine at first glance. She resembled the rumors my father told me about most military women when he was in the Army.

Benson, on the other hand, was the complete opposite. She was older than most of the women in my company but hung in there with us on the obstacle course. She wore her mousey brown hair in a bun, her voice was soft, but could yell cadence loud enough for the recruits in the back of the line to hear.

We marched to and from the chow hall, classes and the obstacle course. Petty Officer Murdock started our training for the marching drill team. After all, that is what the "D" stood for after our company number.

(I was very artistic while growing up. I would spend hours in my room drawing. Whenever we had a break for personal time in boot camp, I would doodle on scratch paper. My artwork didn't go unnoticed.)

Each company was expected to paint a company flag for each drill team. Petty Officer Murdock recruited me and one other recruit to paint the flag. We were given a piece of satin. My piece was pale blue and hers was black. She painted pictures of monsters and ghouls. She wanted to give the fierce competitive point of view to sister companies. She painted the name "Murdock's Monsters". My painting was more in tune with the spirit of the competition. I painted a unicorn with a flowing red, white and blue mane and tail. The unicorn had detailed shading and an anchor tattooed on its hindquarter. Across the front of the flag, it read *Esprit de Corps.* The two paintings were sewn together, trimmed with gold fringe and placed on a flagpole for the flag bearer to carry proudly.

Mail call was the most exciting part of the day we could look forward to the first few weeks. Mom and grandma wrote me about twice a week. Sometime Deirdre took the time to write, her letters usually started out about some cute guy she met. Niki wrote me once; he put it in with a letter mom sent. My father was not much for writing, but I got an eleven-page letter from him once. Some of it he rambled on about the dog or my brother and sister, but the biggest part of it was very touching and special to me.

(Twenty-seven years later, I still have the only letter my father ever wrote me.)

Our company was filling out paperwork for insurance and a strong feeling came over me. As I was checking over the paperwork to ensure everything was correct, I noticed my father's name was listed as the beneficiary on my life insurance. I distinctly remember putting my mother's name on the paper. Just as I saw his name on my paperwork, I seemed to feel my spirit pull away from my body as if I was back home hovering over my father for a few minutes then I returned to my body. It was hard to explain the feeling. As I corrected my paperwork and waited in line, I had the opportunity to call home.

I called my mother. She was happy to hear from me but sounded distressed. I asked to talk to my dad, but she said he was sleeping and she didn't want to wake him. I told her that I felt something was wrong. I left my body and could see my father lying across his bed face down and his left leg was slightly off the bed. He was wearing blue jeans and a red plaid flannel shirt. She assured me that everything was all right but I couldn't help but feel something was wrong. Our calls were limited to five minutes and I couldn't discuss it any further with my mother. I wrote several letters to her and my grandmother, asking them to tell me what was wrong with my father.

It was two weeks before I learned that my father had a bleeding ulcer and was throwing up blood. My mother told me that after she hung up the phone with me, she went into the bedroom where my father was lying and he was just as I described. It sent chills down her spine. How could I have known?

Twelve weeks later, I had one more week before

I completed boot camp and was ready to move on to the real Navy. I got my orders to go to radioman school in San Diego, California. I wrote my recruiter and told him what rate the Navy had assigned me. He was surprised because I had to score high on the ASVAB to get that school. Nevertheless, he cheered me on and told me to have fun with the security clearance that I had to go through.

Liberty was the next best thing to graduating from boot camp. We got a full twelve hours of freedom out on the town in our dress blues. Six of us decided that we wanted to go to Disney World. We spent the day there and met up with some male recruits from our brother company.

(*I don't recommend riding Space Mountain while in uniform wearing your cover (hat). They don't stay on very well.*)

From there we went to one of several Enlisted Men's Clubs. One drink affected me the same as three would anyone else. It was almost midnight when I left the club. We giggled and tried to get our composure before we went on the quarterdeck. We knew that we had to stand at attention, salute and sound off our names. I did pretty well until I got to my name. I just couldn't say it right for the life of me. The more I tried the worse it got. Spelling it was no better, but I did keep a straight face. The watch allowed me to go to my barracks. As I climbed up the stairs, I started undressing so I could jump into the rack the moment I got there. The fire watch was picking up my clothes as I reached the

Wake Up and Die Right

lower bunk. I remember drifting to sleep as the room was spinning. When five o'clock revelry came, I damn near fell out of the bed. It startled me as I was just getting into my REM sleep. I sat up so quick that I hit the bar under the top bunk, knocking myself out. The goose egg-sized knot on my head was the only thing that kept me from being written up because I couldn't perform my duties from the partying from the night before.

A corpsman was standing over me with smelling salt. I had to spend the rest of the day in the dispensary sleeping off my headache. I probably could have milked the time off but I didn't want to miss any days of training because I wouldn't graduate. I was going to make sure I did graduate from basic training in two days. I felt so free being out on my own and far away from home. I didn't want to leave Florida without having a chance to enjoy it.

I knew my parents couldn't make it to Orlando for commencement and I decided to get a hotel with a couple of friends from boot camp and stay a few days longer after graduation before going home to see my family. I told my parents that I had to stay a couple more weeks than planned. I just wanted to be able to surprise them when I came home. I only stayed in Orlando for about two days before flying home. Since no one knew when I was coming, I took a cab from the bus station and had the driver drop me off down the road from my house. Wearing my dress blues, I walked up to our house and looked over the back fence. I saw my father in the

109

backyard talking to the neighbor over the hedge.

I yelled out, "Hey, old man!" saluting my father. His face got pale white and he let out a big yell for my mother to come quickly. I saw her run out the back door to my father, not knowing what was wrong.

"Look what the Navy sent us!" He was grinning ear to ear. My mother put her hands up in the air and let out a squeal.

"Stay there, don't move, I am coming", she said, panicky. Just as she started to go in the back door, she ran back and yelled for me to stay right where I was and ran into the house. My mother flew out the front door with a camera, snapping pictures, one after the other. She cried as she grabbed and hugged me. I motioned for the cab driver to pull up in the driveway. My father didn't want to take the time to go through the house to get in the front yard, so he jumped the fence like a kid.

Grinning with excitement, he yelled to the neighbor, "Hey, my daughter the sailor!"

Mom grabbed my cover when I set it down on the couch, then she put it on her head, began walking around the house singing "Anchors Away." It was a great homecoming!

After two weeks at home, I had to leave for my first duty station in San Diego, California. I arrived early and I checked into my barracks on Friday evening. The next morning I awoke around nine o'clock. Panic-stricken that I was late for revelry I scurried around the room trying to find my uniform.

That is when I met my first roommate, Jessie Vega. She was short, thin and missing her front tooth. She rolled over, opened one eye and mumbled, "What's the hurry?" I told her that I didn't hear revelry and I didn't know where to go. She sat up in bed and looked at me saying, "This must be your first duty station and you're in training school, huh?"

I answered, "How did you know?"

Jessie jumped down off the top bunk, scratching her backside.

"Been there, done it!" All I could say was "Huh?"

Jessie said, "You are in the real Navy now. We work seven to five, Monday through Friday except when we have duty. You haven't even been checked into school, so you don't even have duty yet."

Jessie staggered into the bathroom, closing the door halfway. She turned on the water and splashed it in her face. She came out of the bathroom drying her face off with a military issued towel and inserting her partial dental plate.

"Give me a minute to wake up and I will take you to the chow hall and then show you around," she said.

That evening Jessie took me to the Enlisted Men's Club on base. I got a lot of attention from the military men and liked it. There were Marines and Australian and British Navy personnel throughout the club. I must have danced all night, non-stop that first night.

Monday morning, Jessie escorted me down the hall from her class, to where my radioman training was located. As I entered the room, I felt all eyes upon me. I was the only female. The chief petty officer checked me in and directed me to my assigned seat. He had me fill out some paperwork. It completed filling out my security clearance forms. He told me that the Federal Bureau of Investigation (FBI) had not completed my background check and I would be in transit until he got the okay for me to start my training since a radioman is required to have a minimum of a Top Secret Clearance.

In the meantime, I sent to the training school, worked hard and did what they expected of me. I did so well that I was placed in charge of the class during cleanup, when we had duty. At first, there was tension, but as time went on, these guys were not just fellow sailors; they became good friends.

Over the next six weeks, I went on with my normal duties waiting for my clearance to come through. Then I got a call to go to the Naval Investigative Service (NIS) who was requesting to meet with me regarding a problem with my background check. I was scared to meet with the NIS and FBI. I introduced myself to Special Agent Burton and Special Agent Fry. Burton had a large manila folder with several pages partially out of the folder. He looked at me with a straight face and asked about my father and his writing letters to Russia. "Russia?" I asked, dumbfounded. He laid out copies of several letters to and from my father. There were

Wake Up and Die Right

several black marks within the letter. I was in awe. I couldn't think of anything to say because I was shocked at just the implication. After further investigation, Special Agent Burton said my father was supposed to be writing my aunt. She was the daughter that my grandmother Marlonnia left behind in Russia right after she was born. "The rumors are true," I said to myself. Then Burton showed me other letters that my Uncle Algiris had received from Russia. One agent said, "There was some question about your allegiance to the United States".

"My allegiance?" I asked, surprised. "I don't know what you are talking about!" I said sternly.

Then Burton asked me a hypothetical question. If I were in control of "The Button" that would send missiles to Russia, could I push it if ordered to do so. I knew that arguing with special agents from the FBI would not help my situation. I just calmly said that I would push the button if ordered to do so since I didn't know any relatives in Russia. After completion of the investigation, I was cleared for a Top Security Clearance. Then I could begin training as a radioman.

After a day of extreme questioning, Jessie and I felt we needed to go to the Enlisted Men's Club.

"What you need is a few beers and to meet a nice guy to keep your mind off of the last few days," she said. Jessie introduced me to one of her husband's friends who was station at Ballast Point Submarine Base. Petty Officer Angelo Robino. He was a sonar technician. Angelo was Italian, tall and thin, with a mustache and he had great brown eyes. He joined my table with a couple of friends a few times.

We had been dating for about a month when we checked into a hotel. I don't know why I went with him, but I knew I couldn't go through with doing something that may have been on his mind. He was charming and didn't make a fuss about my sleeping with him fully clothed. However, his patience didn't last when the same thing happened three more times. I gave into Angelo's charm and patience. We made love. He held me all night. I felt secure and happy. By the next morning, I thought about the night before and started feeling sick.

"What did I do?" I kept saying to myself. My nerves were shot by then. I couldn't help but feel guilty. Perhaps because it was my first time and I was far away from home.

Angelo was station on board a submarine, more commonly known as a boat. He would go out to sea for weeks at a time. He went out to sea the next day for a month. Just before he came back in port, I found out that I was pregnant. This was the last thing I wanted to happen and I was petrified to tell Angelo. I confided in the guys that I worked with to get their opinion as to a man's perspective. I told them I going to tell Angelo that I was pregnant that night. For a bunch of guys, they were surprisingly supportive.

When Angelo came back in port, he took me to

a romantic dinner with his best friend and his date. After dinner, we started talking about the last few weeks. His friend snuggled in a corner booth with his date as I put my hand on Angelo's hand. I told him the doctor said we were going to have a baby. He was considerably upset.

"Get an abortion!" he demanded. "I don't want a kid now!"

I responded, "Neither do I, but I can't kill it!"

(Again, here is something that my mother went through when she was pregnant with me. I noticed there as a parallel existence with her and I had to veer away from the same domed life.)

Angelo turned toward his friend and said, "Come on, Leachman, I need a drink." Carlos Leachman was a skinny, pimply-faced, greasy haired, almost dwarf size sailor. He and Angelo walked Jessie and me to our barracks. I felt antsy and couldn't relax, so later that evening I went to the club. I thought I could drown my sorrows so I drank about a half a pitcher of beer before getting tired. I walked unsteadily back to the barracks and dragged myself up the stairs to the third floor. Ever so carefully not to wake anyone, I tried to put my key in the door. The hall was faintly lit with only flashing neon light that was ready to burn out helped me see in the dark. I bent down to put the key into the lock and fell forward, hitting my face on the doorknob. Jessie opened the door just as I fell into the room.

"Why are you drinking if you are pregnant?"

she bitched.

"He wants me to have an abortion. I don't know what to do right now," I said. Jessie asked me if I was going to do it. I told her that I just couldn't have an abortion. Then she said that she would adopt the baby if I couldn't take care of it.

"I can't think right now, Jessie. Talk to me in the morning", I slurred.

I woke up the next day with not only a headache, but my cheek was swollen and throbbing in sync with my head pounding. My feelings were hurt when I didn't hear from Angelo that day but I went to class like usual. Several of my male co-workers greeted me. Jessie had already told them what Angelo had said about the baby. By then I had a very noticeable shiner. All the guys thought Angelo hit me when I told him about the baby. It took about fifteen minutes to convince them what really did happen to my face.

(*That day, I got six marriage proposals. All six wonderful men offered to be the father to my baby.*)

One in particular was Virgil. He stood out with his gorgeous green eyes and long dark lashes. He was due to ship out in a few days and begged me to marry him. These were the same guys who acted as though they didn't like me when we first met. They all offered to be my unborn child's father and it overwhelmed me. Virgil persisted right up until the day he left to go to his next duty station. I told him he would remain special in my heart but I had to know if Angelo really didn't want our child and me.

Angelo was waiting for me when I got out of class the next day. He brought me flowers and asked me to marry him. I asked him if he really wanted to marry me or was it because of the baby. He took a deep breath and said, "Both!" I had mixed feelings about Angelo. I didn't love him, yet. I still yearned for Mason, but Angelo was the father of my child and I had to give him a chance to be a father to our baby.

Angelo was somewhat superstitious and said we should get married on a day divisible by the number seven. So, we married on May 21st in a little church. A few months later, I broke the news to my parents that I was pregnant. We drove cross-country from San Diego to Illinois so Angelo could meet my parents. Everything seemed to be going just fine but there was tension between Deirdre and me. My parents weren't happy for me because, unbeknownst to me, a month prior Deirdre had an abortion. She was going through guilt with a lot of emotional issues. When she saw I was married and pregnant, it caused her to have a lot of bottled up anger explode.

I went into her room trying to talk to her and asked her not to act so badly toward Angelo. Deirdre grabbed a four-foot full-length mirror and swung it at me. She hit me with the mirror full force. It shattered everywhere and I stood there with only minor cuts. I reacted by jumping on her and slamming her to the ground as she tried scratching me with her long nails. I grabbed her hands; I thrust her fingers (*nails down*) into the wood floor, breaking most of her nails. My father had to separate us. The tension was strong. My parents decided to pay for a hotel down the street and called it a late wedding present since we didn't have a honeymoon. We graciously accepted. I saw my parents periodically for the next two days, but Angelo and I knew it was time to go back to California.

When we reached San Diego, we set up house in a new apartment. We found a furnished place that had everything we needed to make it home. The only thing left was baby furniture. It was hard for me to work the graveyard shift when the baby didn't know the difference between night and day. I had morning sickness all the time.

Angelo started acting strangely, the further along I became. He would not let me buy any maternity clothes and told me that I was big and fat. (*familiar?*) I tried to wear my clothes by leaving the pants open and using a belt to hold them up. My grandmother had saved my mother's maternity clothes from back in the fifties and sent them to me. She washed and pressed each outfit with loving care.

I don't think Angelo could accept being married or having a baby. So, he found his own way of coping. Even though Angelo was in the Navy, he sure managed to get away with drinking heavily and smoking pot. He bought magic mushrooms and put it in my spaghetti sauce or marijuana in brownies and even in tea. My pregnancy was hard on me and I feared Angelo and his friend Leachman would be arrested or Angelo would be popped on a urine test, adding stress to my pregnancy.

Every month Angelo would pull duty and stay aboard the submarine. There were times when I would bring him dinner, stay for a couple of hours watching movies in the mess deck. The last time I visited Angelo while I was pregnant was three days before he was to go out to sea for another six months on a WestPac tour (*Western Pacific*). This trip to his boat was a little different. I made my usual walk across the gangplank. There the military watch greeted me. He radioed Angelo that I was topside and going below deck.

I yelled, "Look out below, pregnant woman going down ladder and can't see below me". The sailors knew I was coming and laughed as they watched my belly bounce off every rung of the ladder. Angelo met me at the bottom and escorted me to the mess deck where his crew showed movies for the men who were on duty that weekend. We were enjoying the movie when I felt that I was probably going into labor.

(I *think the movie "Embryo" was playing. A scary movie for a pregnant woman to watch.*)

The chief corpsman had just gone below deck after a night of partying at a base Christmas party. He had a little buzz, but sobers up quickly when he thought I was going to give birth on the submarine. He tried to assess the situation and the best way to get me topside to the hospital. The labor pains were coming close together. The corpsman decided I would have to go topside the same way they load torpedoes, or he was going to have to deliver the baby in the mess deck. "No way," I said. "I will go up the same way I came down." After ten minutes, my water broke.

The chief corpsman had plenty of time to sober up since I had twenty-minutes after my water broke when the baby came. With each pain, my mind was drawn to Mason. While in labor, I yelled out Mason's name. I didn't realize what I had done due to the pain. Angelo knew, but he tried to pretend he didn't hear me cry out another man's name while giving birth to our child, but his crewmembers noticed. Most of the sailors tried to avoid the makeshift delivery room. In just a few more minutes, our daughter entered the world as it may be. Desiree weighed seven pounds thirteen ounces.

(*Her birth certificate shows place of birth "The Pacific Ocean". When actually she was born below sea level since the mess deck was thirty feet under water!*)

She was the most beautiful thing I ever saw. She was so perfect in every way. We bonded immediately. Angelo had less than three days to try to bond with his daughter before he left for his tour of duty in WestPac, but Desiree and I were the talk of the voyage.

After the baby was born, our landlord said we were in violation of our lease agreement, which clearly stated "no children". Angelo went on his tour of duty and I came back to the apartment by

Wake Up and Die Right

myself after the hospital checked me out. I had to pack and find another apartment.

I put most of our belongings into storage and decided to fly home to Illinois for a couple of months while I was on maternity leave. My mother took a bus to the Chicago Airport just to greet her new granddaughter and me. She stood out as the proud grandma when I could hear her shriek, "There's my grandbaby!" As I looked around, I was the only one with a child.

Angelo and I sent tape-recorded letters back and forth and several pictures. We drew closer to one another. When I went back to San Diego, I had to find an apartment that would allow children. I found one just before Angelo came into port. My mother-in-law and nine-year-old sister-in-law decided to come to San Diego the week Angelo came home. They had to share the bedroom with the baby. Angelo arrived back in town a couple of days later and made some of his special brownies and tea just before she arrived. He had his special spaghetti sauce in the refrigerator. I didn't want to eat any, due to the special ingredients he put in it.

Angelo's mother was going to spend time with him on his boat later that evening, but not before she ate a good portion of the "special" brownies before I could get rid of them. The way she was wolfing them down I didn't think she would have room for the spaghetti and "magic" mushrooms that she thought Angelo was so sweet to make us for dinner.

About an hour later, I think she was feeling the

effects of the tainted brownies when she told us she was convinced that she had black lung.

I looked at Angelo and said, "Black lung? You can only get that from working the coal mines, right?" That is when Angelo told me his mother was a hypochondriac. Before they got to his base for the tour of the submarine, she said she also felt she was hypoglycemic. Then when she got a headache, she thought it was a brain tumor. Therefore, her trip to the submarine was more of an adventure than what she was prepared.

(Between Angelo's gourmet cooking and his mother's imagination, she was on a one-way trip.)

Angelo stayed aboard the boat after he gave his mother the tour because he had duty all night. When my mother-in-law came back home she decided to go to bed early because the room was still revolving. She was sure it was her blood sugar by then.

It was 4:05 in the morning; I was awakened by hands around my neck. The faint luminescence of the pineapple shaped night-light only shadowed the figure hovering over my bed. I reached my hand toward the figure's face, anticipating that it was Angelo. Then the deep voice told me not to make a sound and he choked me harder. He asked if there was anyone else in the house. I told him only my mother and sister-in-law along with my six-month-old baby. He whispered, "Sister-in-law?" I stuttered, telling him, "She is only nine years old".

Suddenly he yanked the electric clock out of the wall and tied my hands behind my back. "Bitch, you move or say anything, you're dead!" he snarled in a low murmur. I could feel his hot breath on my face. Rolling me over on my stomach, he grabbed a sweater from the laundry basket, as he blindfolded me, tying the sweater around my eyes so tight that my eyes began to throb. The only thought going through my head at that point was my baby. If I did anything to anger him, my baby would not have a mother. Worse, he could kill her. I prayed silently, "Dear God, help me get through this. Save my baby." The intruder grabbed my arm, yanking me over onto my back. He ripped at my panties away from my body as they were cutting into my thighs. The intruder became angry and straddled my chest. He forced himself on me while he was choking me with his hands, telling me to open my mouth. Trying to open my jaws forcibly, ripping the corners of my lips. I was devastated and humiliated. I was on the verge of passing out when he got off my chest and tore apart the room looking for money. Once again, he warned me not to make any noise or move. I lay shaking on the bed for what seemed like hours. I was afraid to move, fearing he was still waiting inside the apartment. I struggled to get untied from the electrical cord and pulled the sweater from my eyes. I still couldn't move from shock for at least ten more minutes. I threw a robe on and went into the next room to wake my mother-in-law. I asked her to come into the living room. I didn't want to wake Desiree and my sister-in-law, Mandy. I stood in the living room trying to tell her what had just happened; she looked straight at me and said, "My poor Angelo, my poor son!" I was stunned by what she said to me. I stood there in the middle of the living room floor, dazed. I began screaming hysterically. "Angelo? Angelo? Why in God's name are you worrying about Angelo?" She stopped and looked at me and grabbed the phone and called the police.

After about a half an hour, I called Angelo on his submarine. I got the chief duty officer, who at first was not going to allow me to talk to him. I started screaming hysterically into the phone and told him some of what had happened. Only then, he called for my husband to come to the phone. Angelo didn't ask if I was all right. The first thing he did ask was if I could tell if the attacker was black or white. I hesitated in telling him that the subject was a black male. When I told him this, it sounded like he hit a metal locker. By this time, the police started searching the house for evidence. Angelo then began to panic and said, "What do you mean searching the house?" I told him I knew what he was worried about, but the intruder not only took our rent money, he took the rest of Angelo's marijuana.

Our apartment complex was not very big, so we knew the other tenants pretty well. Some of them came to the house when they saw the police. They had found someone had also entered their homes that in the middle of the night. They listed a few things missing, but no one had gone through what I encountered. The tenants seemed to look at me as though I was Darwin's missing link. Many times, I could hear the women huddled up around the pool conversing as to how they would have handled the situation.

One day, I spoke up and told them, "If you love your children, you would have done the same thing I did in hopes that you would be spared and be there to raise them". The gossip seemed to stop until a few weeks later, the night the manager had a little get together with some of the tenants. She and her husband invited me to come up to their apartment since Angelo had to pull duty again.

The managers, Tammy and Jim Whitherspoon, were about Angelo and my age. Most of the couples were also military and in our age range. I was prescribe Valium for my nerves after the attack and was hesitant to go out of the house. I cordially accepted their invitation and a glass of wine from the hostess. I remember going to the master bedroom to use the bathroom because the guest powder room was occupied. Gary Reddick barged into the bathroom. He knew I was in there using it, yet he practically rammed the door open.

Reddick was a loud mouth, unemployed mechanic. He had been drinking since early in the day. I yelled for him to get out of the bathroom.

He asked me, "How about giving me some? You gave it to some bastard you didn't know, or did you know him?" Modesty or not, I stood up, pulled my pants up and with one punch he was lying on the floor. I stepped over him and ran out of the apartment and down the stairs to my apartment. I was so upset and angry that I didn't notice that the manager's husband Jim Whitherspoon had followed me into my apartment.

I ran to the bedroom and grabbed the pearl-handled derringer that Angelo bought after the break-in. Reddick came running down the stairs and heading toward my apartment calling me a "slut". Reddick's wife Glenda was running after him yelling that he was an insensitive jerk. I screamed for him to get away from me or I would shoot his dumb ass. Jim Whitherspoon was trying to get the gun away from me while calling for someone to get Reddick before I shot him for shooting off his mouth. Two of the biggest Marines, who lived next door, dragged Gary away from my door and Jim calmed me down.

The next day the neighborhood was calm. Angelo came home after twenty-four-hour duty. I told him what had happened, telling him that I couldn't stay in that apartment complex. He agreed, so we went shopping for an upstairs apartment.

We found a nice apartment across town. It was actually closer to the base. Angelo's friend Carlos Leachman would come over to the house quite a bit. He was not married and didn't have a girlfriend so he was always looking for a home cooked meal. When our car needed repairs, Leachman gave the keys to his new car to Angelo. I thought it was strange that Angelo was the only one he allowed to drive it but I just thought it was because they had been friends since boot camp.

Carlos Leachman spent the night on the couch often when it got late. Many times, he would bring over steaks for the three of us and even a bottle of champagne.

Angelo had to work until midnight on our anniversary. I was trying to be romantic; I had candles lit in the dining room. I made dinner for the two of us. Angelo and Carlos pulled up in front of the apartment complex a quarter after midnight. I had on a sexy black see-through negligee. Leachman was suppose to drop Angelo off at the house, but decided to come inside. Angelo went into the bedroom and noticed that I was gone. He saw the candles lit and started looking for me in the house. I turned off the kitchen light just before they pulled up, hiding in the kitchen by the sink, waiting for Leachman to leave. I didn't have any way to get into the bedroom except to go right past Leachman. Angelo came into the kitchen and asked me what I was doing. I told him, "Isn't it obvious?"

He smiled and said, "Why don't you go and get some clothes on. Leachman will be here for a while." He then said, "He won't pay any attention to what you are wearing; it is me he wants, not you".

I was fuming as I went into the bedroom. A few minutes later Angelo came into the bedroom and asked, "What would you do if your best friend told you he loved you and wanted to touch you in a way that no other man should?"

I raised my eyebrow. "So what are you getting at?"

Angelo said that Leachman told him that he was in love with him. I asked Angelo, "First, I need to know how you feel about Leachman?"

Angelo said, "Not in that way!" I told Angelo then that I would take care of it. As I grabbed my robe, I went out into the living room, pulled Leachman up by the arm and began pushing him out the front door. I inadvertently knocked him down the stairs trying to get him out of the house. Leachman grabbed the railing to catch himself from falling.

I yelled to him, "When I took my marriage vows, the preacher said may no man put asunder and you aren't going to sunder my husband!" Leachman never came back over after that night.

Desiree was the only thing that kept me going day to day. As special as she was to me, she did have a bad habit of screaming, seemingly for no reason. Things became more stressful for Angelo and me. The doctors couldn't tell me why she screamed so loud and long. It always happen around four o'clock in the morning. The same time as the intruder broke into our apartment and I was assaulted. Angelo didn't have the patience for her as I did. Many times, I would come home from work and I would see handprints on her face. He would give me some story that she fell off the couch and he tried to catch her, smacked her accidentally when grabbing her. At first, I thought it could be possible that is what happened, but it started to become more frequent.

One morning, I got off the graveyard shift. I was tired and had just gone to bed. I heard Desiree screaming and crying differently. I heard Angelo yelling at her, then there was a thump, thump and she quit crying. I ran into the bedroom, watching in horror as Angelo on his knees straddled over Desiree. He was beating her head into the floor. Somehow, I grabbed Angelo. I lifted him up off the ground. A surge of adrenaline was rushing through my veins. I had him so high in the air that his feet were dangling and hitting my shins. I threw him in the corner of the room. He started charging in my direction ready to backhand me. I told him, "Go ahead and try it. You may kill me, but you won't be leaving without me hurting you!" Just then, I picked him up once again and threw him out the second-floor picture window. The neighbor called the police and they were pulling up into the driveway as Angelo flew out the window and landed on top of the patrol car. I yelled I want a divorce and he yelled back, "No problem!"

The police came charging up the stairs into the bedroom. They saw me hovering over Desiree. She lay stiff as a board, not moving. She was just looking at me. Her little hands curl tightly as if she was gripping something for dear life. It was obvious she was in shock. The police released Angelo and me. He went to his sub. The next day I started to sell our belonging so I could transfer back home to stay with my family for a while since I couldn't stay in the barracks with a child.

Once I got temporary orders back home, I sold everything we owned. Angelo surprisingly came to the apartment and said that he wanted to try a second chance for our relationship. I told him it was too late. When he hurt our daughter, there was nothing left in our marriage. As I sold most of the things that we had so I could move home, we were preparing the divorce papers.

(This was a turning point in my life. I went from being a victim to fighting back the only way I knew how.)

I moved back to my hometown where I stayed with my parents briefly until my father died of a heart attack a few months later. My mother was such a wreck over his death. She didn't know how to write a check, balance a checkbook, or know what bills had to be paid or even how she was going to pay them. He never told her. Mom couldn't handle Desiree's constant screaming and asked us to leave.

It was during the blizzard of 1979 when she asked us to leave her house because she couldn't handle the baby crying with her nerves the way they were at that time. I didn't have much money and had very limited resources after paying other expenses that came out of my paycheck. I could only find shelter in the bathroom of the YWCA. They didn't allow children in the rooms, but for a small fee, they would allow us to stay in the public bathroom until the snow let up. I used an expansion gate to keep Desiree from getting out of the bathroom. I laid my faux fur coat on a pile of clothes in a large suitcase for Desiree to sleep in. I wrapped her up and held her close to me. The blizzard was so bad that there were snowdrifts five feet high. I carried Desiree over my head when I had to go outside. Once I fell in a snowdrift, struggling to keep Desiree safe from smothering. She looked like a little blue tick in her snowsuit. The only part of her exposed to the weather was a small portion of her face and her little red lips and nose.

My grandmother kept telling me to give her up for adoption because it was going to be a burden on me to raise a child without a husband or money. I told her that I wouldn't do it. Not unless I couldn't take, care of her or feed her. She was all I had. She was my inspiration.

After a few months, I was able to get back on my feet. The Navy allowed me to travel. I got orders that I was going to be attached to Naval Air Station Agana Guam for several years. I wasn't state side for about four years but the next time I went home to visit, I received a strange phone call. It was Mason Templeton. He said that he was divorced and had two children that he had custody of, a three and four-year-old. I told him about Desiree and that she was four-years-old. He asked if he could see me again. Trying not to sound too eager, I agreed to meet him. It was Independence Day and I had the same feeling of butterflies at the thought of seeing him again, some eight years ago. I had one question for him.

"What in the hell happened to you?"

He replied, "Long story".

I asked, "How much of it has to do with your father?"

"All of it." he replied.

I had a fluttery feeling when we met at his sister Angela's apartment. This once handsome man was now worn and sickly looking and scruffy. Mason had gotten out of the military three years earlier. He had gain a considerable amount of weight, balding and wore wolverine boots with holes in the sides. I still saw the man that I fell in love with back in high school.

(I guess it is true, when you truly love someone, the flaws that others see go unnoticed.)

He told me how his father interfered every time we got together. I was prepared for anything Mr. Templeton had to say about me. My grandmother used to have a habit of cutting out local articles from the papers and sending them to me about the things going on in Loves Park and in Rockford. I collected a few interesting news clipping about Mason's father. I showed Mason the clippings where his father was fired from his job at the school district.

Chas Templeton was charged with having sexual contact with both a child at the school where he worked at as a boiler technician and with Angela and their younger sister Jenna. Mason's jaw dropped when he read the articles. He said that he had no idea and called his mother to ask her about the article. She confirmed the stories were true, but it was better to keep it in the past. She told him, "Leave things alone".

Mason and I started to see one another on a regular basis. Soon we were living together so he didn't have to live with his parents and go by his father's rules. One rule, of his dad's house included him not seeing me.

I helped raise his children and he helped me with Desiree. With three little ones, Mason and I were careful to have safe sex, but four months into our relationship after making love, the next day, I started feeling nauseous. "No, this can't happen to me again", I said to myself.

Around Thanksgiving, the doctor confirmed that I was going to deliver around April or early May. I started to whimper at the thought of another child. Mason was so excited that he picked me up in the doctor's office and swung me around.

(That was something different from what I was expecting.)

There were complications throughout my pregnancy. I was not expected to carry the baby full term. I lost a lot of blood during the fourth and fifth month. I was sure I lost our baby and was calling out for Mason. I left the bathroom, to lay down on the bed. He was distressed as he reached for a mangled fetus. Mason took me to the hospital immediately.

Kerrigan Rhea

I was five and a half months pregnant when I lost the baby! Somehow, I knew that I was still pregnant. Dr. Gorkinski wanted to perform a D & C when he didn't hear a heartbeat, but I refused. I told him that he had to do an ultrasound to prove to me that there was not a baby. During the ultrasound, I could see a very busy baby moving around inside. Dr. Gorkinski said that they must have been fraternal twins and this baby appeared to be doing just fine. It saddened me that I had lost our child, but it was a relief to know its twin was healthy.

In late April, I gave birth to an eight-pound four-ounce towheaded little girl. We named her Jade. She looked just like Mason. She had his ears, big blue eyes, Templeton hands and feet. Mason's family never acknowledged Jade as their granddaughter and that really hurt.

(Not so much for me, but I hurt for Jade as she got older and tried to have the Templeton's in her life.)

His parents, well actually his father, never really accepted me either for the same childish reason as when I was a child.

The following Thanksgiving Mr. and Mrs. Templeton wanted Mason to come to their house for the holiday.

(Mason's ex-wife, Minerva, was trying to locate him by hiring a private detective. With the help of her PI, she got Mason's children as they were playing in the front yard. When they went to court, it was more or less whoever had physical custody of

the kids was nine/tenths of the law. She got full custody of them. Mason never saw his kids again until they became adults.)

I told him to go ahead and spend the holiday with his parents. Desiree, Jade and I would go out to eat for Thanksgiving at a nearby Denny's restaurant. Mason had mixed feelings about leaving us to spend the holiday with his parents but I insisted I wanted to be a bigger person than his father was.

Just as Christmas started to approach, Mason asked me to marry him and I accepted. It wasn't' the most romantic proposal. He was on the toilet and yelled out, "Let's get married".

We eloped by going to my chief communications officer's house in Glenview, Illinois where I was stationed. Our wedding date was easy to remember because it was on Pearl Harbor Day, December 7. Things didn't start out on the right foot.

Bobby and Tammy Grateman bought our wedding cake. It was a chocolate sheet cake with an off-white butter cream frosting with tiny purple flowers and white roses. Tammy put it on long-stemmed wineglasses from Italy as pillars. My flower bouquet was a fur muff with silk purple and white flowers and baby's breath.

My dress was very simple looking. It was a beige suit and skirt. The jacket was trimmed in gold. We hurried to get dressed to go down to the courthouse as I polished my nails, blowing on them to dry and admiring the iridescent mother-of-pearl polish.

In my haste to go out to the car, I grabbed my jacket that had been lying on the couch. As I was putting it on Tammy yelled, "Svetlana, what is all over your jacket?" I took off the jacket to look at it and by the smell; it was obvious that Bobby and Tammy's dog Popeye hiked his leg up on the couch and all over my jacket. I was devastated and asked, "What else could go wrong?" I glared at that one-eyed, old fart of a English bulldog as he stood on the back of the couch looking out the window as if to say, "How did you like that?"

The drive to the courthouse seemed long, since my heart was pounding with excitement that I was going to marry my true love. I was pouting as we got out of the car and walked up the stairs of the courthouse. The guys walked together as Tammy and I followed behind. They were having man talk, laughing and teasing me. They joked that this is usually when Mother Nature intervenes and ruins the honeymoon. "Stop it!" said Tammy. "That isn't nice; you will jinx everything by saying that! Loni already thinks just the date has a curse on it!"

"Come on Tammy, I have to go to the bathroom before we go see the judge," I said in an annoyed voice. As I went into the stall, Tammy heard me yell out to her, "Oh shit!"

"What?" said Tammy.

"Well, all I can say is, I have been jinxed!" I replied. "Can you get me something out of the machine, Tammy?"

"I would if there were anything to give you."

She snickered. "It is empty!"

"I guess toilet paper will have to do for now," I mumbled.

We met up with the guys and gave them a funny look. Mason said, "What?"

"You two just had to joke about it, didn't you?" I replied.

"Nah-h-h, you don't mean... Are you sure?" Mason naively asked. As I turned around to walk away, Mason started to bust out laughing.

"What is so funny, Mason?" said Tammy.

"Bunched-up toilet paper is working its way up Svetlana's back!" Bobby and Mason were laughing so loud; the security guard had to come over to ask them to quiet it down as I raced back into the bathroom to correct the problem.

After ten minutes more snickering, we signed the registry. We listed Bobby as Mason's best man and Tammy was my maid of honor. As we went into the judge's chambers, Bobby took out a tape recorder he carried inside his suit pocket and set it up as the judge was putting his robe on.

"What is the recording for, Bobby?" Mason asked.

"To commemorate the moment for your grandchildren to hear," he replied. Tammy piped up, "If they still have tape recorders in the future."

"Sh-h-h!" the judge's assistant whispered. "We are about to begin."

We managed to get through most of the ceremony. However, when it came time to exchange wedding rings I was horrified. My hands were sweaty inside the fur muff. They were as swollen as the rest of my body that month. As I pulled my left hand from the fur muff, I noticed that part of the muff was attached to my still drying fingernails. The judge grinned as I tried to pull the pieces of fuzz off my ring finger. We all tried to keep straight faces as Mason tried pushing my wedding ring on my swollen finger. It sounded like a chant from Bobby, Tammy and the judge, saying, "Push, push, push".

The judge then said, "I pronounce you man and wife; you can kiss the bride", as the tape recorder "clicked" for the end of a memorable tape.

I couldn't believe we made it through the day. I just wanted to get back to the house for a strong drink and piece of my wedding cake. When we got to the house I noticed Popeye was nowhere in sight. Probably because he knew, I wanted to give him a swift kick in the rear for what he did to my suit jacket. Tammy said, "Let's get some pictures of you two cutting the cake. Oh my God! The wedding cake!"

"What do you mean the wedding cake, Tammy?" I threw my piss-soaked jacket on the floor and ran to the table. "The whole middle of the cake is gone!" I shrieked. "Surely, this is a sign that our marriage is doomed", I said.

My wedding may not have been something out of a *Cosmopolitan* magazine, but none of that mattered, I had the love of my life. Or did I? Mason's parents were not going to accept our marriage. It hurts that they never acknowledged Jade. All I could do was try to shelter her from any cruel remarks that Mr. Templeton would say about her.

As the months went by, I started to see another side of Mason. He started working for the local police department as a reserve. He seemed to enjoy it, since he was military police while in the Army. I really didn't care for his supervisor, Don Dickerson. He resembled Fred Flintstone, only he was missing his four front teeth and he had the same large knobby nose and square blockhead.

I found it hard to believe it when Mason said he and his wife Daphne were "swingers". Daphne didn't look that much better. Her voice was like HR Puff-N-Stuff's character "Witchipoo". The best of imaginations couldn't visualize Fred Flintstone and Witchipoo as swingers. Daphne worked in a massage parlor. Naïve me, took a while before I learned that she did more than massages!

Jade was about five months old, Desiree about five years old when one night Mason came home around three o'clock in the morning. I always kept a .357 Magnum under my pillow when he was working nights. Usually he would call out to me as he came up the stairs of our townhouse to the bedroom to ensure that I didn't shoot him, thinking he was a prowler.

Mason came into the bedroom, kissed me and said that he felt like being romantic. "It's three in the morning. Mason, how do you think I can get motivated while I'm half asleep?" I said as I yawned. He lightly touched my leg, gently rubbing it and said, "Let's do something different this morning".

"What do you mean different?" I said.

"I want to handcuff you and blindfold you." He grinned. (*I only agreed to be handcuffed in front.*) As I heard the clicking sound of the handcuffs getting tighter around my wrists, he blindfolded me. As soon as he tied a scarf around my eyes, I started to shake. I had the same feeling as I did when the intruder broke into my apartment in San Diego. I became anxious and apprehensive. Mason said that he had to use the bathroom to clean up and would be right out. He told me to lie back in the bed until he came out.

As I lay in the bed, my body was trembling with fear and flashbacks. I could hear my heart beating fast when I heard a noise from the corner of the room. Then there was a feeling of a presences and pressure at the end of the bed. I yelled out to Mason. He answered me from the bathroom, yet it felt as though someone was getting onto the bed. I sat up and pulled the scarf away from my eyes. I was eye to eye with a toothless Fred Flintstone with no clothes on! I reached under my pillow and pulled out the .357 Magnum. The long silver barrel was gleaming from the reflection of the moonlight glaring through the blinds. I pressed the barrel tightly up against this pungent, wannabe cop's head. Don started yelling for Mason louder than I was yelling for him to get in the bedroom now!

I heard the toilet seat hit the commode as it fell away from Mason's butt. He hobbled into the bedroom with a trail of toilet paper stuck to his fanny and pants around his ankles to find me still cuffed, holding a gun to Don's head.

Mason watched as Don urinated on the end of the bed. "You move, asshole, you are dead!" I snarled with clenched teeth. He never said a word after that. Peeing on the bed was a good sign that I had his attention. For almost thirty minutes, Mason tried to get me to put the gun down. The more he talked to me the harder I pushed the barrel up against Don's head. It was not until I cocked the hammer back that they both knew I was serious.

I was so angry that I could have easily shot him and Mason for putting me through that. Eventually Mason talked me into putting the gun down. Still furious, I threw the gun on the bed and it went off. Don didn't waste any time running out of the room and to his car butt-naked! I demanded that Mason take the cuffs off me before I broke them. The adrenaline was pumping through me, I am sure it would not have taken much for me to snap the restraints.

About ten minutes later, the phone rang. Mason answered it. Don called to say that he left some of his police gear in the townhouse and asked Mason to meet him downstairs. Then I could hear Don asking Mason, "Damn, Loni scared the shit out of me! Do you think she would have really shot me?"

Mason's eyes looked over at me at the top of the stairway as he slightly turned his back to me and whispered to Don, "Hell, yes, she would have shot you. She cocked the damn hammer!"

For the next hour, I sat in the bed, rocking back and forth counting to ten and then again backward. I was prepared to shoot both of them but held back because of my kids. I loved them too much to go to prison for a double homicide.

Times were nerve wracking between Mason and me for some time. It was not until I got orders to be station in Jacksonville, Florida that I started talking to him again. Perhaps getting away from "Fred Flintstone" and starting over in another state would bring us back together.

I went ahead to Florida and bought an eighty-foot mobile home and had it set up for when Mason came into town. He worried about finding jobs because he had to quit so many of them just to follow me to my next duty station. Mason found it hard to be a military dependant husband. He needed to find a job that would understand the short employment record.

Mason got lucky when he was hired at the Department of Defense (DOD) at my base after the first week he got to Florida. He looked dashing in his base security uniform. I worked on the same base in communications at the time. About a year later, I started to have abdominal pain and was hemorrhaging so much that I needed blood transfusions almost every two weeks. It was obvious some-

Wake Up and Die Right

thing was wrong. It was cancer.

It was difficult for me to take care of the girls while I was having this medical issue. We had a nice couple in the trailer park directly behind us offer to help. Doug Whipple and his wife Mallory had a four-year-old girl, April. Doug was in the Air Force and went out on several military training maneuvers. Mallory was home alone a lot. She got along with my children and offered to keep them as long as I needed. I spent several weeks off and on in the hospital, finally having surgery. Mason depended on Mallory to take care of the girls so he could work the crazy hours he had been assigned. It was during this period she and Mason started having an affair.

A neighbor sat down with me when I came home from the hospital and said she couldn't take it anymore. She showed me love letters that Mason wrote Mallory and vice versa. She said that Mallory asked that she keep them for her so that Doug would not find them.

I confronted Mason and Mallory about the letters. I was weak and still unable to get around and they laughed at me. Mason announced that Mallory had just learned that she was pregnant and he was moving her into our trailer. If I didn't like it, I could leave. I never felt so much pain throughout my body as I did that day. I just wanted them to stay away from me while I tried to recover.

Mallory said she was too scared to wait at the house when Mason was not there. So she would stay at her residence with her husband, who had moved another woman into their trailer. When Mallory was staying with us, I tried to make both her and Mason think I was nuttier than a fruitcake to keep them away from me. I did the next best thing. When they were sleeping, I would take Mason's revolver, when he woke the chamber was open and the gun barrel was facing Mason's head. I took the bullets out, laid them next to the gun. When they would wake up in the morning, sometimes the gun barrel was on the nightstand pointing at her.

It was about one and a half months later that I decided I was not going to take any more crap from them. Mason had to stay on the base for a twenty-four-hour shift. Mallory was getting her belonging together to go back to her trailer. The last thing Mason told me before he left for the base was, "If you don't like it, leave".

(Déjà vu again but I was going to do one better than my mother did when she was told that.)

I smiled and told him that he won. I would leave. The kids and I would be gone when he came home. He said, "That is great, it is not soon enough for me". He then got into his car and left for the base. Of course, I was feeling a bit destructive by this time. I took the remaining personal effects that were Mallory's and began singing to myself and throwing her things out my trailer onto the front yard. I heard her screeching as she grabbed the phone, standing in her doorway, calling Mason at the base. She doubled over for special effect for the neighbors to see her holding her stomach and yelled, "Oh oh, if I lose this baby because of you, bitch, I will have you arrested!" I looked at her and smiled. "I guess Mason can just make another one!" Mallory was so livid that she got in her car and left for the rest of the day.

Now the next part of my plan was to get the movers to the house and get this house on the road before Mason got off work. Luckily, I had kept the wheels on and the movers were available when I called. I had the trailer on the road going across the state line by dusk. Mason didn't know that I had received new orders sending me to Georgia and that our trailer was on its way there by the time he got off duty.

(*I told you I would do one better than my mother.*) ☺

I got a call at work two weeks later when the same neighbor who told me about the affair said that Mason was dumbfounded when he came home to all his belongings lying on an empty lot. She said that she laughed about it, especially when she heard Mallory tell Mason that she was through with him since he didn't have a place to live. Then she over heard her tell him, "By the way, this baby isn't yours!" She told Mason that she was going to kick out her husband's new girlfriend and stay with Doug.

By now, Mason was looking for our home and me. It didn't take much for him to track me down. There were not too many trailers on the interstate going to Georgia that time of the year. He showed up on my doorstep, very humble. I let him return home only to make it clear that I was filing for a divorce. I told him that I would give him the trailer since he punched holes in it and threw me through the walls. We stayed together, actually happily, right up until a year after we were divorced.

By this time, the military was giving me a medical discharge because they thought I might not make it through the cancer. I didn't want to get out of the Navy after ten years. It was the needs of the military and I was no longer useful. During the last few years of my service, I had worked out of my rate as a Master at Arms (or known as military police). I loved the work and was good at it. I was determined to become a police officer.

My last duty station was on a ship at the Florida/Georgia line. I decided to stay in the south when I was discharged. My first job when I got out of the Navy was at the local sheriff's office in Horse Stomp County, Georgia. I was hired to work as a dispatch/correctional officer. The jail was run down and there was not much holding it together. Horse Stomp County was building a new jail just across the main office. It was not until the inmates managed to tear down what was left of the old jail that the new jail unexpectedly opened. I had a crash course in training as a correctional officer as well as training the other correctional officers coming into the jail. I read all the manuals, rules and regulations. Soon I became a supervisor.

Wake Up and Die Right

I booked in suspects as the local police and deputies brought them to the jail. My first contact with a seasoned criminal was a pint-sized Haitian man who put in writing on a tank order what his sexual requests were and included me. Of course, this was to rattle me. I responded by visiting him in what we called the "Bull Pen".

(*A large common area away from the inmate cells. Some of the inmates were playing cards as they sat on a cold metal picnic type of table welded to the chains in the concrete floor.*)

The sex-crazed inmate saw me approach the electronic door. He jumped up and greeted me with his contemptuous grin. He asked if I got his request. I replied, "I did get it. I want you to know that I will not stand for such disrespectful behavior." The inmate ripped open his shirt, looking over his shoulder at the other inmates as they watched intensely.

"Does my hairy chest turn you on, Officer Chekov?"

Before I could think my answer out, I responded, "Honey, I have more hair on my pillow that has fallen out of my head than you have on your chest!" The Bull Pen inmates busted out laughing.

After a year, I found it hard to baby sit adults. I decided to put them in jail than take care of them after they got there. I was hired at one of the city police departments. I began working at Crestview Police Department as their only female officer. The department had a reputation of only hiring one female at that time because of their Good Ole Boy attitude. Raised in the Midwest, I had no idea what that meant so I willingly became known as the "Token Female".

Chapter 6

Lady In Blue

I found that the South didn't take to Yankees, let alone a female Yankee. The other officers teased me about my accent, but I thought it was they with the accent. I found that there was a communication problem almost immediately. For the first couple of months I rode with a training officer. Billy Bob Red Feather was his name and his police radio call number was 1644.

He would say, "Tern the winder dawn, it's hotter than a cat dipped in alcohol and set on fur." Officer Billy Bob Red Feather was all country, from the cowboy boots he wore to the .44 cal Magnum on his gun belt. He loved fishing, boar hunting and eating crawdads. About six-two and a smidgen overweight, Officer Red Feather told tales of the town in which he was born and raised. You may be thinking that the last name Red Feather is not too common around the south. It happens that Billy Bob was a Native American. He was from the Cree Tribe and a cowboy wannabe. Sure, he stood out among the rest of the Southerners born and raised in Horse Stomp County but not as much as a Yankee would. He knew just about everyone in town. My first night riding with him he let me know that he knew all the good places to eat. Granny's Kitchen was a favorite of most of the officers. Billy Bob's exclusive taste buds preferred gator tail, grits and red-eye gravy and sweet tea. Eating like that every day for the past ten years could explain the roll of blubber hanging over his gun belt.

After riding with Billy Bob for about a month, he told me he was going on vacation for a couple of weeks. He said I was "learnin real well" and didn't think I needed to ride shotgun with anyone until he came back to work. So, he handed me the keys to his patrol car.

This particular night one of the dispatchers was off duty and wanted to ride along with me to get an idea what it was like on the road so she could be more insightful to the officers' needs.

I welcomed the company when I learned Chief Dispatcher Penny Applegate wanted to ride with me. We hadn't been riding very long when I got a call. I had a little problem understanding the dispatcher's reference to a possible fire. Penny translated and we wound up in a wooded area. It turned out some chap was smoking wild boar in his homemade smoke house and the smolder attracted the attention of the neighbors. I notified the dispatcher of the situation and that I was going back on patrol.

As we were heading back on to the main road, my high beams caught the reflection of two woodland creature's eyes. I wasn't sure what type of woodland creatures but I couldn't swerve fast enough to keep from hitting one or both of them. Penny and I heard a thump, bump, bang, then thump, bump, bang. The noise didn't seem to go away and the vibration of the thumping and bumping and banging gave us the strong impression that something was stuck in the tire well.

I pulled the car over to the side of the road. Since my flashlight was still charging, there wasn't enough light to see anything. I told Penny that we needed to go into town where there was better light to see what was stuck under the car. I started to pull forward and that sound started up again. When I got to a traffic light, the noise stopped, but as soon as I started moving, we could hear it again. I drove to an all-night convenient store that had florescent lights along the front of the building. As I pulled into a parking stall, customers either going inside or leaving the store commented on the noise. We got out of the patrol car, Penny let out a squeal. I ran around the passenger side of the car and a possum's head fell out from under the tire well. Its tongue was hanging out of its mouth, but I couldn't find the rest of the animal. I didn't notice it at first, but there was a funny smell radiating from the car. The smell was getting stronger but I wasn't sure, where it was coming from or what it was.

As I was examining the car an old man walked up to us and stood there a few minutes. He turned his head a moment to spit out the juice from the wad of snuff in his cheek.

"Yep, y'all got a problem with that dad burn wild-smellin par-fume."

I looked at him and said, "Pardon me, do you know what that smell is or where it is coming from?"

He rolled the wad of snuff to the other side of his cheek and put his thumbs under the suspenders of his overalls. "Yep, that there smell is comin from y'alls ve-hick-ul. Yep, juz what I thought, a wild kitty, pole cat some folk calls them."

"What is a pole cat?" He shook his head and said, "Y'all ain't from around these here parts." Penny piped up and said, "I think he is trying to say you ran over a skunk."

"Skunk? How do I get the smell to go away?"

The old man shook his head and said it just had to wear off. I looked over to Penny and asked her if she thought the smell would go away before Billy Bob got back from vacation in two weeks. Penny said she wasn't sure but we could try to put the car through a couple of car washes and buy some air fresheners for inside. So, we put the patrol car through four car washes and sprayed every flavor of deodorizer.

I parked the car in the back lot of the police department. It sat out in the parking lot for the next

Wake Up and Die Right

---

two weeks in ninety-degree humid heat. I had hoped the smell would dissipate before Billy Bob noticed it. I got to work early for the evening shift because Billy Bob was coming back to work that night. I wanted to catch him before he got into his patrol car. Penny was standing by the communication door when I came inside the department and asked her if she had seen Billy Bob. Before she could answer my question, I heard him on the radio saying he was back at the station.

"What's he doing on the radio so early?"

The dispatcher said, "He is training a new guy named Slick Rutherford and he was showing him the city limits and the main areas that we patrol".

Penny and I looked at each other and walked toward the back door to greet Billy Bob. He was walking in the door, rubbing and blowing his nose with a tissue. The new guy came in seconds later and he was rubbing his eyes. I ran up to Billy Bob and told him I needed to talk to him about something. Before I could say anything else, he said, "Man, someone needs to tell the new guy to lay off the after-shave. He stinks like a fruity wild animal." Then I could hear the new guy talking to one of the ranking officers and asking if all the patrol cars had such strong air fresheners. Penny and I giggled as we told Billy Bob what happened while he was on vacation.

"Hell, I wuz goin to have a little talk with the boy about hi-gents. If he dabbed a little red gravy behind his ears it would give him a better smellin par-fume."

Billy Bob was a good sport about the car but said he had his own home remedy for getting rid of unwanted smells. He sprayed the car with vanilla. He didn't use the imitation extract, but fresh vanilla beans. He put a couple of small empty tobacco pouches with crushed vanilla beans in the car. I like the smell of vanilla, but I had no idea that would help the smell to go away.

Billy Bob said, "Shucks, my ole granny and granpappy ran a funeral home. They had vanilla everywhere. Granpappy said it would get the stench out of anything and he had a few stinkers in his funeral home in the past." It didn't take long before the car was drivable again.

(To this day, I use vanilla in my house and car.)

Lesley Lester was the nightshift supervisor. Modestly aging, Lester fancied himself as a ladies' man. He was tall, thin with a square jaw, a pompadour hairstyle and a pencil thin mustache. Lester was known more for spending time in the convenient stores and motel lobbies talking to female clerks than doing police work.

While Lesley Lester had his eye on the convenient stores, Billy Bob had his eye on local restaurants and food. After watching Billy Bob eat dinner, I could only stomach some coffee and toast during his gourmet meal.

We heard radio traffic from Lieutenant Lester: "1602, Crestview...I will be out with a blue Ford Mustang with a female occupant at Orange Drive and Honey Dew Circle. It looks like I got a Dewy," he said in a professional manner. I haven't gone through the Police Academy yet, so I still was not familiar with the codes or slang. Billy Bob saw the puzzled look on my face.

I hesitated to ask. "What's a "Dewy?

He piped up and said, "The lieutenant is out with a driver under the influence of alcohol." Every so often, I could hear the dispatcher call Lieutenant Lester to check and see if he was all right. Each time that he answered

"10-4 Crestview", he sounded out of breath. Billy Bob said,

"Let's head out that way in case the lieutenant is having some problems. He has been out on that stop for fifteen or twenty minutes."

"1602, Crestview, I am 10-95 with a female."

"1602, 1644, can you 10-23 the PD," he said. Billy Bob replied, "10-4". I looked at Billy Bob and he smiled.

"Before you ask, Loni, the lieutenant has a female in custody and asked that we meet him at the Police Department. I am sure he wants her run on the Intoximeter."

We arrived at the department before the lieutenant. I watched as he brought in a pretty brunette who was teary-eyed. She didn't smell or act as though she had been drinking. The woman looked as though she was recently become tousled. Her shoulder length hair was tangled and her clothes were wrinkled as though someone had grabbed her by the collar and twisted the neckline. She had black streaks of mascara under her eyes. It was up to the Intoximeter if she would be charged with DUI.

(As science progressed, so did the outdated machine to test for breath alcohol. Back in the early 1980s, this particular Intoximeter reading could be manipulated one way or the other.)

The young girl shook and looked over at me and whispered, "Please help me. You have no idea what this officer said to me. He told me he would ruin my military career if I didn't have sex with him. He could guarantee that I would have a DUI reading from that machine if I refused. I haven't had anything to drink. I am a diabetic and he took my medication. Please help me," she cried.

I was astounded. I couldn't fathom what she was trying to tell me; could really be happening. I was new to the department and I just didn't know the circumstance of the arrest.

I watched as Billy Bob performed the test. The young lady was brought to the temporary makeshift cell that looked like a barbaric version of a dog kennel. The cage had rusted hinges and smell of rotting food, just inside the back door of the department. Lieutenant Lester smiled and put his arm around Billy Bob. I overheard him tell Billy Bob to meet him in his office. Billy Bob did just as he was told, taking the Intoximeter slip with him. A few minutes later Billy Bob came out of the lieutenant's office holding the Intoximeter slip dripping with coffee.

Wake Up and Die Right

He avoided making eye contact with me as I observed him perform another test and attach the new reading to the woman's file. I watched as Lieutenant Lester walked out of his office with that demonic grin that unnerved me. He seemed somewhat harmless. Yet there was something about him, a sinister look. Call it woman's intuition because I couldn't give any other reason for feeling that way about him.

For the most part, Lester was quiet and kept to himself. He would only have to look at a fellow officer and they seemed to be able to communicate through telepathy. With just a glance, I would see the officer nod his head in acknowledgement, never saying a word.

This night was going to be the start of many similar nights to come. Over time, it seemed Lieutenant Lester's arrests were only women. He had released male prisoners who had been in the back of his patrol car if he saw a pretty female he wanted to stop. It was usually young, naïve women from eighteen to twenty-six years of age, but this particular female would become a real problem for the lieutenant later on.

He went ahead and charged her with DUI. According to the second Intoximeter test, she blew point fifteen grams percent, which is almost twice the legal limit. Billy Bob called the Newcomb Naval Base for security to pick her up, as protocol required. Lieutenant Lester handed me her file and told me to fingerprint her. I took her out of the cell and she was shaking. There was still no smell of alcohol on her breath and she didn't act like anyone intoxicated.

It had been less than an hour since her arrest. I have never seen anyone sober up that quickly after blowing a point fifteen grams percent. I looked at her file and saw that her name was Justine Foxx. She was a nineteen-year-old seaman (E-3) stationed aboard the USS Oakridge submarine tender. I noticed that the first printout was not in the file, which really made me feel guarded.

She whispered to me, "I know it is hard for you to do anything. You seem as confused about what is going on as I am. Please remember everything that has happened. I might need you to help me." She squeezed my arm just as the military police arrived. Lieutenant Lester met them in a very professional manner. Billy Bob just walked away from them, looking down at his feet. I could hear Lieutenant Lester tell the military police that Seaman Justine Foxx gave him a hard time. He said she was coming on to him. She tried to talk him out of arresting her. When it didn't work, she started accusing him of trying to seduce her. As each word rolled off his tongue, he stared directly at me, as if in anticipation that I would say anything to the contrary.

Justine was placed in handcuffs after I finished fingerprinting her. She turned her head to look back at me as the military police escorted her out the door of our department. Still visibly upset, she gave me a half smile as I nodded my head to her. Billy

Wake Up and Die Right

Bob grabbed my arm, tugging on my shirtsleeve to follow him, then said, "Come on, we need to get back out on the street." We both quietly got into his patrol car. Neither of us said anything to one another until we got our next call.

About a week had passed when one of the dispatchers called. "Crestview 1610, 10-19." I acknowledged that she wanted me to return to the office. I was riding by myself at that time and I was turning into the back of the department. I saw Lieutenant Lester leaving as I pulled into the parking lot. He glanced over at me and he continued to drive away. As I entered, the dispatcher on duty, Kelly Nelson, appeared upset. I asked her what was wrong. She said she needed a bathroom break because she didn't feel well. She asked if I could watch the radio for her because some of the officers were out on calls or traffic stops. I agreed as she ran to the bathroom. I could hear her coughing and gagging several times. Kelly returned to the dispatch station after ten minutes. She was wiping her face with a wet paper towel.

"Are you all right, Kelly?" I asked, very concerned.

She shook her head yes then said angrily said, "No! No, I am not all right! I don't need this shit! I am about ready to walk out of here and not look back. If it weren't for the fact that I need this job, I would be gone."

"My God, Kelly, what in the hell happened?" I blurted out.

She said things first started happening about a week after she began working at the department. "Chief Jones always makes little snide comments in a roundabout way that could be construed two different ways. Most of them are sexual in a nature," she said.

Chief Horace Jones was a short, pudgy man with severe pockmark face. His nose is best described as similar to actor Karl Malden. His hair was greasy, thin and wispy. Large flakes of dandruff covered his clothes and the top of his desk.

Jones mask the stench of body odor with cheap cologne and breath mints from the Dollar Store. He definitely was not a pretty sight to look at, let alone smell. He too thought of himself as a ladies' man, just like Lieutenant Lester. In fact, they seemed very close to one another. It was almost as though each had something on one another. Each dangled their secret over the other's head like a pork chop to a hungry dog. Both had a grin to go with the encrypted words they spoke.

Kelly told me that there were several times when Chief Jones would criticize her for her attire. Many times, he would tell her that she looked like a tramp or a slut. She was offended and said that she was only wearing jeans and a cotton shirt.

"Nothing revealing. My pants aren't tight," she stammered.

"Things started to get worse when I started to get obscene calls while on duty. Sometimes it was just heavy breathing and then there were times that it was a woman screaming at me, calling me a slut and a whore. The calls kept coming, one after the other, tying up the police phone lines." she sighed.

"Were you able to recognize the voices of the persons who were calling?" I asked.

She said, "At first I didn't recognize them. Eventually, I learned it was Horace Jones and his wife Beulah."

"How can you be sure that it was the chief and his wife calling you?" I said in disbelief.

"Well, besides recognizing their voices, I kept complaining to Captain Barnes, who had Kapers investigate the harassing calls. Kapers had a phone trap put on the police telephone lines. One night, I activated it repeatedly. The female would be screaming at me, saying stuff like "Why don't you leave and get another job, you slut!" Sometimes I could hear a man's voice in the background egging her on as she was calling me a whore. Then I started to get the same type of calls at home. A few weeks later I got letters too!"

"No shit? What kind of letters and calls are you getting at home?" I said in amazement.

"Well, one letter read, 'You will get what you deserve. Bitch, bitch, bitch!' Detective Kapers came in the next morning with a computer readout that he had gotten from the phone company. He asked me if I knew whose number showed up on the printout. When I told him that I didn't recognize them, he said it was Horace Jones' phone number from his houseboat that is docked in the next county.

I documented the date and time that I got the calls and when I activated the trap. Each time it was Horace Jones' number!" She started sobbing.

"What did Detective Kapers do with that information? Did he confront the chief with it?" I asked.

"Well, he went to the captain and told him about it. The captain said that he was surprised about the calls still coming since the chief knew the phone would have a trap on it. He said that he told the chief about the calls coming in on the police phone lines and needed to get a trap on it earlier in the day. Captain Barnes thought the chief and his wife would be the last persons he could imagine making calls," she said.

Then she went on to mention a newly hired officer, Gil Jackson. Kelly said she called him into the office when the prank calls kept coming into the department and interfering with her answering 911 calls. He pulled the tapes from the taped lines and listened to them. He was so flabbergasted! Officer Jackson could hear a drunken woman on the line calling Kelly all kinds of dirty names and telling her to leave her husband alone. Then you could hear the chief yelling things like "You tell the bitch, she has been trying to get into my pants since the slut started working for the Crestview Police Department!" Kelly repeated what Jones said.

"What happened to Officer Jackson? I haven't met him yet." I said. Kelly snickered.

"You won't ever meet him. He turned in his gear that night and said this place was a loony bin and he was out of here! The chief has already hired someone to take his place. His name is Suwannee Pendergrass."

"Pendergrass?" I said, surprised.

Kelly answered with a frown. "Yes. Why, do you know him?"

"Kelly, two months ago I helped transport him to a cocaine rehab from the Horse Stomp County Sheriff's Office because he flipped out on his wife! He has simple battery charges pending in Savannah."

Kelly shook her head and said, "He will fit in this place real good with this bunch. Getting out of cocaine rehab on a Friday and start working at a police department arresting dope heads on the following Monday!"

"Enough of that; what happened with the prank calls? Did you ever file a complaint or tell Mayor Hanson what has been going on?"

She looked at me and said, "I am not sure who I can trust around here. I asked him to come by one evening when I was working so we could talk. He came by after a big party but was intoxicated himself. He demanded the keys to one of the patrol cars so he could go for a ride with the lights and siren on. I would not give them to him; he snapped at me and said that he had as much right to those keys as any other city worker. I didn't know what to do, so I called in Sergeant Riley on the radio, but the mayor left by the time the sergeant got here. I need my job because I have a three-year old who has some serious medical problems and the bills are astronomical. I can't afford to lose my job right now."

I asked her, "Are you afraid of losing your job?"

She said, "Most of our co-workers know what is going on and I feel like they do their best to protect me and support me without jeopardizing their own jobs. I always feel like they want to do something to help me, but they don't know what to do."

The things Kelly was telling me was a lot for me to take in. I asked her what she was upset about when I first got to the office. She asked me if I saw Lieutenant Lester leaving when I came into the parking lot. I told her that I did see him in passing.

"What happened?" I asked.

Kelly said, "Lieutenant Lester just tried to seduce me. He came into the department and went into the chief's office. He called me to come inside a few minutes later. When I walked in there, he…he…grabbed me by my shoulders and tried to kiss me. I struggled with him and managed to push him away from me. I told him not to ever touch me again! He just looked surprised when I said I didn't want anything to do with him. I ran to the radio and called you to come to the office. He left like nothing happened."

"Well, Kelly, I am not sure what to do myself. There has to be someone you can trust to help with the stuff that is going on within the department. I am a single parent too and I need my job to put food on the table as well. Let us just keep this between ourselves unless we can find someone who will be trustworthy. The wrong person getting this information can cover it up and we will look like fools." I went back out on the road but told her to call me anytime she felt scared or needed a break.

About a month after Lieutenant Lester arrested Seaman Justine Foxx, she had to make an appearance in court. Foxx showed up for court but had her supervisor and her company commander. She went before Judge Collins and told him that she was going to plead not guilty and wanted to have this hearing before him.

Judge Collins said, "I received a phone call from Commander Ellis and I'm familiar with this case. It will be set for a hearing in my office this afternoon. I expect Lieutenant Lester, Chief Jones, Officer Billy Bob Red Feather and Officer Chekov to be present." There was a lot of tension in the courtroom. By that afternoon, the judge heard what everyone had to say about the night Lieutenant Lester arrested Seaman Foxx.

Judge Collins said, "It pains me to say that I do feel that there has been some inappropriate behavior within the Crestview Police Department. I don't see that there is sufficient evidence to warrant severe disciplinary actions against Lieutenant Lester. However, I do feel that it does warrant further investigation on the department and their practices. As for the tampering of equipment to register a false reading, I am inclined to have disciplinary if not prosecute Officer Red Feather."

The judge lowered his glasses halfway down his

nose. He leaned forward in his seat and said, "Son, when I learned that the military took both breath and blood on this young lady after she was returned to the Navy's custody and both tests indicated there were no drugs or alcohol in her body, I was ashamed of the Crestview Police Department and you!"

Then turning to the chief the judge said, "Chief Jones, I expect that this officer's Intoximeter license will be terminated! Is this clear?" Chief Jones looked befuddled, but agreed with the judge to pull Officer Red Feather's Intoximeter license. The judge then turned to Justine Foxx and the base commander. He apologized for the conduct of the two Crestview officers and dismissed the case.

The walk back to the department was tense. Lieutenant Lester just beamed as he left court. Billy Bob just looked at the ground as we walked, kicking pebbles. We all knew that Lieutenant Lester ordered Billy Bob to change the test results. Lester was almost gloating, knowing that he managed to get away with his shenanigans once again.

(Seaman Foxx later hired a private attorney to represent her in a wrongful arrest suit and the Crestview Police Department settled the case for seventy-five thousand dollars. Several officers from the department had testified saying, "Lieutenant Lester is not one of them. He has power at a presidential level and abuses it." One officer went on to say in court, "This guy had so much clout it is scary.")

Kelly was just about to start the evening shift and saw us walk into the office. She motioned for me to come over to her. Kelly asked about what happened with Lieutenant Lester.

Before I could answer her, she said, "Wait, I can tell you what happened. Nothing, right?"

I told her that the judge didn't have enough clear evidence to warrant any disciplinary action, but he was sure something was crooked within the department. Then I said that Billy Bob lost his Intoximeter license.

"That doesn't surprise me," she said. "The one I feel sorry for is Billy Bob. He is a good cop. He's trying to get through a few more years so he can retire. It isn't the first time Lt. Lester has had Billy Bob change the outcome of the intoximeter reading. Any other time Billy Bob runs it like it should be run. Everyone is afraid of Lt. Lester, even the chief. You should watch how much Chief Jones shakes when Lt. Lester comes into the room. He plays like they are best friends but he is shaking in his boots when that man walks through that door and just stares at him," she whispered excitedly.

There is something about Lt. Lester, where everyone avoids him. Now Billy Bob may have his whole career may go up in smoke because he felt pressured to do what he was ordered to do. Kelly was tired of having her share of misery from this department. She had so much bottled up and nowhere to go with it. It will be only a matter of time, when I am pulled into the nightmare. Kelly grabbed my arm again, said she can't take it any more. She has to tell someone what happened when Lester left the office the other night.

"You know the night that you came into the office and I was upset and you saw him leaving?" I told her I remembered. "I didn't tell you everything; he told me that he was going to show me the proper way to search a female suspect, in the event I am asked to search an inmate. He pinned my hands up against the wall and spread my legs. Then took his nightstick and ran it slowly down my side and over my breasts and my inner thigh. He explained that women are notorious for hiding weapons in their pants."

"My God, Kelly, why didn't you tell someone earlier?" She looked at me and said, "He has a way of saying and doing things to look like you did something wrong and then makes you believe it. According to him, he was being professional and I was reading something into it. That night he told me that he loved me."

"You have to tell someone, Kelly. That is not proper. A rookie would know that."

"Loni, this is why I am telling you first. I am leaving. My dad is a GBI agent and told me that this is the most unprofessional department he has ever seen and he wants me out of here. I am going to go back home. The chief told one of the dispatchers that he has to find a way to get rid of me before I file a suit against the department.

I am telling you all this because you need to

Wake Up and Die Right

watch out for yourself. This department has not ever had more than one female officer at a time. You are a token female. Just like, there is only one token black officer. You are in the South. That is the way it is done. The good ole boys have issues with women. Every female before you left either being harassed or put into a position to have to performed favors to keep their jobs until they could get away. Even the call number 1610 is reserve for only women officers.

I am not the only one going through all of this. Talk to Dana Randall; she has more horror stories than I can tell you. She even went to Mayor Hanson about what is going on here. This is my last night here and I just wanted to make sure I got my personal things together. I don't plan of being back after today."

(Kelly didn't come back the next day. There was a lot of talk as to why she left so suddenly.)

The Chief said, "Good riddance to a troublemaker. She left before I had to fire her for coming up with stories. Right, Lieutenant Lester?" Lieutenant Lester grinned and winked at me. My skin felt like it was crawling with fire ants. I just looked at the two of them with a straightforward glance and went back out on the road just pondering what Kelly told me.

A few weeks passed and things seemed quiet on the graveyard shift. The chief would come out in an unmarked car at night just to see what the officers were doing. Dana Randall was dispatching that night. I only met her once but Kelly told her that she could talk to me if she had any problems. I couldn't do much to help her either but would be truthful if they decided to take the situations to another level.

I heard the chief on the police radio calling for certain officers to check out suspicious vehicles that appeared to be under the influence. He kept calling in license plates and had most of the officers tied up on calls with DUI suspects.

I was on a call reference to a shoplifter at the local IGA grocery store. The suspect hid a bottle of vodka and a six-pack of beer under his coat. I made an arrest and headed to the department to book my suspect, Leland Lee. I called into the dispatch to let her know that I was done at the scene and, as protocol, called in my mileage and that I was transporting a subject. I called several times and didn't get a response. The Horse Stomp County Sheriff Department dispatcher was listening in on our calls. She took the information and continued trying to raise Dana on the radio.

When I arrived at the department, I saw the chief's unmarked car. I brought the prisoner in the back door and put him in the cell. I walked to the dispatch office, but Dana wasn't there. Then I could hear the lock turning and the door open in the chief's office. Dana came out of his office and ran past me to the break room. The chief was looking down as I neared his office and zipping up his pants. It was obvious that I startled him.

"Damn zipper, I have to get that thing fixed. It

keeps sliding down and I am not aware of it." I didn't say anything to him but thought he should be the one to get fixed. Then he walked out of his office toward my prisoner.

"So, Loni, what do we have here?" I told him Lee was a shoplifter and I was in the process of booking him. The chief started talking to my prisoner, looked back at me and said, "When you are done booking him, let him out on his own recognizance. I am feeling charitable tonight." Then he walked out the door, got in his car and left.

I knocked on the break room door, asked Dana if she was all right. At first she didn't answer, but after a few more knocks she opened the door. The look on her face was all too familiar to me when I saw Kelly come out of the bathroom the first time I saw her. She apologized for not answering the radio and walked back up to the communication station. I booked my prisoner and released him on an O.R. bond per the chief's order. When I was done, I went to the communication station and asked her what happened. Dana looked worse than Kelly did when I first saw her upset because of Lt. Lester. Dana couldn't even answer the radio calls so I stepped in and responded to the officers' calls.

About a half an hour later, Dana told me what had happened. She said the chief had deliberately preoccupied the officers on bogus DUI calls so he could be alone with her. He called her into his office and said he had her evaluations ready and had to go over them with her. He got up and locked the door. He said he didn't want anyone to come in the department and overhear them because evaluations are a private thing. At first, he talked about the evaluations but she noticed that he didn't have the paperwork before him while talking to her. Then he told her that she could go places within the department if she continued to work hard. Then he stood up and said she had to "work as hard as this!" He then proceeded to expose himself. Dana said she freaked out and froze. She said if it was not for me coming in the door with a prisoner, she did not know what was going to happen. She told me that she was going to the mayor about the stuff going on within the department. I just told her to do what she had to do to protect herself. I went back on patrol wondering what I had gotten myself into by coming to this department.

Later that week I heard Dana had a meeting with Mayor Hanson about the chief and Lieutenant Lester. She met with the mayor and brought her mother and their attorney. I didn't see Dana for about three weeks. No one really seemed to know exactly why, but I did have a chance to ask her about it when I ran into her at the local gym.

"What happened when you went to the mayor?" I asked. She said that her attorney taped the meeting with the mayor and told him every detail of the things going on within the department. Mayor Hanson's face got red and he acted shocked. He said he would do something about the chief.

"Well, Dana, has anything changed since you

Wake Up and Die Right

---

and your attorney met the mayor?" I asked.

She said not much had changed. The chief was more nitpicky and giving her a hard time about little things like the cord to the phone being crooked and that she didn't know how to hang it up the phone properly. However, no one had confronted her about talking to the mayor.

By the end of the month, Dana said she was looking for another place to work. She couldn't handle the chief coming up from behind her, grabbing her arms, kissing her on the neck and cheek. She said she pulled away and reminded him that she would go back to the mayor's office if he didn't leave her alone to do her work. After that, anytime he came into the communication station, she would excuse herself or call for an officer to come in and watch the radio. Dana mentioned that there were times when the chief would run wants and warrants on the mayor's political opponents. She became skeptical of this when he never documented the criminal histories in the log.

Frequently he would come into the communication station and offer to give the dispatchers a break and would run inquiries for officers' requesting a driver's history while on a traffic stops. The chief would log the names down.

She made mention he was not certified on the terminal and knew that the whole department could loose their certification to even have access to the terminal if the NCIC learn he was doing that.

This morning, Chief Dispatcher Penny Applegate came into the office looking tired and a little disorientated. I asked her what happened to her and she said that she was working a lot of overtime since Kelly left and then last night Dana quit.

"Quit? Why did she quit?" *(As if, I didn't know.)*

"I don't know all the details but she got a job with another police department."

"In Horse Stomp County?" I asked.

"Yes, but I don't know how she did it when it isn't too professional to just up and quit working when you are supposed to start a shift. Someone called for references and the chief told me to give her raving recommendations," she said in an annoyed tone. "I am working all this overtime and the city won't even pay me for it!"

"Isn't that illegal?" I said abruptly.

"Sure it is, Loni, but who is going to make them pay me for it? No one!" I shook my head and told her that I had to get back out on the road. I had a split shift today and was leaving for the police academy on Monday.

I teamed up with a young officer named Benjamin Madden. He was tall and a little hefty. He had black curly hair and a baby face. He and his wife moved here from Poe County, Georgia. He was a police officer up there and wanted a little more excitement. His wife's name was Alice but she liked to be called Allie. They made such an odd couple. She was barely ninety pounds, with freckles, short dish water-blond hair with dark roots and a tight perm and not very endowed. She looked like more

Wake Up and Die Right

like his child than his wife. Allie had a deformed left hand; she told me she got it caught in her grandmother's wringer washing machine when she was five years old.

Ben was funny and loved to joke around. He was like a brother to me; we hit it off the first day. I got along great with his wife Allie. They were renting in the trailer park where Captain Barnes and his wife who were managers of the trailer park.

Frequently, when new officers moved into town needing a place to live, they would rent from the captain. Tenants would often have a block party and cookouts.

Ben, Allie and I would have a bar-b-que at their house on the weekends with our kids playing together. He loved to cook out on the grill and usually made more than he could eat. Ben often invited some of the other officers that weren't married and didn't get a home-cooked meal too regularly. I mentioned that Billy Bob loved food and thought he would enjoy a good bar-b-que.

Billy Bob accepted the invitation almost before Ben could invite him. Allie and I were setting up the yard for the kids to play some games. We made a makeshift volleyball net. Billy Bob walked over to where I was hammering wood into the ground to anchor the poles. He had a hamburger in each hand and a beer tucked in the pocket of his bib overall pants.

"Whatcha bangin into the ground?" He said with his mouth full of hamburger.

"I'm hammering a stake into the ground." He looked puzzled as he chewed faster so he could swallow to speak.

"What -cha hamm-er-in a good piece of meat into the ground for?"

I stopped what I was doing and said, "Billy Bob, I'm not hammering s-t-e-a-k in the ground, I am hammering a s-t-a-k-e in the ground!"

Billy Bob said, "I don't care how you spell it, I can worsh it, cook it and still eat it".

It took me a few minutes to clarify what I was doing. I felt like we were having an Abbott and Costello conversation about "Who's on first base, what is on second", and so on.

I left for the Police Academy just after Christmas. I had to drive into the next county every day, about forty miles one-way. I would be tired coming home after I picked up the kids from the sitter, Rowena Rodgers.

She was a police officer's wife and had two small boys of her own. I never knew her husband's real first name but everyone called him "Animal" Rodgers. Animal got the nickname because he got into a fight with a subject who got his gun from his holster one night and they were in a tussle. Animal bit the guy's earlobe right off! Thus, he got the name Animal.

Animal was a strange sort of guy. He stood six foot five inches and loved to show off his smile since he had all his teeth capped. I rode with him one night. He liked to drive and loved high-speed

Wake Up and Die Right

chases. This particular Sunday night it was boring with not much was going on. We were leaving a convenience store after drinking a couple cups of coffee to keep us awake. As we were getting into the car Animal spotted some guy in a silver Toyota Camry making an illegal u-turn where the sign was posted.

He kept yelling for me to hurry up and get in the car so he could catch him before he got onto the interstate. I barely got in the car when he put it in reverse. I hadn't quite gotten the door closed, let alone my seat belt on. As he backed the car up and pulled forward, I was still struggling to pull the door closed, but the force of gravity was going against me in doing it. Animal made the u-turn with the blue lights flashing and sirens wailing. I was still trying to pull the door closed. Just as he made the u-turn, I was pulled out of the car, with only my ankles still inside as I hung onto the door handle for dear life. I watched the blacktop pavement rush past my face as I tried to grasp a hold of the armrest. I felt my fingernails scraping across the corduroy fabric. I couldn't even get a word out as I was gasping for air while hyperventilating. Then I heard Animal start laughing as he grabbed what little of me was still inside the car. He pulled over to the side of the road and pulled me the rest of the way inside the car. I was thunderstruck for a few moments, just sitting there listening to the big oaf laughing like a hyena. A few more minutes later after he wiped the tears from his eyes, he asked if I was all right. I looked straight ahead and calmly told him to take me home. He asked me why I wanted to go home. I told him again to take me home.

Animal said, "Awe, come on, Loni, why do you want to go home? You're all right."

"No, Animal, I am not all right. If you must know, I need to go home to change my clothes," I replied.

"Change your clothes?"

I turned my head, looked straight in his eyes, and said, "If you must know that too, I wet myself after your little driving stunt!" Then the laughter really started.

"Sure, Loni, I will take you home, but I hope the seats are Scotch guarded."

That was the last time I rode with Animal, voluntarily. He kept my little secret between us. Well, only after I threatened to blackmail him by telling the rest of the department about the hooker he picked up one night.

He had arrested her for prostitution but that didn't stop him from flirting with her. Sheena was a very good-looking woman, with long blond hair, big brown eyes and pouting lips. She was tall, thin, shapely and buxom. I caught his eyes roving her long legs in her micro mini skirt. It was obvious that he was peeking at her cleavage as she leaned over the desk to sign her paperwork. I could hear Animal as he inhaled her sweet perfume as he was fingerprinting her.

He told her she had to spend the night in jail and

would go to court in the morning. He assured her she would be able to bond out at that time. Animal asked me to strip search and bag up her belongings while he did the report.

I agreed to do it but whispered in his ear, "Wouldn't you rather do the strip search?"

He had a big grin and said, "Yes, but I don't want her yelling sexual harassment. I will wait until I meet up with her sometime while I am off duty and it is a more personal atmosphere, if you know what I mean."

I escorted Sheena to the jail shower area and told her to give me her clothes so I could bag them. Sheena proceeded to take off the long wig, eyelashes. She had silicone implant breasts that where tucked into her size D bra. As she washed the makeup off, I could see a faint beginning of a five o'clock shadow. As she obliged further, when I unconditionally found out that she was really a he!

I ran out of the shower area and told Animal he had to strip search his prisoner. I told him that the little hottie that he was going to meet up with on his personal time had something more going for her than just long legs and a big bust. The grin he was wearing while writing his report disappeared. He looked at me with bewildered eyes and said, "Are you trying to tell me she is a dude?" It was my turn to laugh hysterically. All I could say was "Yep!" Animal and I never talked about that incident again, but every time I picked up my daughters from his house, he would have this nervous look if he saw me talking to his wife, but I assured him my conversation was strictly about my children.

Once I got my girls fed and spent some time with them, I would go into my room and start working on my police studies. So often, I would call Ben at eleven p.m. to help me study for tests. There were times that we were on the phone for hours, sometimes until two o'clock in the morning. We went through the laws and statutes. Allie was so sweet. She let us carry on our conversation throughout the night. Many times, I would bring her flowers for allowing me to borrow her husband to help me study. Of course, I had to drop off a six-pack of Pabst Blue Ribbon beer for Ben to show my appreciation.

On the weekend, I listened to the scanner. I heard Hanover and one of his cronies were helping the sheriff's office with a felony warrant in our city for a drug raid. Slick Rutherford jumped in on the radio and wanted to be a part of the action. For some reason the Feds were in town and were, a part of a big sting and major take down. The sheriff's office asked Hanover and Slick to cover them. Slick wanted glory, so before everyone got into position, Slick charged into the residence on Skunk Creek Road. The warrant was a no-knock warrant (*meaning the police can break down a door*).

Slick charged into the wrong house. He broke in the door from the back, screaming and yelling for everyone to hit the floor or he would shoot them. The homeowner was a ninety-two-year-old woman who kept a .22 caliber shotgun by her bed like any

Wake Up and Die Right

good Southerner. Slick and Hanover grabbed the woman and threw her to the ground, breaking not only her left arm, but as they put pressure on her upper back with their knee, Slick's knee allegedly slid down her neck as she was face down. One of her shoes was lying sideways across her throat. The pressure on her neck broke the frail woman's windpipe. Luckily, for Rutherford and Hanover, the paramedic's where standing by for the raid. They got to the elderly women in time to perform a tracheotomy before she suffocated. That was some good gossip for a good month. There was supposed to be an investigation into the matter but somehow, it just disappeared.

I regularly stopped into the police department on the weekend while I was going to the academy to say hello to the remaining dispatchers and some of the officers. I enjoyed coming in to talk to Ben and Victor Kapers and of course, Billy Bob. They always gave me pointers for passing tests at the academy.

Sergeant Francis Hanover was working the evening shift. He was a nice-looking man from a blind women's point of view. The officers nicknamed him "Fannie" because he had such an appetite for young women's backsides. Hanover had groupies following him; these women loved men in uniform. He did look somewhat debonair dressed in his blues and wearing a gold badge and rank insignias but you can't make a silk purse out of a sow's ear.

One night I was waiting for Ben to come back

into the office after answering a burglary call. I noticed Hanover and some of the other officers had a tendency to spend a lot of time in the evidence room. I asked the dispatcher on duty if there was a big bust and they were logging in evidence. She rolled her eyes and started laughing.

"You mean you don't know? Take a better look at what they are doing in there and see for yourself," she said in a sarcastic way.

I walked toward the evidence room and smelled a familiar smell. It was pot! They were in there smoking marijuana from the evidence room. Hanover came out of the room laughing. He wore a strong stench of marijuana all over him. His eyes were glaze and said he had the munchies and was going to an all-night diner to get something to eat.

"That's evidence!" I said. Hanover got up close to me and said he was just checking to see if it was the real stuff. Then he started laughing again. I heard what sounded like a beer can top open. I looked inside the evidence room and there was Officer Mannford Mauzer. He barely made the height requirements to get on the department. He looked like a troll with his large nose and excessively long hairs growing out of his ears. They were disproportionate in comparison with his beady eyes. Mauzer wore a crew cut but looked like one of those wishing troll dolls that I had as a kid. I think we called them "Wish Nicks".

Mauzer was off duty, wearing civilian clothes and drinking beer confiscated from my shoplifting case.

"That's my evidence you're drinking!" I said.

(*I am not sure how much beer Officer Mauzer had ingested, or if it was the pot, but he was three sheets to the wind when he came out of the evidence room.*)

Hanover told the other officers to leave and he would lock up the evidence room.

"What about my shoplifting case? Those guys drank my evidence."

I asked Sergeant Hanover what I was going to do about my shoplifting case since the evidence was gone. He just said, "Shit happens. If you tell anyone anything, you are the one who is going to look bad. The chief will believe me over you."

Officer Mauzer was barely able to stand next to Sergeant Hanover. Bam! Thump, thump. Mauzer fell, hitting his head on the report writing desk to his left. Hanover and Rutherford helped him up.

"You need to call the ambulance. He hit his head pretty bad," I said to Hanover. He said there was no need for that and pulled out the first aid box and put a Band-Aid over his eye to match the other band-aids on his right cheek and his left hand.

Hanover smugly said, "Now you know why we call him Mummy."

Officers were amused by his wit. Mauzer left the department to go over to Rufus Odell's house later that evening for a party. He was so wasted, that he left his weapon in Rufus' garage. Odell's thirteen-year-old stepson found Mauzer's 9 mm pistol while getting beer for Rufus and fired 18 rounds through a garage door and into a neighbor's home.

That wasn't the first time Mauzer drank so much and lost his gun. The next night while drinking in a Horse Stomp County nightclub, he left without his jacket, which contained his back up gun that was loaded. A bartender found the weapon and called the Horse Stomp County Sheriff's Office because he thought the Mauzer was to intoxicated and disruptive to give him the gun back. It turns out Mauzer never knew he was missing it until a deputy went to his house the next day to give it to him.

As I started to leave the department, an officer called on the radio, asking the sergeant to meet him at 438 Spinnaker Circle. He had a woman who wanted to make a complaint about Lieutenant Lester. I stopped to listen to the radio traffic. Things started to get interesting when they changed the radio channel to block out scanners. Only the dispatcher could hear the car-to-car conversation other than the officers.

Hanover met with the female complainant, Darlene Lawson. Lieutenant Lester had pulled her over for not making a complete stop at a stop sign just before he got off duty that night. She said he told her that the only way she was not going to jail was if she made it worth his while. Ms. Lawson said she just now got up the nerve to say anything as to what had happened. She told Hanover, "He propositioned me. I refused! Then he frisked me and put me in the patrol car as he went through my purse looking for my identification. I had over eight hundred dollars in my pocket book to pay my rent tomorrow and now it is gone!"

According to the dispatch logs, Lieutenant Lester didn't call a traffic stop into the dispatcher for that area. She said he didn't write a ticket nor book her. Lawson said he let her out of the car and gave her a verbal warning. She didn't notice the money was missing until she got to the Winn Dixie grocery store ten minutes later to buy the money order for her rent. Ms. Lawson said she looked through her car to make sure the money hadn't fallen out. She was adamant that Lester was the last person who had her purse.

I left the department and met up with Ben and Victor at the local Denny's parking lot. They were listening to the call from the young officer.

As I pulled up, I heard Victor say, "Another one bites the dust."

He was referring to Lieutenant Lester. I told them, "That's nothing; let me tell you what happened with Sergeant Hanover and Officer Mauzer". I filled them in on the raid of the evidence room and asked, "What will this do to my case?"

Kapers said it was not the fist time a case was dropped because evidence was destroyed or missing. "That is the way the good ole boys play at a Southern police department," he said, shrugging his shoulders.

I told Kapers and Ben that I couldn't just let them ruin my cases. "I got the guy dead to rights! It was a good arrest," I nobly said to them. "They can't keep getting away with the things that they do. I need to call someone, but who isn't corrupt in this department?"

Kapers answered by saying, "That isn't a good idea. Didn't anyone tell you? Officers' home phones are tapped. Nothing is personal within the Crestview Police Department. They will use what they can against you and for them. If they can't find anything, they will make it up as they go," he said.

Kapers told me about Bubba Bansheer. "He works at a small, privately owned phone company and is the one who puts the clips on the phone lines for the police department or for anyone with money. I overheard Chief Jones on the phone with Bansheer. He said that he owed him another favor and wanted to get some stuff on the mayor. That meant burning the mayor. I am sure he tapped the mayor's phone. That's how he found out Mayor Hanson was gay. He was setting up a rendezvous with one of his lovers. I think the chief is blackmailing him."

Kapers didn't go into much detail but he said he knew the chief was also blackmailing Bubba. Bansheer was a divorced, single father of two. He had custody of his teenagers, fifteen-year-old son Beau and fourteen-year-old daughter, Beverly. It seemed that Bubba liked a couple of Beverly's girlfriends. One of Beverly's friends gave birth to a little boy about a year ago. The chief called Bubba into his office based solely on his suspicions as to who the father may be. Bubba couldn't handle the confronta-

Wake Up and Die Right

tion and admitted being the father of the child. Now he was in debt to the chief, tapping phones (*without a warrant*) any time the chief wanted one. He had him taping the mayor's phone so he could try to find something where as he has control over the mayor. Jones knew that the mayor wanted to get rid of his fat ass, especially with all the complaints from the dispatchers. Chief Jones was looking for some job security. He wasn't going to tolerate a gay mayor having control over him for much longer.

Sometimes Ben and I would talk on the phone and the next day it seemed that everyone knew what we had talked about that day. That was when I believed Kapers was right about the phones being tapped. Chief Jones smugly asked me about a certain relative that I had talked to that week. He didn't hide the fact he was recording conversations and that it was Bubba who was doing it. Chief Jones took pride in bragging about his connections with certain individuals to get information. He liked being a name-dropper.

From that time forward, Ben and I would use code to talk on the phone, to throw off potential snitches. We worked out a certain code to meet at the Circle K but it was really to meet behind McDonald's across the street so we can watch who went to the Circle K looking for us. I learned a lot that weekend.

Monday morning I went back to the academy. It was the last week of training before graduation. Starting Wednesday, we had preparation for three nights. Each police department put their cadet officers up at the Gator Inn Hotel down the street from the academy.

I didn't care much for the instructor Festus Peabody. Kapers told me to beware of him because he was very tight with the chief.

Our class had about thirty officers from different cities within a hundred-mile radius. They divided the class up. Half of us went to the firing range for night shoot. The other half went to the felony night traffic stops. I noticed that I was the only female within the group for traffic stops. When it was my turn, I demonstrated the proper procedure for a traffic stop and made a simulated suspect arrest. The training assistant, McCoy, was assigned to role-play as the suspect in my traffic stop. Prior to each traffic stop, the instructor gave their assistant a scenario for the suspect to act out.

In this case, I disarmed him of a weapon on his ankle and a knife in his boot. As I handcuffed him, I continued my search and found that he had yet another small caliber weapon in the crotch of his pants. I informed Instructor Peabody that there was a gun in the crotch of Officer McCoy's pants. He told me to get it! From that point, I assumed that it was a test to see what I would do. I informed him that the suspect was handcuff, I was not in danger, my partner was in route to me and he would retrieve the gun. Peabody sternly told me to reach into McCoy's pants and get the gun. I told him that I refused to do it because I knew it was a ploy to embarrass me in front of the other officers. I continued my simulated arrest and put McCoy in the back of the patrol car. The vehicle front seat were pulled all the way back so far that McCoy's knees were up against his chin; therefore, he couldn't have access to the weapon with his hands cuffed behind his back and to his belt.

Peabody became angry with me and said, "Your partner isn't coming. Put your hands down his pants and get the gun!"

I became incensed. I thought about the things that were going on within my police department and I blurted out, "We're both police officers. I did a good search. If it was a real life or death situation I would not have hesitated to get the gun."

At this point, Instructor Peabody said he was going to kick me out of the academy. I leaned over and whispered into Officer McCoy's ear.

"I am onto you and Peabody's little game. If I am forced to put my hand in your pants, I promise that my finger will find its way to the trigger of the alleged concealed weapon. Even though the gun has blanks, we both know that there will be sparks that shoot out of the pistol and you may feel a burning sensation."

McCoy started sweating and loudly blurted out, "It was a good search. I am in no way capable of getting to the weapon that is hidden in my pants." Peabody was enraged!

When we took a break, I immediately called the Crestview Police Department and asked for Victor

Kapers. Penny Applegate answered the phone and told me that Victor had been promoted to Detective. After a few minutes of conversation as to what was going on at the academy, Kapers gave the phone to Captain Barnes. Kapers said the captain had more influence than he had. Barnes told me to continue with all my classes unless he told me something different. He said that Instructor Peabody didn't have the final authority to kick me out of the academy. My throat was dry and I could barely swallow from nerves, but I did as the captain said.

I went back to my hotel room to relax after a stressful evening. There was a knock at the door and one of the role-players, a Georgia State Trooper, was leaning up against the doorway. He stood almost seven feet tall and was skeletal looking. He told me Peabody sent him to my room and thought I'd be receptive to some company.

I looked at him and said, "What kind of company were you expecting?"

He looked like a Cheshire cat and said, "The only kind that is fun".

I didn't bat an eye before I spun him around and told him to get his ass out of my room. I immediately got on the phone again trying to call the captain. When I couldn't get a hold of him, I called Ben and Kapers. They told me to hang in there. Since it didn't work as Peabody was expecting, I shouldn't let my guard down.

I was sitting on pins and needles. I worried that I was going to be kicked out of the academy for

Wake Up and Die Right

---

some sexist thing. I went to class the next morning as if nothing had happened. Peabody just gave me a dirty look, but didn't say anything to me. He tried to avoid eye contact. At break, I called the captain and asked him what was going on. He told me to relax; everything would be all right. Peabody thought I would be upset enough to leave that day, in which case I could have been kicked out of the academy. It didn't work, but he wasn't going to let some long-legged female win a battle without another sneak attack.

News about how my day had gone spread like wildfire back at Crestview Police Department. There was something going on in town that was even more interesting than my perils. The gossip was about the city engineer, Casey Long.

Casey was cocky and flamboyant. He thought very highly of Mayor Hanson. So much that there were rumors of them being lovers.

He had been missing for almost a week when his body was located in Tallahassee, Florida near a swamp. I stopped by the police department over the weekend after I read about the Leon County Sheriff Department finding Casey's body. Our office was working with Florida to help solve the case. We were given copies of the crime scene photos. Victor was doing some investigation into the case and learned that prior to Casey missing; he'd had a deep argument with Mayor Hanson.

When looking at the photos, it was obvious Casey had been beaten systematically. Tire tracks from a pickup truck indicated someone ran over his head a couple of times until it was mush. He was also shot in the groin and a baseball bat was shoved up his rectum. Victor said the murder looked like a personal vendetta. Perhaps there was more to Casey and the mayor's relationship. On the other hand, this could be the something the chief had on the mayor for job security.

There was a rumor that the mayor's phone conversations were intercepted, supposedly by accident, when his cell phone discussion was picked up by the police radio. On the other hand, Chief Jones could have received a little help from Bubba Bansheer.

Everyone knew the mayor was a homosexual even though he was married and had two sons. No one dared come out in the open and say it to his face. After all, he was running for governor in the next up coming election. We all knew his marriage was for show because he wanted to go high into politics like his father before him.

The former Mayor Hanson senior had a well-known homosexual reputation also. In most cities, homosexuality is accepted, but things are much different in a bible belt like Georgia. They are so behind on the times. Unfortunately, for Mayor Hanson Senior, he was found dead and naked, thirteen years earlier. He was discovered lying on top of a little more than forty thousand dollars cash in the trunk of his car. His murder was never solved.

Former Dispatcher Kelly Nelson called me that

Wake Up and Die Right

weekend and wanted to meet me somewhere since she didn't trust the phone lines. We talked about Casey Long. She told me that she knew there was something between Casey and the mayor for some time. She saw Casey a week before he went missing. He confided in her that they had been lovers but the mayor dumped him so he could run for governor. The Hanson told him it would be political suicide for him to have a homosexual relationship.

Casey revealed to Kelly he was in love with Mayor Hanson and his heart was broken when he dumped him for power and money. Out of anger, Casey said he told the mayor he was going to tell his wife that they were in love and go as far as tell a newspaper reporter who was covering the mayors political career.

(*He knew the mayor's wife was well aware of Hanson's homosexuality. Especially since her pregnancy was artificially inseminated due to Hanson's dislike for women. The mayor's father paid her handsomely to keep up the charade of a happily married couple.*)

Kelly said Casey's biggest mistake was when he threatens to go to the newspapers about their affair. He told her the mayor was furious and said something to the effect that he would not live long enough to tell anyone. The next thing Kelly knew, Casey was dead.

She said she never told anyone but me because it was no one's business but Casey's and, of course, the mayor's relationship. Now Casey's murder changed everything.

I asked, "Why are you saying anything now?" Kelly said she had started getting calls from the chief all of a sudden. The phone calls were not the same as before. She said he was taking an interest in Casey and wanted to know what Casey told her before he went missing.

"How does he know that you saw him before he went missing?" I asked. She said she saw Penny Applegate the day she was having lunch with Casey. Penny started playing super sleuth and calling her when the chief and Lester couldn't get anything from her. Kelly thought Jones and Lester figured she would open up to her former supervisor. She said the calls started some time after the funeral.

Kelly mentioned that Penny was asking questions like "Do you think the mayor killed Casey? You should talk to the police."

Kelly said she told Penny she didn't know anything and she wasn't going to stay around town to find out, let alone be in the middle of it.

"I am leaving sooner than I planned. I am getting out of here before I am next to end up dead for knowing too much. Next week I am getting married to a military man and moving to Colorado," she said excitedly I asked her why she wouldn't want to go to the police to solve Casey's murder.

Kelly responded, "Yeah, as if Georgia's Key Stone Cops are going to make a case against the mayor when they have two detectives that are nothing more than dope head drunks trying to solve a homosexual's murder. That is a laugh!"

I knew she was right. Everyone in Horse Stomp County was afraid of the mayor for some reason. Casey's death made matters uncomfortable when anyone had to meet with Hanson.

I went back to the academy in preparation for graduation. Surprisingly, I made it! I was now a certified Georgia police officer and one that knew too much when it came to the department. Kelly Nelson's words "end up dead for knowing too much" kept going through my head. I wasn't sure if I was more afraid of the Crestview Police Department or Mayor Hanson.

Ben and I were teamed up as partners. Our first call was an officer needing back up with a DUI suspect who pulled a gun on Animal and Detective Kapers at exit 62 off Highway I-95. A half an hour earlier there was a high-speed drag race approaching 100 miles per hour. According to one of the Horse Stomp County deputies, the actual speed may have been closer to 120.

It turned out to be two off-duty Crestview police officers implicated as the perpetrators. While a sheriff's deputy was on patrol on the I-95 Highway, the deputy spotted two vehicles barreling down the highway at a high rate of speed. One vehicle stopped prior to exiting the off ramp. He was later was identified as Detective Archibald Riddle of the Crestview Police Department.

When we arrived, I could see Animal had blocked the other car off from leaving and was on the loud speaker trying to talk to the suspect. Weapons were drawn. I couldn't get a good look at the black male as Ben and I tried to maneuver our way behind the suspect. The closer we got I realized I knew the assailant. It was the department's senior detective, Rufus Odell.

He was intoxicated and barely able to stand up. Animal was talking to him as Rufus was flailing around with his weapon. Odell's unmarked patrol car was embedded in a streetlight. Hel was cussing and staggering around the car. Kapers jumped him and knocked him to the ground and Animal cuffed him. Odell didn't appear to have any injuries and refused treatment from the rescue unit on the scene. He was transported to the police department where Kapers ran him on the new, updated Intoximeter. At first, he refused to blow into the tube but later changed his mind and blew a point thirty grams percent. That was almost four times higher than the legal limit.

As for Archibald Riddle, he just received a citation for speeding and drag racing on the interstate. The deputy didn't test him for DUI since our department already had the embarrassment of one detective under the influence and possible aggravated assault on police officers. The chief was hot under the collar when a citizen who was listening on the scanner, called Mayor Hanson out to the scene.

It was obvious Archie had been drinking prior to his drag race with Rufus. The chief ordered Archie and Rufus to go through mandatory detox for alco-

Wake Up and Die Right

holism. However, things were going to be handled a little differently for Archie and his racing partner.

We thought for sure they were going to lose their certification as police officers. Aggravated assault on four police officers, trying to leave the scene of an accident and a DUI on top of all of that, is pretty serious charges compared to just speeding and drag racing. To my surprise (*no one else's*), it didn't happen. The NAACP showed up while Rufus was sitting in the (*dog cage*) cell. Everyone at the department acted as though they were walking on eggshells. The Crestview Police Department was scared to death of the NAACP.

(*This was because the department had a well-documented history of being overly zealous when arresting people of color for no legal reason.*)

I am not sure what happened but Rufus never went to jail other than when they first brought him to the department. He kept his job. He was not placed on suspension for his actions.

Rufus had his own blackmail list on the upper echelon to get away with aggravated assault. He was just one more person on the department that no one could touch. Surely, he, along with the lieutenant and chief, had something on the mayor to be able to get away with such blatant disregard for the law.

There was something strange about Rufus Odell. I am not sure what the qualifications was to become a detective at that time he was promoted, but I know something just was not right with him. Besides the obvious drinking and pointing a gun at his co-workers.

I turned in a report about a burglary for him to investigate and he would call me into his office to tell him what was in my report instead of just reading it. This happened every time a report was turned in and he was assigned to the case.

I noticed that Victor Kapers worked most of the cases lately. I told him I was getting frustrated about being pulled off the road to come into the office to go over my reports.

"Are my reports written that badly?" I asked. "Everything was already in the report for him to start his investigation."

Kapers started laughing and said, "I forgot, you are pretty new around here and don't know."

"Don't know what?" I asked.

"Rufus is illiterate."

"What are you talking about? How could he go through the police academy and be promoted to detective if he can't read?" I said with bewilderment in my voice.

"Officer Chekov, Detective Odell can read just enough to fake it. His police certification is grandfathered into effect. That is why he hasn't gone to any other department."

"So what you are telling me is when he calls me into the office to go over my report it's because he can't read it?"

"Yes, you got it." he said.

I just looked at him and had to ask, "Does everyone in the department know this?"

Wake Up and Die Right

Kapers sighed and said, "That is how it is here, Svetlana. You have three things going against you. One, you are a Yankee. Two, you are a woman. Three, your name is foreign. You will be under a microscope and no matter what you do, it will not be good enough because that is how the 'Good Ole Boys' do it."

I was thunderstruck for a moment, and then asked, "You're not from Horse Stomp County, are you?"

"Nope," he said in a slow Southern drawl. "I'm from the South but a lot further north."

"Well, Detective Kapers, are there any more like Rufus Odell? I mean, grandfathered as police officers?"

"As a matter of fact, one other, Archibald Riddle.

"Another detective?" I said. "What are the requirements to become a detective?"

Kapers chuckled and said, "Archibald Riddle is known for his drinking on duty and driving a patrol car as well. He and Sergeant Hanover take turns drinking up the evidence. One day last week there was a DUI bust and the suspects had a couple of large bottles of vodka. Riddle and Handover drank themselves silly, then filled the bottles with water and put them back in the evidence room. Rufus went in the evidence room, took home the same bottles, and found out that they were filled with water. Boy was he livid!"

I tried to do my job, but I found that Kapers was

right about the three things going against me. I was constantly rib for the way I talked, but some of the things they said didn't make any sense to me either.

Captain Barnes' sidekick, Lieutenant Jimmy Jack, asked me to go out to the car and get a crack pipe out of the "pocket of the car" that he confiscated from a transient. I was looking inside the doors where the pockets were and I couldn't find the crack pipe anywhere. I told him that I couldn't find it. He asked me where I was looking for it.

I told him, "In the pockets of the car doors"

He sternly said in such a twang, that I just couldn't take him seriously, "Y'all ain't from around herea, are ya? The pocket of the car is over herea." Then he opened the glove compartment.

"The glove department! Why didn't you just say the glove department?" I asked.

He snorted then turned around and as he started walking away, he said, "Y'all have a lot of learnin to do. Women dun't belong on the streets. You must be one of them les-beans to want a man's job."

I sarcastically responded by asking him what a "les-bean" was. Then I realized I really made him mad when he called me a dumb bitch. I understood the words that were coming out of his nasty mouth. I didn't like it, but I understood it. It was obvious where this was going so I just backed off my snide remarks.

Ben and I went back out on the road. He couldn't believe that I was so brazen to say something like that to Lieutenant Jack. Actually, I was

Wake Up and Die Right

surprised that I said anything like that to him. It just seemed to flow out of my mouth. We laughed about it and completed our shift.

The next evening was a Sunday. It was just getting dark when Ben and I were coming into work, and we passed the Banister Chevy Dealership on Tater Street. I watched as a dark figure in dark clothes walked around the closed dealership looking into the vehicles, a black Corvette in particular. I told Ben that I had a strong feeling we were going to have a stolen car tonight. I couldn't wait for roll call to get over with so we could stake out the car lot.

Roll call had some interesting passed-down information. Sergeant Hanover said one of the local beauty shops in the Ferguson Square Mall had a broken window. He described it as a hole a BB gun shot out the size of a rolled-up newspaper. He said to patrol the area because there was no contact number to notify the owner.

The next pass-down information was cocaine missing from the evidence locker. It was the major cocaine bust where Detectives Archie Riddle and Rufus Odell made the arrests six months ago. The department had some concerns as to what they were going to tell the court when in a week Riddle and Odell needed to produce the evidence for trial since the suspects wouldn't take a plea offer.

As Ben and I left the squad room, Ben said, "I wonder who is going to explain to the judge how cocaine is missing from the police department? It isn't like you can replace it with talcum powder or, like Hanover, replace vodka with water and still make a case."

I responded, "I remember when Archie made that big bust. Rufus was trying so hard to jump in and take some of the credit. Since he couldn't write, he had to rely on Archie to put his name on the police reports when Archie thought it was convenient to have him listed as a witness. There were bags of cocaine scattered all over the squad room that day when they were taking inventory."

Ben said, "Yeah, I remember it too. One of the bags had a hole in it and some cocaine got on the countertop and good ole Archie brushed it with his hand; then I watched him act like he had the sniffles and was going to sneeze but inhaled what was on his hand."

I replied, "You saw that too, huh?

Ben and I got into our vehicles after roll call and decided to go out toward the Ferguson Square Mall to see how the window was holding up. When we got there, I didn't see the newspaper-sized hole. I didn't even see a hole, but did see some glass on the ground. So Ben and I got out of our patrol cars to take a better look.

Ben spoke up and said, "No wonder you didn't see a newspaper-sized hole, the whole window is gone!"

I told Ben I was going to step inside the window and see if I could find something with the owner's name on it to notify her of the broken window. I

Wake Up and Die Right

---

stepped over the huge picture window glass pane. On the east wall there was a business license hung up over a workstation. It had the name of Denise Connor. I saw the roll-a-dex on the receptionist's desk and took a chance that Ms. Connor's name would be in there. Sure enough it was. I called her. She said she lived about an hour away but would be en-route. I let her know that I couldn't stand by that long but would frequently cruise by her business to ensure no one went inside. She agreed to meet me in an hour unless I was on a call.

As Ben and I left the small hair salon, I told Ben I was going to head over to Banister Chevy. He said he would head that way too, but to run radar. It was about time for the bars to close; traffic would be heading north from Florida and we could catch some deweys.

He got set up to run radar about a block from the dealership. He said he could see the car lot from where he parked. As I was heading toward him to run radar, he called me on the radio.

"What kind of car were you looking for?" he said

"A black Corvette, why?" I replied.

Ben got back on the radio and said, "I just saw a black Corvette coming off the dirt road at a high rate of speed and heading this way. He is just south of Banister's Chevrolet."

The adrenaline was building up as I neared the dealership and noticed the black Corvette was missing from the lot. As soon as I told Ben it was gone, a black Corvette pulled out in front of me. I didn't know if it was the same car, but I was going to follow it. As I followed, it picked up speed. Ben locked the speed in at sixty-five miles per hour in a thirty-five zone.

He yelled into the radio, "We have PC (*probable cause*) to stop the vehicle for speeding."

I sped up to get closer to the vehicle to see if there was a license plate. As I got close enough I could see that it was a Banister Chevrolet temporary dealership plate. I can remember calling into the radio to Ben "BINGO!" I turned on my blue lights and siren; then there was a high-speed chase.

"1610 Crestview, I am in pursuit. 10/80!" Ben acknowledged that I was in a high-speed chase with the Corvette. He radioed that he will be in pursuit as well.

The subject had no intentions of stopping. He put the pedal to the floor and shot past four cars in a matter of minutes. I was having trouble catching him in a four-year-old Crown Victorian. He crossed the state line and went over a hill. By the time I got over the crest, the Corvette was on the side of the road, the doors were open, and no one was around. He had run out of gas and ran on foot.

"1610, Crestview, I got the vehicle stopped one mile over the state line, requesting backup."

Lieutenant Lester and Sergeant Hanover were listening to the chase on the scanner. Florida units offered the use of their dogs to catch the driver. I called into the station.

Wake Up and Die Right

"1610, Crestview I have a stolen vehicle, a 10/99 vehicle."

The dispatcher came back. "Crestview, 1610... I doesn't show that there was a car stolen on my pewter."

I was frustrated and replied, "Crestview, it was stolen out of the Banister Chevrolet car lot and I chased it into Florida".

The dispatcher came back by saying, "Crestview 1610, Lieutenant Jack and Sgt Hanover said no assistance is needed by Florida cuz we haz no proof the car was stolen."

I was so agitated that I had to take a couple of deep breaths. The Florida trooper laughed. He said he would help me get the Corvette back to Georgia and called a wrecker; my dispatcher had radioed me and said since there was no proof it was stolen, I could not get a wrecker. I told the dispatcher to send a wrecker and I would pay for it myself if the car turned out not to be stolen.

While waiting for the wrecker, I started to inventory the vehicle. I noticed several twelve-packs of soda and at least twenty keys to cars with Banister Chevrolet tags on them. When we got the vehicle back to Banister's I started looking around the lot. I found the door open to the main office and it had been ransacked. It looked like we also had a burglary. The dispatcher contacted the owner, Bobby Joe Banister; he came out to the scene.

Detective Kapers was called out to process the scene. He had to drive at least sixty miles one-way to come back downtown. He wasn't on call or duty; it was Archie and Rufus who lived two blocks away and were on call, but they couldn't even talk on the phone after having a bar-b-que party at Rufus's house. Archie had his wife drive him to the Banister's dealership. He got out of the car. His eyes were glassy and he kept sniffling.

Ben grinned as he looked over at me and said, "I bet I know where that missing cocaine went."

When Detective Kapers arrived on the scene, he said he had things under control and Ben and I could go back on patrol. That is when I got a call from the dispatcher to meet Denise Connor at the beauty salon.

Ben and I both arrived about the same time. Ms. Connor was hysterical. She was visibly upset and said she knew who did this to her store. I pulled out my note pad and proceeded to ask her questions as to why she thought she knew who broke out her front window. She had such conviction in her voice and eyes when she said it was Francis Hanover! I asked her if she was sure. She said she had no doubt in her mind. I was hesitant to tell her Sergeant Hanover found the window broken. At that time, the hole was not as big as it was now.

She said, "It was him all right! He came around here yesterday, hitting up the small business owners to buy his security system and staff. I refused him on the spot. When I did, he told me that without his system, someone could break my storefront window and mess things up. He did it!"

Wake Up and Die Right

Ben and I were trying to calm her down because she felt the whole department was in on sabotaging her place of business. She demanded a police report in the next day or two for her insurance company. I told her it would be complete within three days. That gave me time to write it and my supervisor to review it.

I put everything in the report as she stated. I tried to stay neutral while writing the report, but we are taught to write the witness's statements and that is what I did. Ms. Connor handed me a Marlboro cigarette butt that had been flicked inside her store. She had cleaned the floors before closing. The butt was sandwiched between some broken glass. To me this meant the person who broke the window left the cigarette butt inside of the business when it had the newspaper-sized hole and the rest of the window was broken after the butt was thrown inside.

DNA wasn't that well known at the time this happened, but if it was I don't think the person who left it behind as a calling card would have done so, especially if he was a police officer.

The next afternoon, Ben and I got a call at home; we were ordered to go to Chief Jones' office. He wanted to discuss our reports in reference to the beauty salon. Unexpectedly, we both got third-degree interrogations by Archibald Riddle and Rufus Odell. They accused us of setting up Francis Hanover. No matter what I said or did, they managed to turn it around. Rufus started questioning me about my reasoning behind the vendetta to get

Hanover. I had no idea what they were talking about, but that didn't matter to them. Rufus said he thought it was because of the young woman who accused the sergeant of "rape" in his patrol car while he was in uniform. He felt I was siding with the victim.

(That caught me by surprise! Odell was telling me how I was out to get revenge on Hanover for raping some poor woman and I learned about the whole thing just then from him.)

What I didn't know was how it fit in with the fact I knew he was trying to start his own security business. He had been soliciting some of the businesses the day before the incident involving Denise Connor's window. Some of the other businesses within the Ferguson Square Mall confirmed that the sergeant was really pushing his security company. While he was on duty, they said the sergeant was almost threatening them saying something would happen if they didn't buy into his company called "Extreme Security".

Odell didn't seem very interested in that bit of information in my report. It was amazing how Odell started out interrogating us, and then virtually told us all about a young woman whose vehicle broke down off the highway. How she and a friend were waiting for a wrecker to come and tow her car to the nearest garage. Hanover pulled up and offered to stand by as she waited for Schakelford Towing. He then invited the women to sit in the patrol car to keep warm since it was getting cold out. The young woman, who later was known as Willow Smith, took Hanover up on his offer while her friend decided not to get in his patrol car.

Hanover mentioned that he had to patrol Cat Tail Swamp area and asked Willow to go with him. She agreed and they left her friend behind. Apparently, they engaged in sex. According to Sergeant Hanover, it was consensual and according to Ms. Smith's attorney, he forced himself on her. The attorney demanded a police report be made and some disciplinary action if not criminal charges on Sergeant Hanover.

Ben and I told Rufus that a vendetta was the farthest thing from the truth.

"First, everything we put in our reports was what Ms. Connor and the other merchants told us and we reported it as such. Since he was the detective, it was his job to investigate and figure out "who done it". Second, not knowing all the facts about Sergeant Hanover allegedly raping someone (*at least until he told us*) I would be inclined to believe Willow Smith," I said sternly.

Ben and I left the office to go back home as Rufus just stood there looking at us dubiously as he pondered whether he told us too much.

That day, court was session in the Horse Stomp County Courthouse on Archie's big major drug bust. Things started to get elating. Ben and I just started the day shift when we were pulled off the road again to go on another special detail. This time it was because the district attorney wanted the cocaine as evidence in court. We were told to deliver it since Archie and Rufus had conveniently forgotten it. I knew this was going to be enlivening when Archibald Riddle had to explain that most of the twelve pounds of cocaine he had in the evidence locker was gone.

(Transporting that large amount of cocaine required two officers. Well, I was going to cover my ass in the event Archie acted surprised that it was not all there.)

We checked out the cocaine from the evidence room and had the proper chain of custody to transfer it to court. Ben was yakking all the way to the courthouse, laughing and saying how he couldn't wait to see the look on the judge's face when they saw that there were only four and a half pounds of cocaine left. This was the biggest drug bust in the history of Crestview Police Department at that time. In fact, it was the biggest single bust in Horse Stomp County. We were curious as to why Ben and I were pulled off the road to deliver the cocaine. Not that we mind getting out of the city limits but we all knew someone was going down for this and we felt perhaps we where being set up by the chief or Hanover.

Just as we were pulling up to the courthouse, I saw the district attorney swiftly walking toward us as he took long strides in his steps. The look on his face was haunting. The veins were popping out on his neck and forehead. His nostrils flared and he was snorting as he took each step.

Ben looked at me and said, "It looks like we don't have to tell him about the five and a half pounds of missing drugs."

District Attorney Fletcher walked up to us and said, "Take it back, at least what is left of it! Make sure it is under lock and key until the GBI (*Georgia Bureau of Investigations*) has a chance to investigate the Crestview Police Department!"

Ben said, "Then you know?"

Fletcher bellowed, "I knew about the shortage but what really was the icing on the cake — it turns out Archibald Riddle is not a certified officer and can't take out a felony warrant, let alone make a felony arrest! The department thought Archie was grandfathered into the department even though he had been certified some twenty years earlier. What they overlooked was the fact that he had a separation from law enforcement for more than ten years and had no more arrest powers than John Q. Citizen would have. Riddle will have to go back through part of the police academy to get his certification."

District Attorney Fletcher went on to say, "It didn't even help with Detective Rufus Odell on the case because he couldn't read the police reports to refresh his memory of the case. It was obvious that he was not even there! Drunk or sober! So go on, get out of here, take what's left of the so-called 'evidence' and sign it over to the Horse Stomp Sheriff's Office!"

Ben looked over at me as DA Fletcher walked away and grinned. "They can't blame us for this one, now can they?" He said smugly.

The sheriff's office was just behind the courthouse. We brought the cocaine inside and asked for their evidence custodian. The sheriff was standing next to the receptionist desk and walked over to us.

"How are y'all doing today," he said with a political smile. Ben spoke up and told him what District Attorney Fletcher told us to do and why. The sheriff's smile got bigger and he mentioned that he was wondering how long it would be before the GBI would be investigating our department. I think he was pleased with the fact the mayor would be getting involved in this mess, he and the sheriff were political rivals.

Mayor Hanson used what ever he could against the sheriff when one of his own deputies was under investigation. The sheriff thought he was hitting below the belt by bringing out something that he himself was not responsible. Mayor Hanson fought vicious when it came to politics and the sheriff learned from the best. Now it was the mayor's turn to know how it feels, especially since the sheriff is hoping Hanson's association with Casey Long's disappearance will go public, but this will have to do for now.

Ben said; he told the sheriff that we don't know anything we just work there. The sheriff's smile got bigger and said he understood it is a bit of an embarrassment on the department.

After we signed over the cocaine to the sheriff's office, Ben couldn't help start laughing again. He

Wake Up and Die Right

---

laughed so much; he had me stop at a convenience store so he could go to the bathroom. While I was rubbing my jaws from laughing along with him, I decided to get a fountain drink at the back of the store when I saw Officer Slick Rutherford come inside the store wearing civilian clothes. He and Ben used to work at the same police department in Poe County, Georgia. Slick was hired on at the Horse Stomp County Sheriff Office before coming to the Crestview PD. That was just after Deputy Willie Niles's arrest.

Slick was a roly-poly, nerdy-looking guy and another one with his belly hung over his belt, wore military issue style glasses.

(*Ben and I called them birth control glasses, because no one in their right mind would have sex with him, hence the name.*)

Every department has a "Barney Fife" and he was the Crestview's Fife, only more sinister. Everything outwardly about him was just like the character on *The Andy Griffith Show*. The way he would pull up his belt and sniff while distorting his face. For some reason he fancied himself as a super sleuth. I leaned back against the counter and watch Rutherford in action. He loved to flirt with the clerks (*even though he was a married man*) by giving some cock and bull stories how the department couldn't do anything without him. He went on to talk about some news article in the paper about Deputy Willie Niles and said he (*Rutherford*) was working undercover but acted before the top brass gave him clearance. He has to face a minimal punishment, in other words an official slap on the hand. He told the clerk that he didn't notify the right authorities fast enough.

I knew he was the real crook. Then Ben came out of the bathroom. Rutherford looked startled and stopped talking. I walked up to the clerk to pay for my drink.

"What is this you are talking about Willie Niles?" I asked as I was sipping my drink. He reached for a paper in the newsstand next to the door.

"Here, read it in today's paper for yourself", he said smugly.

I paid for the newspaper. I got back into the car and told Ben to drive while I read the article. As I read it aloud to Ben, he was getting irritated. ***The headline was <u>Officer's Drug Money Theft</u>. The article read, "An investigation of the Horse Stomp County Sheriff's Office with then Deputy Slick Rutherford's involvement in the theft of 'drug money' has been completed. District Attorney Nichols is considering taking action against the Horse Stomp County deputies.***

"Rutherford was suspended with pay for his alleged involvement in the incident. Lieutenant Lester of the Crestview Police Department conducted the 'internal affairs investigation' for the Horse Stomp County Sheriff's Office. His findings were kept secret until testifying to the grand jury.

Wake Up and Die Right

"During a January 15ᵗʰ 1988 theft trial of former Deputy Willie Niles, Rutherford admitted that he withheld the cash from the any law enforcement agency, which he found along a dirt road after a high-profile traffic stop in which drugs where suspected was made by Rutherford. Nothing was found on the suspects or in their vehicle and subjects were sent on their way.

"Rutherford admitted to taking at least $30,000 in cash in a plain plastic bag lying by the side of the road after a traffic stop. Rutherford stated to authorities he was working as a self-appointed undercover agent for the Sheriff's Department to catch "bad cops".

"Later at the Horse Stomp County Sheriff Department, Rutherford said he asked Willie Niles, he found the money and asked what he though they should do with it. Rutherford said Niles recommended they keep the money in which Rutherford testified they did.

"March 10, 1988, Superior Court Judge Snodling agreed with the District Attorney Nichols to give Deputy Rutherford immunity from criminal prosecution to testify against Deputy Willie Niles. Rutherford has since been hired as an officer for the Crestview Police Department after tension between deputies at the sheriff's department and himself.

"Defense attorneys for Niles fought assiduously against the prosecution after Assistant District Attorney Kyle Cavenal filed a motion for

amnesty because Rutherford's testimony is 'crucial' in the trial against Deputy Willie Niles."

"Ben, that little weasel set up Willie! He was the one boasting how he got away with a little over $95,000 not $30,000! I knew he got suspended from the Sheriff's Office but I had no idea he was still getting paid and managed to conveniently leave the Sheriff's Office and get hired onto our department after he testified," I said angrily.

"So he was the one the newspaper was talking about. This month's article is the first time the papers actually gave names, replied Ben."

Ben told me that while he was on the Poe PD, he worked side by side with Slick. Ben best described Slick as "the biggest brown noser to the brass". For some reason he was well liked by them, probably for being a snitch. Ben said that when Slick left Poe County, he was under investigation for furnishing drugs to a female inmate. Poe County deputies served a search warrant at his home but Slick had already moved out and only his former roommate and fellow officer still living at that address was arrested.

Phone records showed Slick had at least two-hundred collect phone calls coming from the jail to his house. Of course, Slick's name was not on the phone bill. His roommate had to take the fall for that too. Even though the calls were recorded from the jail, they couldn't distinguish if it was Slick talking to the girls.

"Aw, come on, Ben, you would think that in this

day and age, forensics could identify his voice," I said.

Ben responded by saying, "The best I can figure, I don't think anyone believed it was he who was having sex with the female inmates for drugs".

Ben cringed and shook his body as if he had touched something gross. He went on to say there were no real names used for the phone calls and none of the inmates would testify against him, so they could only charge the roommate.

"Poor investigation if you ask me," I said.

Ben thought it seemed strange that he got away with all that and bounced from one police department to another with no aftermath. For some reason Georgia police department heads kept hiring him. He was totally useless as an officer, but great as a crook and as a yes man! Someone was working overtime covering up.

(*Now he is at our department and very tight with Lester and Hanover two of at least twelve biggest crooks that wear a badge!*)

"Ben, I heard rumors; Hanover has done some dabbling into fraudulent schemes. He was in charge of some National Police Group and was withdrawing funds and making purchases of fifteen thousand dollars for his personal use from a bank account of the Georgia Chapter of the National Association of Field Training Officers. They made him the treasurer. The investigation lasted for five months and all he got was unpaid administrative leave. He doctored the books so well, leaving several different trails to look at, that they do not know who took the money."

Ben said one-day Crestview Police Department would get their just desserts.

Chapter 7

Good Cop, Bad Cop, Dead Cop

Ben and I had been working close for about three years. We sat back and just observed what was going around us, from the way things disappeared within the department to the way some officers excelled. They are the ones that had something immoral on one or more of our superiors. We started documenting what was happening within the department on both paper and tape recordings. I found it easy to conceal a mini tape recorder in my brassiere. Many times, I tape recorded the sexual overtones or derogatory statements that Sergeant Hanover and Lieutenant Lester would say loudly to one another. A good portion of the time it was aimed at me. However, there were times it was aimed at women in general. Many times, they would pretend to be a friend and invite officers to go to lunch with them, and then try to humiliate them. Unfortunately, I was one of those officers.

I had to work a double because we were shorthand, due to the flu going around. The lieutenant and Sergeant Hanover would play nice guys and invite me to meet them at Kooter's Bar and Grill. I let my guard down that day and told them I would meet them. When I showed up at the eatery, I saw them sitting at a table that clearly seated only two people. I was not going to let them know that I was embarrassed by their little joke. They looked at one another and made smug grins; I just pulled up a chair and squeezed the chair in between them. The server asked if we wanted a bigger table and I could see it in their eyes as they were about to say "no".

I chimed in and said, "No thank you...I just stopped by to let these gentlemen know that I can't meet them."

I gracefully left with my pride still intact. Of course, they didn't see me get into my patrol car and choke back that sinking feeling that I was getting right about then. I felt my heart begin to palpitate and my face flushed in a matter of minutes. I am not sure it was so much from the mortification as to how much I was seething.

The only thing that brightened my day was when I got a laugh seeing the chief spend more time trying to find smut and dirt on his endless number of adversaries. He only did this to look good in the eyes of the mayor until he could backstab Hanson's political career.

I have to say I did have some enjoyment when the chief suspended Sergeant Hanover for two days because of a traffic ticket. It was an old Georgia law on the books for adultery, which he charged Hanover. Horace Jones said it served him right where as Hanover was dumb enough to be caught cheating on his wife with a married woman.

Ben learned, apparently, the other woman's husband filed a complaint with our police department after the traffic incident, which generated a thirty-page report. Several rumors started to trickle into the investigation, where Archie was the lead detective for Internal Affairs (IA). As it turns out, not all the allegations were substantiated. (*H-m-m-m, I wonder why?*)

However, one incident investigated was captured on Hanover's dashboard camera. This made it hard to avoid the evidence. A year prior to this investigation Hanover conducted a traffic stop last June, which led to an initial Internal Affairs investigation on Hanover. He acknowledged he stopped a red Mitsubishi belonging to his former lover's son; he refused to call for another officer even though the teenager asked for one. Hanover didn't give an unlawful act as the reason for the traffic stop. He just wanted to talk to the young man to give his mother a message, since she refused to answer his calls.

The woman, also married at the time, ended their relationship but he wasn't happy with her decision. She feared Hanover would stop her or other family members just to be vindictive. Her fears came true when her son was stopped. The investigation revealed a number of things wrong with his traffic stop of her son.

In addition to the dashboard camera evidence, Hanover was suspended without pay for another two days for a traffic violation when he ran a red traffic light in the next town while returning from Superior Court. The Wolfbane Chief of Police, Harold Buckie, might only have a three-man police department in Wolfbane, but he did not take crap in his town. He was going to play it by the book with Hanover. When Chief Buckie pulled the sergeant over, he observed a familiar nicely clad young woman sitting in the front seat of the patrol car. Hanover tried to schmooze Buckie when he said he picked up the young woman after court where she had just filed for divorce from her husband.

(*Unknown to Hanover, her husband happened to be one of the three officers on the Wolfbane PD and Buckie's stepson*).

Chief Buckie radioed Chief Jones and told him to come down to his department to pick up the City of Crestview's patrol car. Hanover had a suspended driver's license for traffic violations out of Florida.

The two police chiefs discussed the sexual misconduct of Hanover. It was unbecoming as a city employee because it violated a 1901 Georgia law. Although rarely enforced, it made adultery a crime. Buckie said it was still on the books and he was going to pursue it. After all, one of his finest officers was so upset over the incident that he could not come to work, so the chief felt he had to file an official complaint on Hanover.

Chief Buckie said the matter would be submitted to the Horse Stomp County District Attorney's Office for further review. Hanover called the news media; they learned the prosecutors announce they would not take any action against Hanover's sexual indiscretions, but it was all over the news. However, the case was forwarded to the Georgia Peace Officers Standards (P.O.S.T.) and Training Board.

(A group that oversees more than 10,200 sworn peace officers)

The Board's executive director said the agency agreed with the steps taken by Crestview P. D. and would take not further action.

The detective's report stated that while on duty, Hanover engaged in misconduct by running a red traffic light and improperly used police equipment when turning on his blue lights and siren to run the traffic light without cause. They also stated that during the course of duty, Hanover met a Wolfbane police officer's wife, with whom he later admitted having struck up a four-month relationship that ended after his misconduct charge.

The Crestview P. D. admitted that the affair violated a Georgia law that makes adultery a Class three misdemeanor punishable by as much as thirty days in jail and a $500 fine. Therefore, he got a slap on the wrist (*again*) and was told, next time don't get caught! At least Ben and I had something to talk about when we would meet in one of our secret rendezvous spots the department had not deciphered from our code.

Ben could see that I was a bit pissed with what Hanover put me through and then getting away with breaking the law, yet he had the audacity to humiliate me with a lunch invitation. It was clearly nothing more than an invitation to be burned by him and his sidekick, Jimmy Jack. Nevertheless, Ben had a way of always making me feel good and laughing it off.

He said something to the effect of "Their loss of great company. I can't imagine the two butt brothers having a female getting between them anyway."

We joked about it for about a half an hour while at lunch and then went back out on patrol. I got a call to come into the station and meet with the chief. My guts were in knots at the thought of seeing him. Ben reminded me to turn on my recorder and just see what he had to say.

Just as I got to the department, I pretended to play with my locket that my little girls gave me for good luck. I turned on the recorder and went into the chief's office. He brought up the topic of the academy graduation that I went to for Officer Knap last month.

"Yes sir, I remember going to his graduation. You asked me to go for support of the department," I answered, confused.

"Yeah, yeah, I did tell you that", he said in an "I don't give a shit" tone of voice. "I got a complaint from Instructor Festus Peabody as to the way you were dressed. He said you looked like a tramp or a whore."

At that moment, I didn't feel too ladylike and replied with a burst of energy.

"What the fuck are you talking about?" The chief was quite taken by my tone and cussing.

"Well, he said your attire was very unprofessional and you were an embarrassment to the department."

This time I looked straight into his eyes and leaned over his desk.

"Again, what the fuck are you talking about?"

Horace Jones just answered by asking me another question. "What did you wear to the graduation?"

"The same thing I wore for the Christmas party back in December. Both you and your wife complimented me on my dress. There wasn't anything about it that looked inappropriate!"

"I saw your dress?" he asked. "Yes, it was a simple sweater dress that was long sleeved, v-neck, not low cut, no cleavage. Not to mention the dress came to the middle of my calves!"

The chief jerked his head back and looked down at some papers that he was fumbling with and said, "Well, if Peabody says it was inappropriate then it was not the proper thing to wear".

I looked at him stunned. "I wanted to wear my uniform and you told me to wear a nice dress for the occasion."

"I guess I was wrong. According to Peabody, you are banned from going to any further functions at the academy."

"Chief, that is pure bullshit! What is going on here?" I demanded.

Jones told me he would find the underlying cause in this matter. He said I was excused, but mention there was one more matter he had to discuss with me.

Jones said there was an ongoing investigation for the rumors that I was having sex with nine out of ten officers within the department. He even named Ben as one of the officers as part of my entourage of lovers along with any new recruits. My alleged tryst location of choice was the Cat Tail Creek (*where Hanover allegedly committed rape*) and I would have my way with defenseless men who carried guns.

"Why would you have an Internal Affairs Investigation for some bullshit rumor like that?" I asked.

Jones sneered at me and said, "Because most of these officers are married and if any of this is true, it is conduct unbecoming of an officer and you could be demoted and suspended".

"Me!" I said abruptly. "If the rumors are true, it is they who should be written up for their conduct. I'm not married! This is the farthest thing from the truth and you know it! The person who is starting the rumor should be disciplined!" I raised my voice.

It was becoming clear to me, he was trying to intercept any possibilities of my getting any rank by saying I was sleeping my way to the top of the department. Of course, he tried to sound sympathetic to my cause and said Lieutenants Lester and Jack along with Sergeant Hanover were behind it.

I demanded to know the names of those who accused me of having affairs.

"I have a right to know who my accusers are! I learned that in the academy. And who are these so-called reputable married officers?"

Chief Jones said I was correct and had that right about my accusers in his sugarcoated voice; he named several officers including the captain and Lieutenants Lester and Hanover.

Later that afternoon I requested a meeting with Lester/Hanover in their office that they shared. The captain was present. We went down the list of names the chief had given me. One by one called the officers into the office.

Each time I recorded their statements as I asked each one outright, "Am I screwing you? Have we ever had sex at Cat Tail Creek, or anywhere else?" Each officer answered the same as the last, "No!"

It started out as a process of elimination. From nine out of ten officers, eight out of ten, seven out of ten and so on. You should have seen the look on their faces when I asked Lieutenant Lester, Sgt Hanover and Captain Barnes the same questions I asked the officers. Needless to say, not one officer accused me of having a fling with them. The Internal Affairs Investigation was terminated at that point.

I was fuming again when Ben ran into me in the squad room. I told him what had happened. He looked as confused as I was. "Where did they come up with the Cat Tail Creek shit?" he said.

"Your guess is as good as mine, Ben."

Then I told him that there was a grand finale. I told him about the police academy incident where I was question about my attire for graduation.

"I saw what you wore. What is the big deal? Loni, you know Peabody has a boss. Spector, Darrin Spector, the director of the academy. You should contact him."

"You are damn right, I will. I am going to write a letter because Peabody is too cowardly to put his complaint in writing to the chief. While I am at it, I will bring up what he did on the felony night stop when he ordered me to search Officer McCoy by putting my hands down his pants or I would be kicked out of the academy! Ben, when is this stuff going to stop? How much are they going to throw at me? I'm overwhelmed with the lies. If it wasn't for you and your support, I would be totally lost," I said in a very heartfelt way. I hugged him as I cautiously looked around.

Several times, I started the letter to Darrin Spector and several times, I tore it up. I would just get so upset, I sounded like I was just ranting and raving like an idiot. It wasn't until Ben came over to my house and we went over what I had already written that I calmed down enough to sound like I was halfway intelligent. As we talked, I would write and re-write what had already been written, when we were done talking, I had a very eloquent letter to the police academy director.

Wake Up and Die Right

It was about two weeks later when I got a call from Spector. He recalled meeting me after graduation and said he remembered my attire.

"I recall the dress because of its unusual color of blue. In fact, that stunning color of blue caught my wife's eye and she was commenting how charming you looked and that no one would suspect you are a cop."

He told me, "Don't worry; I will look into the matter".

Spector kept his promise and called me personally. He first called the captain and the chief, telling them to put me on the conference line with them.

He started out by saying, "I want to make sure this is perfectly clear. I conducted my own little investigation here at the academy and found that Festus Peabody is the one who has brought shame to the academy. He has not only insulted Svetlana but he has insulted other female officers and that will not be tolerated! I have a list of inappropriate conduct and complaints that could warrant termination."

Once he was done, he said I would be receiving an apology from not only Peabody, but also the academy. Spector kept his word and I did have a letter written on Academy letterhead. He ensured the chief of police and Captain Barnes received a copy of the letter.

However, it was useless since the chief joked around with the officers in the squad room. He had already gotten on his male chauvinistic high horse and spread the rumor throughout the department of my scanty dress and the embarrassment I put on the department before Darrin Spector completed his investigation. None of those officers ever heard about the apology I got in writing. Therefore, it was just one more thing to add pressure to my questionable career and respect for my rank and as an officer.

For a short time, their focus turned to a less known officer, Mannford Mauzer *(the troll)*. He was usually in the company of Sergeant Hanover since he had worked for the Crestview Police Department. Mauzer had been recently indicted in a public corruption case, but resigned before police could question him. Prosecutors released information to the media on how he was link to the case.

Mauzer was charged in a ten-count indictment alleging he used a police database to make illegal records checks on the witness and an attorney involved in a state securities fraud investigation that Detectives Riddle and Odell where investigating. The latest report released shed light on Mauzer's link to Hanover's fraud scheme with the account of the Georgia Chapter of the Police Benevolence Association. It looked like Hanover had done it again; everything appeared to show he was untouchable.

When Mauzer testified he was ordered by a supervisor to obtain information about the fraud scheme. Mauzer refused to identify his superior. The public worried it could be any ranking officer within the department or even the mayor. Ben and I

Wake Up and Die Right

---

knew it was Hanover. Mauzer left a number of items in his locker, some of which were found in a search of Hanover's home.

Mannford Mauzer was convicted of stolen property, disseminating criminal histories and hindering prosecution by not turning over names of those involved. He was sentenced to ten years in a federal prison. This made Chief Jones very nervous that GBI would find him out, or that Mauzer would make a deal with the district attorney. That is when Ben and I knew Horace Jones was neck deep in Hanover's escapades.

Mauzer was the fifth Crestview officer in six months to face allegations of wrongdoing. Most had dodged the judicial system and Sergeant Hanover had fared particularly well since it was determined that he used his marked patrol car to pull women over just to ask them out on dates after his last incident with the dash camera.

Archibald Riddle and Rufus Odell, both conducting internal investigations on officers, were now under investigation for the mishandling of evidence in forty-five criminal cases, several suspected sexual predators and some drug dealers they knew personally. Odell's inability to read, let alone write, left a lack of chain of custody paperwork. Between him and Riddle, they would just let work pile up to go home and have a few drinks at noon. Then their breaks went from noon to five o'clock in the late afternoon. Of course, they didn't come out at night. On the other hand, if they did, it was difficult to see who was holding up whom.

Lieutenant Lester was under investigation by the GBI (*Georgia Bureau of Investigation*) for sexually abusing five young girls. Lester's statement to the press was "They were asking for it" as he beamed from ear to ear. "Don't let their innocent looks fool you. I have stuff on them. They wanted it! That isn't a crime."

Lester met his latest victims on the Internet. A girlfriend of one of the girls told her mother of the two victims. Her parents in turn notified the girl's parents, who searched her room for evidence that may confirm or deny Lt. Lester's indiscretions, before calling the police. That is when they came across the officer's love letters to meet at a secret location, which started a new investigation. The other three victims were initially suspects as drunk drivers and arrested by Lester. He was the second officer caught in this act by his own dashboard camera; Lieutenant Lester made traffic stops and was caught on tape negotiating their bond with sexual favors.

The public indicated they were wary of the Crestview officers' recklessness. The mayor had been bombarded with complaints about the department, many of which indicate they will "take care of business" themselves if they are pulled over by one of the city's officers.

Chief Jones said the public's attitude toward the department left some need for concern for the remaining honest officers. (*He included himself in that category.*) Therefore, he sent Ben to Jacksonville, Florida to pick up the new bulletproof vests for the department. Everyone eagerly awaited his arrival in the squad room. Lieutenant Lester, while on administrative leave with pay, checked off the names of each officer to receive a vest. Each vest was measured for perfect fit. The chief walked into the squad room and pulled out the last vest. It was mine. It was placed on the squad table standing up. He was making jokes with the other officers as I walked into the room.

"Check this out," he said, pointing to the breastplate in the vest. "If Loni got shot in the chest, the bullet would ricochet up her nose and blow off her head!"

Laughter was heard all the way into the communication room. It stopped abruptly when I entered the doorway. I looked over into Captain Barnes' office, walked in there and closed the door behind me. I asked him if he had heard what they were saying in the next room. He acknowledged that he had. I told him that this had to stop. I was tired of being the butt of their sick, jokes and they were pushing for a lawsuit. As I opened the door to his office to leave, I found both Lieutenant Lester and Sergeant Hanover standing outside the door eavesdropping. They walked past me as if not noticing me standing there and then walked into the captain's office and started looking under the desk. Captain Barnes asked what they were looking for under there.

Lieutenant Lester smugly said, "We were just looking to see if Officer Svetlana Chekov was still under your desk".

The captain looked puzzled and asked, "For what reason would she be under my desk?"

Then Sergeant Hanover said, "We thought she would be giving you a blow job!"

Just as Hanover made that statement, I heard a click! The recorder stopped. I looked around to see if anyone else had heard the clicking sound. I heaved a sigh of relief when I realized I was in the clear.

I played the recording back to Ben when we got off work. He said, "You know, with a few more tapes like these, you will have enough for a discrimination suit. Jones is so busy with all the criminal cover up; he won't know what hit him when you throw a civil suit at him."

That was exactly what I decided to do. It wasn't as if I could go to another police department. I tried leaving, but Jones or Hanover did everything they could to discourage them from me being hired. In other words, I was "black balled" like so many other honest cops trying to get out of here. I was tired of the corruption, the good ole boy games and their rules. I was going to file a suit if it meant losing my job while trying to do it. I had Ben, even though he was a man, he had insight to the smut that Lieutenant Lester, Sergeant Hanover and Chief Jones were putting out.

Ben had his own problems at home besides

worrying about the police department always trying to burn someone for doing their job. Allie had been seeing someone when Ben was working. He told me about it and said it didn't really bother him; it was the idea of someone else raising his daughters that bothered him the most. Allie was very slow and naïve and it didn't take much to talk her into anything. He suspected that was how she met this guy, Grayson.

Ben said that his biggest problem in his marriage was Slick Rutherford and his wife, Darla. He said that Allie lived in a foster home; Darla's parents were her foster parents. She and Darla were close and Slick used her to his advantage.

Good ole "Barney Fife" the second, he was such a sneak. He made corporal after he burned Willie Niles. Anyone who was there when the incident happened knew Rutherford was the one who kept a good portion of the money but got cold feet and turned it to his benefit. He made rank after he paid off the chief, Sergeant Hanover and Lieutenant Lester when he got to our department. Lester seemed to take a real shine to Rutherford. I don't think it was just the money but because he could manipulate him so easily to squeal on other officers. He played undercover cop. What Willie Niles did was wrong. What Slick Rutherford was doing was even worse.

Slick and Darla followed Ben and Allie to Horse Stomp County after he was burned over the theft and testified against his former roommate in Poe County. He could only make it as a police officer by hanging onto Ben's shirttails and manipulating Allie to get what he wanted from Ben. Slick was incapable of thinking on his own. He was like a puppet; someone was always pulling his strings and putting words in his mouth. If that wasn't bad enough, he made police situations worse when he let the rank go to his head.

Slick insisted we call him "Corporal". He needed to hear us confirm his power. We chuckled about the authority high he was having. It was stronger than any drug he was taking.

Right after our little laugh, Ben and I got a call of a closed diner burglary in progress. The suspect was still inside the building. There were some visible signs that the suspect kicked in the bottom quarter panel of the back door. Yet the "corporal" decided to try to break in the front door, which was double glass and had a huge chain through the handles. I watched as Slick put his hands on his gun belt and adjusted the gig line of the buckle, and then sniffed a little as he made faces when he cleared his throat. He turned sideways and rammed his shoulder into the glass doors. He bounced off the doors as if he were made of rubber. His hands were at his side as he shook his wrists. He snorted again and shook his head as if he were dazed. Again, he rammed the glass door and again bounced off.

Ben and I snickered as I walked up to him and said, "Yo, Corporal, wouldn't it be easier to break in the door that was already broken into by the suspect?"

Wake Up and Die Right

Slick looked at me as if to say he was going to suggest that. When we walked around the back of the building, Ben kicked out the rest of the bottom half of the panel on the door, leaving the top part of the door and the doorframe intact.

Slick said, "One of you will have to crawl in the hole of the bottom panel and open the door and let the rest of us inside".

Ben spoke up and said, "There is no way I could fit through there and as for you, Corporal, your ass will defiantly get stuck trying to fit through". Then they both looked at me and said that I would have to be the one to go inside the building.

"Yeah, right! How do I know that the perpetrator does not have a machete and will chop off my head as soon as I poke it through the hole?" I said reluctantly.

Someone had to do it so I did. I crawled inside and opened the back door for both of them. Ben was left-handed, I was right, so I usually aimed toward the right and him to the left when entering a potential scene. He carried a shotgun as we secured the building, I shined the flashlight and he would aim wherever it shined.

Ben kicked the swinging door to the women's bathroom and my mag-light shined on a grungy transient trying to hide under the sink. He smelled like fecal matter and marijuana. His clothes were stiff and dirty; they could almost stand up on their own. His hair was wild looking and his face and hands were weathered. I aimed my gun on the transient, covering Ben as he reached under the sink and picked up this man in a dirty tattered trench coat off the ground and up against the wall. I am not sure where Slick was while we were taking the guy into custody, but once the cuffs were on the transient, Slick became brave and physical with him by slamming him up against the wall and on the floor. He flung him around like a stuffed toy.

I yelled out, "Yo, Corporal, don't you think we need to finish securing the scene to ensure there are no other transients inside?"

Rutherford grabbed his gun belt and adjusted it, sniffing as his mouth crooked to one side with every sniff he made. "Yeah, yeah, good idea, I got him covered."

Ben gave the all clear sign for the bathroom. I found another transient hiding behind the bar, lying down on the empty shelves. He was a frail, aging man who didn't smell or look much better than the first transient. I scared him so bad he started having an asthma attack and the paramedics had to be called.

I could see that the two men had been staying in the building for some time. There was decayed food and wrappers lying around the establishment. Since there had not been any running water or electricity for some time the toilets where full and filled the eight commodes to the top. The stalls were streaked with fecal handprints and old newspapers that where used as toilet paper piled in the corner of the bathrooms.

Wake Up and Die Right

Slick took the transients into custody until we could transport them to the county jail. We went back to the office to do the paperwork. When we were done, Ben mentioned that he was getting hungry. We decided to head back to the convenience store to grab one of those gray hot dogs and a drink. I always made a point not to look at the hot dogs when I was eating them. They were ugly. I made sure to put lots of ketchup, mustard and pickle relish on it to cover up the color of the food but it was tasty. I noticed that the clerk was flirting with Ben and he seemed to like it. The clerk told him when she got off work and asked if he would like to meet up with her.

He just said "Maybe" and walked back to his patrol car.

"What was that all about?" I asked.

He said that he had been tempted to go out with her but just didn't have the courage to do it.

"Are you nuts? You are still married," I said.

"Listen, we both know Allie is cheating on me. Strangely enough, it does not bother me. I wasn't going to tell you this, but she wants a divorce to move in with that guy she is seeing," Ben said

"Darla introduced Allie to Grayson and told her she could do better than me." Therefore, Allie fell for it. Ben said she was planning to take most of the stuff in the house and move into his house a few blocks away.

"How do you really feel about it, Ben?" He just said it left him open to date once she was out of the house. He did get custody of a couple of dishes, two sets of silverware settings and a glass. She didn't leave him very much furniture. Just a recliner to sleep on, but he said he'd make do with what he had. I told Ben that I felt bad for him but he said he didn't have to worry about Slick manipulating Allie to find out his personal business. He told me Allie loves to talk and she tells everything that goings on between them. Ben was careful not to tell her anything about the department.

We no sooner got our food and drink when there was a call to come back to the department to see Chief Jones. The chief wanting to see us was puzzling. We couldn't figure out what dilemma they where going to put us in the middle. It didn't take too long to figure out what was going on; we were going to be the patsy again, for what Sergeant Hanover had done.

The next day chief was in his office along with Lieutenant Lester and Sergeant Hanover. I overheard them talking and Hanover told the chief he had to do something about Ben and I. We knew too much.

As we walked in the office, Lester and Hanover had that "I am going to get you and that you won't even know what happened" look on their face.

Chief Jones ridiculed us about the hair salon and the report we made. Ben showed his temper, which was something I had not seen too often.

"Look, chief, we wrote what was said to us and it is up to those nitwits you call detectives to figure out what really happened. We don't know.

The chief said he was going to have to conduct an internal investigation on us.

"Us?" said Ben. "What the hell is the matter with you and this department?"

The chief excused us. "I think what pisses me off the most, Ben, is the fact that Hanover and Lester are involved."

The next day when I came on duty, I heard that a Georgia State trooper had stopped a couple of vehicles and requested the nearest agency to assist him. That would be the Crestview Police Department. I jumped in my car and Ben rode shotgun. Lester got in Hanover's car and headed out to the scene. When we got there, Trooper Skinner had three vehicles pulled over and there were drugs in the first vehicle. Ben and I took the third vehicle and the sergeant and lieutenant took control of the second vehicle. I noticed as Hanover started to search the vehicle he pulled out a small handgun. He was overheard telling the elderly, retired New York businessman, Wilson Moore.

"Did you know it is against the law to carry a handgun in the state of Georgia?"

The businessperson blurted out, "It isn't my gun."

Hanover said, "Then I guess you will not need it". He took custody of the gun and let him go on his way.

"Ben, Ben, did you hear that? It's not illegal for a citizen to carry a handgun in the state of Georgia!

What the hell is he up to?" I whispered firmly.

Ben responded, "You know and I know what Hanover did was bullshit and he will get away with it, but if we do anything to report it, it will backfire and we will get the blame. Just stay out of it!"

It was about two weeks later that the chief called me into his office again but this time to ask me about Hanover. He said Hanover was an embarrassment to the department and showed me a letter from a New York attorney who, in the letter, stated she represented a Mr. Wilson Moore. The letter said he was pulled over on the interstate earlier this month. He wanted his handgun back. The letter went on to say that, he felt intimidated when the sergeant told him it was illegal to have a gun in the state of Georgia. The chief indicated he wanted me to do an internal investigation on Hanover.

"Me? Why do you want me to do the internal investigations? Why not have the captain or lieutenant conduct the investigation?"

The chief said, "It wouldn't be a fair investigation and I believe you would call it as it is for what it is worth".

I was somewhat flattered but very apprehensive of the chief. However, I started to conduct the investigation and would give all the information to the chief and let him make a decision. Of course, there had to be a catch. I couldn't let Hanover or Lester know that I was conducting the investigation.

The first thing I needed to do was to find the

gun. Hanover said he couldn't find it. He told the chief Wilson Moore said it wasn't his gun and didn't want it, so Hanover had it confiscated. The proper procedure would have been to log it in as evidence. However, there was no record of the gun signed into custody. Lieutenant Lester and Sergeant Hanover were not exactly willing to discuss anything with me.

I called Mr. Moore and recorded our conversation. He stated that the sergeant and the lieutenant were very rude and had made smartass comments about him being a "Yankee" and said they could "make" or "break" his day. Moore said he heard about officers in the south being corrupt and didn't want to take a chance one of them would shoot him. He got my attention when he said Lieutenant Lester asked if he had any money. When Moore asked if he was trying to take a bribe, Lester grinned as he was smacking his chewing gum and told him, "Naw, y'all might need it to get outta of jail." Then Hanover saw the gun in the open gun case in the backseat. Moore said it was an antique and belonged to his deceased father and he was on his way to Florida to give it to his son. When asked if it was his, he did tell the officers that it was not, but before he could explain that it was his son's, Hanover took the gun. It was not until he got back to New York when he started feeling like a victim. Then he contacted his attorney and she wrote the letter telling the chief to return the gun.

I made a copy of the tape and gave one to the

chief. I also let him know that the gun was missing and not in the evidence locker as it should be.

The chief was angry and said. "Find out where that gun is!"

"Chief, wouldn't it be more appropriate you asked Hanover and Lester?" I asked.

His reluctance made me think the chief was afraid of the sergeant and lieutenant for some reason.

"Gee, I can't imagine them having anything on him", I said to myself sarcastically. I told the chief that I would start working on locating the gun Monday morning. I would just keep working on places to look for it over the weekend.

Monday morning during roll call, it was mentioned that we were one officer short for the shift. Over the weekend, Slick shot himself in the leg.

"What happened?" I asked.

The captain said it was an accident; he was pulling a small caliber gun out of his ankle holster and it went off, piercing the calf of his leg. The dispatcher called the off-duty Sergeant to go to the scene. I thought it was strange for Hanover to come out to the scene when there was a sergeant on the watch for that shift. I call it woman's intuition again, but I was wary so I asked the captain if I could read his report. He let me read it. Two officers had arrived on the scene; their reports sounded pretty much the same. Then I noticed that the serial number of Slick's gun was listed. It looked very familiar. I compared it with the letter from the New

York lawyer, which included the serial number, make and model of the gun.

"Bingo! A match." I heard Hanover got a call to go back on duty. One of the paramedics came into the police department and asked how Slick was doing. He said he was one of the responding units. I asked him if Slick talked to him about the incident.

"Yeah, he was more worried about contacting Sergeant Hanover because he said it was Hanover's gun. He gave it to him to use as a backup gun. He was practicing pulling it out of his leg holster, which was new and still stiff and when he pulled the gun out of the holster, his finger was on the trigger."

I whispered to myself, "Bingo again."

I brought this new information to the chief. He said that he would handle it from there. He just asked that I didn't say anything to anyone about what I found. Apparently, some time that day, the chief must have brought it to Hanover's attention what he knew. The next thing I knew I was in the captain's office. Hanover and Lester were standing there. Lieutenant Lester was screaming and calling me names. He said I had no authority to start my own investigation on a senior sergeant. That is when I could see the chief was up to something. He planned this whole thing out for it to back fire on me. Ben was right. The chief knew they would go ballistic and turn the table of their guilt to my doing what they thought was an unauthorized investigation. I never mentioned to them that the chief asked me to conduct the investigation. I held back in the event I was wrong thinking the chief was really out to get me. It turned out he told them he was the one who initiated the investigation.

I told Ben what had happened with my little investigation. He said he couldn't believe this was a real police department! I told him, from then on, I was-recording any conversations that I might have with any of these people. Ben said he was going to do the same thing. It is a shame when a police officer has to resort to recording conversations to cover their ass in their own department.

Ben went into the squad room and heard all the scuttlebutt. Apparently, Lieutenant Lester, Sergeant Hanover and the chief would take turns dogging out different officers and city employees, especially the mayor and his sexuality. Ben was recording everything. Lester and Hanover were talking about how to get rid of the new black officers that the city council made them hire.

(*The department had acquired three more black officers per the mayor and city council's instructions.*)

"They are totally useless. No black officer will ever be promoted within this department. There goes any competition for us."

Then the chief looked over at Lieutenant Lester. "Yeah, I know your goal is to have my job and Hanover is out to get yours."

The Chief said, "Then my head is on the chopping block". They laughed about it.

(How I could ever imagine I could get a promotion?)

"No blacks or women will ever be promoted in this department. Women should be bare foot and pregnant. Thank God the mayor hates women more than we do in this job," the chief said.

Then the mayor walked into the squad room. The chief's sneer turned to a nervous smile as Ben could hear him stuttering and falling all over himself verbally.

The mayor had picked up the conversation and said, "There is no way in hell that will ever happen".

They all laughed and continued talking as though Ben wasn't in the squad room.

Ben discreetly walked away to his patrol car. He radioed me to meet with him so he could tell me about their conversation in the squad room.

"We need to get an attorney with everything going on. There is too much corruption in this department and it is about time it comes out."

Ben called the PBA (*Police Benevolence Association*) Chapter President Billy Diggman in Atlanta from a pay phone. Diggman told us to talk to Victor Kapers; he was one of his representatives.

"Victor Kapers? He works in our department," Ben replied.

Diggman said, "You're right; he isn't advertising the fact that he is a part of the PBA until we can get a chance to work with the other officers within the department. Your chief refuses to allow us to the department. Don't worry, Ben; he will you and Svetlana."

Ben called Kapers and told him that Diggman told us to contact him. Kapers knew a lot of the stuff going on so we didn't have to go into much to fill him in. He said he would arrange to get an attorney assigned to us and start making a case.

Kapers advised, "Always use a pay phone. Never call from home."

Two PBA attorneys, along with Diggman and Kapers, met with Chief Jones several times about the way they treated me were the ranking staff made jokes that were derogatory in a sexual nature and promotions. Jones was frustrated to learn I was aware of their conversations. I was never privy to these pre-law suit consideration meetings, but I heard the chief was upset to hear some of my recordings of him and the mayor making comments that I could never be promoted because I was a woman. That got their attention and not long after that conversation there was an order that no one could have tape recorders inside the department. Within a week of their encounter, I got a promotion. I didn't go up through the ranks but straight to sergeant! I was the first woman in the history of the Crestview Police Department to make any type of rank. Token female or not.

In the meantime, Ben and Allie were having some rough times. She told him that she was leaving him for good and would take his little girls. He was heart-broken over his daughters. He still contended he didn't mind that she was leaving. She came to the house that night and picked up the rest of her belongings.

They got into an argument when she brought her new boyfriend in the house. Ben told her that was heartless for her to do that to him. She started screaming at him and throwing things and slapped him in the face. He grabbed her, spun her around, and then pushed her away from him. She was mad and left to call the Crestview Police Department. She told Corporal Slick Rutherford that Ben had assaulted her. He took her to the magistrate judge's office and a warrant was issue on Ben for misdemeanor simple assault that Ben choked her.

(*You could be charged with assault if you spit on someone in the state of Georgia.*) Only she told the judge (*with the encouragement of Slick Rutherford and the Crestview Police Department*)

There were red marks on the right side of her neck that were not there when she left Ben at the house. The warrant went to the Horse Stomp County Sheriff's Department. Rutherford went back to the department and filled in Lieutenant Lester and Sergeant Hanover what had transpired with Ben and Allie. Hanover called the warrant section of the sheriff's department, trying to get a deputy to pick up Ben while in uniform at the beginning of his shift in the morning. The sheriff said he wouldn't do it and called Ben about the warrant. He told him he could voluntarily come to the sheriff's office and turn himself in so he would prevent any further em-

...ent. The sheriff said our police department ...going out of their way to put him through hell.

(Neighboring police agencies were familiar where Crestview's loyalties lay and considered some ranking officials as nothing more than what the rest of the public do, "KEYSTONE COPS.")

It was the next morning when I got a call from Ben. He called to say he was in the "Sheriff Barney Bateman's Hotel".

"What are you talking about, Ben?" I said.

"Jail, Loni, jail", he sighed.

"What happened to you? Why are you in jail?" Again, he sighed.

"Loni, just see if you can bond me out of jail! I will fill you in later, but I will tell you that the Crestview Police Department was behind convincing Allie to press charges on me as well as setting me up and trying to have me arrested in uniform just to humiliate me. If it is the last thing I do, I will get back at Crestview PD."

I contacted Kapers about Ben. I didn't have to tell him about what the department did to Ben because the news of the warrant and Ben's arrest spread like weeds after a rainy day in the south. Everyone knew about it, or our department's version of what happened. I met with, Magistrate Judge Watkins, to set a bond for Ben. I asked the judge what the police had as evidence. Watkins opened the folder and showed me two Polaroid photos of Allie. I saw the photos of Allie's neck and it was obvious that Ben didn't choke her. He was a southpaw and had huge hands. Her own deformed fingers made the marks on Allie's neck. I told Judge Watkins, "This is bullshit judge."

Then proceeded to explain why I knew it was not true. The judge told me that he was leery anytime the Crestview Police Department is involved in anything, present company excluded. He said that is why he was making the bond low enough for me to get him out of jail today.

I bonded Ben out of jail within an hour of leaving Judge Watkins office. Ben was doing all right but was more angry than upset.

"Slick took advantage of Allie being a dumb ass and twisted what happened to get brownie points with Lieutenant Lester and Sergeant Hanover, that brown noser did it again!," he said angrily.

Victor Kapers set us up a meeting with a PBA attorney in the next county. It wasn't safe to have the meeting in Horse Stomp County. The attorney was very well known throughout the state as well as in Florida and North Carolina. Victor called us and told us that Attorney Odie J. Halbrook was expecting us tomorrow at six o'clock in the evening at the Beaumont Hotel. Odie Halbrook was feared though out the state. He tried the first RICO act and several suits against various police departments and won all of them.

Halbrook was an eminent man, six-five, around two-hundred and thirty pounds. Odie was very distinguished with his dark hair and gracefully graying around the temples. His suits where tailor made for

...se physique. He wore a size fourteen shoe ...ere always spit shined to show his reflection ...n top of the toes. Odie spoke with a deep resonance voice where he could easily have been a crime show narrator.

Victor, Ben and I met with Mr. Halbrook until after midnight. He assured us that something would be done about the injustice within the Crestview Police Department. He said that we had laid the foundation of the case with all our notes and tape recordings. It would only be a matter of time. (*Something one of us didn't have.*)

By the time, we got back into town it was almost one o'clock in the morning. Ben dropped me off at my house and went on to his. I called him after he got home and asked if he was all right. He told me that he was fine, but it seemed strange walking into an empty house. He still claimed not to care that Allie was gone and that he was okay since she left. He said he was getting tired and had to get up early for work. I asked him if he would be all right going back to work. Ben laughed and said he wouldn't give them the satisfaction not showing up. I hesitantly asked if he had any thoughts of doing anything stupid. At first he responded by saying he wouldn't shoot anyone if that was what I was asking. I told him not necessarily. I wanted to make sure he wouldn't do anything to himself.

He laughed, if I think he was going to shoot himself over this he said, "NO, anyone who kills themselves is a coward and that is something I was

Wake Up and Die Right

not. I've told you in the past, the same thing, besides if I were going to do myself in I would just put a gun to my head and get it over with so there isn't any second thoughts. Don't worry about it Loni, my goal is to burn Crestview and the two of us will be rich when we get done with them, he said excitedly."

We hung up and I walked slowly to my bedroom and plopped on the bed fell asleep. I was so beat; I lay on the bed still wearing my clothes. Someone was banging on my front door; I looked over at my radio alarm clock with its big, bold red numbers indicating it was two in the morning. I shuffled my way to the door, but not before, I grabbed my 9mm from its holster.

(*Grabbing my gun was just a habit as a cop, always being prepared for the unexpected. Besides, it was 2 a.m.*)

Peaking out the peephole, I noticed it wasn't anyone important, just that puny excuse of a brown nose, Slick Rutherford. He was in uniform and said he needed to talk to me.

"What the hell do you want, Slick, at this time of the morning?" I asked.

"I want to know what you and Ben saw an attorney about in Savannah," he said, stammering as he shifted side to side.

"What are you talking about, Slick?" I sarcastically asked.

"We know you and Ben went to see an attorney. Are you going to tell me what went on over there?"

I looked at him as if he were crazy. "Now what would make you think we saw an attorney?"

He became very intense. "Damn it, Loni, you know that the phones are tapped and there are higher ups that want some answers, now!"

I told him, "Like hell I have to say anything to you. Get the hell out of my house."

I proceeded to push Slick out the door. He stood in front of the door and he said, "You will regret it, Svetlana, mark my words, you will regret it!" I abruptly turned and stomped off toward my bedroom and went back to bed.

The next day, Ben was to work the day shift. When I turned on my scanner and didn't hear his voice on the radio traffic, I thought that was very strange, especially when I heard Rutherford still out after working the graveyard shift. I called Ben's house several times, but no answer. Then I called the chief dispatcher at home.

"Penny, have you heard from Ben?" I asked, concerned.

"The strange thing is, Loni, he never showed up for work today and never called out. I have been listening to the scanner all morning, also. I called the office and talked to Sophia, who is on duty right now. She said Ben never showed up for work and the patrol sergeant had Rutherford work over. Loni, do you think Ben was too embarrassed to show up for work after being arrested?"

I told Penny that Ben would never do that, he was pissed about Crestview PD's part in pushing

Allie into pressing bogus charges for something he didn't do and then trying to have him arrested in uniform. He would show up just to annoy Lieutenant Lester, Sergeant Hanover and the chief.

"I am going over to his house in a few minutes to see if he is all right," I told Penny. "I have this strange feeling, almost a premonition. I can see him lying on the floor face down. Penny, I have this gut feeling something happened to him and he is dead!"

Penny replied, "Loni, that sounds morbid, but I have somewhat the same feeling." She said she would meet me there.

He only lived about two blocks from my house so I got there before Penny arrived. Ben lived in a little blue house with white trim and a white picket fence. He had a porch extending from the large picture window in the living room all the way to the master bedroom. It was a beautiful August Sunday and most people kept their windows open to air out the house, since it was almost fall.

I stepped up onto the porch and knocked on the front door. There was no answer. I could see through the sheer curtains into the living room where Ben's recliner was positioned in the southwest corner of the house. I didn't look closely because I could see him faintly through the picture window. He appeared to be sleeping in his underwear. I didn't want to humiliate him more by letting him know I saw him in his skivvies. Therefore, I stepped away from the picture window and knocked on the door some more. When he still didn't answer, I walked down the porch to the window to his empty master bedroom. He had the window open so I yelled to him through the screen. There was still no answer. My arms and legs tingled as I hesitantly opened the screen door. I noticed the inside door was cracked open. Something told me not to touch anything so I bumped it open with my hip. As I stood in the archway of the door, a tall lamp with a wide lampshade was obscuring my vision where Ben slept. I could see his feet but nothing else. I continued to call for him, again so I would not embarrass him when he awoke. When there was no answer, I crept into the house where I saw Ben not sleeping, but DEAD!

I was somewhat shocked not to see a gunshot wound to his head. In fact, his gun was nowhere around him. There was an emptied can of gun cleaner lying next to the right side of his recliner. It was a very disturbing scene. I stood there distressed when looking around the empty house. Sugar bowls where emptied and all the cupboard doors and drawers were open and appeared to be ransacked.

His body was arched and lividity was present so he had not been dead but four-or-five hours. I could see that the headrest of the recliner was pushed up toward the top of his head instead of resting at the base of his head. His underwear was twisted. I immediately left the house as I began to scream with anger. I screamed so loud that when Penny arrived she said she could hear me a block away. She later described me in the police report as crazed with grief. I was more angry than grieving at that point. I knew that he had been murdered and there would be a cover up.

Penny had her teenage son with her. He ran to a neighbor's house to call the police. The first officer on the scene was a rookie. He was new to police work and had not gone through the academy as of yet. I would not let him through the door because he had no experience or training to handle a death scene, let alone a homicide. The only other officer available was Slick Rutherford. If looks could kill, he would have been dead at first one glance I gave him. I made sure the captain got a call at home since he lived close by and the chief lived in Florida. He in turn called the Horse Stomp Sheriff Department to be unbiased in the case.

(It was common practice, for another department not to handle a case that involved their own personnel.)

I stayed at Ben's house until Deputy Carnes arrived on the scene with a camcorder and camera.

I drove recklessly to my house, shaken and scared. I was upset over Ben's death, but feared that I would be next. I knew I had to contact someone from the PBA I had to keep my wits about me to remember not to use my home phone. I drove to the nearest pay phone down the street to call Victor Kapers, not only as a friend of Ben's but also as a PBA representative. Then I called the PBA President Bill Diggman and left him a message about Ben. I called my attorney Odie Halbrook and hysterically left a message begging him to call me. When he did call all I could say was "They killed him, they killed him" repeatedly.

The department gave me time off work with pay since I was so devastated. In the meantime, Ben's body was transported to Atlanta to the GBI for an autopsy. The preliminary autopsy was done locally but when I read the report, I thought it was very strange. There was no mention that Ben had a missing toe, let alone only one testicle. I was sure the Crestview controlled the coroner's office, besides its officers.

The department said he died of an overdose of anti-depressants that belonged to Allie before the coroner's report was complete. The autopsy didn't show a high enough level to come to that conclusion.

His funeral was closed casket. The mortician talked to me after the services. I asked why he had a closed casket. He said Ben was purple and black from the chest up and would have been unidentifiable. I knew that a rookie cop would be able to figure out that what the mortician said was true, that Ben had died face down, moved after death. My premonition was right when I visualized him dead face down in his house.

Things started to take another turn. Chief Jones had a copy of the death scene video taped. He kept it in the bookcase where he stored his training films. Periodically he would take it out the first few months of Ben's death and say he was going to show it to people as if it were a collection of horror films. Penny Applegate was one of the people who viewed the macabre film. She said she could see how Ben's house was ransacked more so after I left. She said the sugar bowls I saw earlier had been emptied out onto the floor. I am sure they were looking for the mini tape recordings that Ben and I had. His phone was dusted for prints, as everything was thrown about.

The chief called me into his office my first day back to the department after a two-week leave of absence. He told me that he knew I was attempting to make a long distance call on Ben's phone when I found his body.

(I didn't touch anything inside the house, especially the phone. However, why would the chief say that? What was he trying to do, make a new scenario of what happened to Ben? What he didn't know was that I knew Ben didn't have long distance service. He would ask me to call his mother in Florida so she could call him. Again, I felt this was some type of a set up.)

I was sure Ben's autopsy would point to the Crestview PD and perhaps to certain people within the department. Until then, I was in fear for my own life. I had to come up with a way to detour any possibility I would be the next one to have an unfortunate demise.

I had a Will drawn up with copies of all the tape recordings that I had, along with some very detailed information about the department and its personnel.

I made no bones about having all this information in my Will, so in the event of my death it would go public, there were other copies of the tape recordings not to mention other letters and tapes that would surface. I thought this would buy time for me until I could get out of the department. I tried to cover all the grounds to bring out the department's carelessness.

I was so obsessed about Ben's death that I couldn't eat, but I looked forward to sleep. So many times, I had dreams where Ben would come and talk to me. It was so real. I felt he was trying to tell me how he died. I felt I was so close to finding out what really happened to him. The only comfort I have accepting his death is to know that the people who are guilty of his passing may get away with it in this lifetime, but will not in the next. I know that God's hands will be upon them in time.

Chapter 8

Starting Over

Bad cops still managed to filter their way into the department Sergeant Nate Boggs was one of them. His deceitful beginnings were to bed his subordinates' wives while their husbands were out on patrol on the night shift. He, like so many officers before him, fancied himself a Casanova. That is something that tends to miscarry. They are legends in their own mind.

Boggs, a weightlifter and a steroid user, went into confrontational rages on a daily basis. Sure, he was the one to instigate them but always wanted the last word. A couple of times he went a little too far with his exploitive nature.

Two years earlier, Sergeant Nate Boggs repeatedly called and harassed Officer Bart Tanner by calling his cell phone and making statements such as, "I can see you" and "I'm coming to get you". The calls occurred after Tanner discovered his girlfriend at the time, who had been convicted of drug trafficking and Boggs was the arresting officer. He would taunt Tanner by telling him that his girlfriend and he were having an affair. Tanner retaliated by informing Boggs wife of the affair, which only fueled the fire that Boggs had already started.

The late night threatening cell phone calls continued, so, Tanner requested a police report to be made so he could take out a restraining order against Boggs. In the report listed two fellow police officers as witnesses to the phone calls. While making the report with officers about the unwanted phone calls, Boggs happened to call his cell phone while Tanner was at the police station. Tanner put the calls on speakerphone for the officers to hear the threats and they recorded the calls.

Boggs bullying voice repeatedly warned Tanner: "It ain't over. ... I'm coming to get you ... You can't hide from me. I will get your women."

The incident report indicated Tanner had complained to police about Boggs several times in the past. It wasn't until the fellow officers heard Boggs threats and confirmed his number from the emergency roaster. Boggs was reprimanded for his actions.

That didn't detour Boggs. While in charge of another new recruit just out of the police academy, Officer Derrick Tucker, Boggs went back to his old ways and this time it got out of hand. Tucker was a nice clean-cut rookie who had only been married for a year. Tucker called his residence only to have

Wake Up and Die Right

Boggs recklessly answer the phone while he implied that he was in heated passion with the young patrol officer's wife. Dispatchers could hear Tucker, as he demanded Boggs to leave his home and wife. Boggs only promoted the situation by threatening the patrol officer that he would leave when he was finished with business.

Tucker was devastated and came to me to say he was going to confront Boggs. He said that Boggs told him that he would blow him away if he tried anything. As much as I tried to convince Tucker to control his emotions, he took off in the patrol vehicle. Before I could call for back up and get into my car, only the faded blue lights from the top of his squad car could be seen in the distance.

Within a few blocks, Tucker was in front of his residence. While sending officers to his home, I was calling Boggs intermittently on both the radio and then his cell phone. In a matter of minutes, I arrived on the scene. I could hear a shot fired. Backup officers ducked for cover. The muzzle flash came from the direction of inside the house. Return fire came from Tucker's gun. There was a blood-curdling scream from Boggs. "You fuckin shot me," he yelled in a high-pitched screech. At least fourteen more shots were fired by officers on the scene before Tucker and Boggs were subdued. Boggs was bleeding from his shooting hand.

As I tried to assess the scene, I noticed droplets of blood. They led from where my patrol car was parked to where I was standing. Then there was a searing pain in my body. I was shot! It was unclear as to where the shots fired were coming from but I knew that if the Crestview Police Department were conducting the investigation, no one would know who shot me. Captain Barnes was acting chief that night and arrived with Mayor Hanson at his side.

Oddly, or was it traditionally, no charges were filed against Tucker or Boggs. Tucker quit the department while Boggs was given desk duty until his injury healed.

I was on convalescence leave for the next six weeks. I had a lot of time to think when I was suddenly served a notice that I was being terminated for the incident with Tucker and Boggs. Crestview PD held me responsible for the incident because I was the senior sergeant on the shift that night. I am not sure what I could have done to stop the situation but it didn't matter because Chief Jones, Lt. Lester and Sergeant Hanover had already started an internal investigation on me while I was in the hospital. It wasn't as if I didn't see this coming for some time.

I thought, why come up with such bogus charges. Then it came to me, my Will! That is it, if I died due to complications from the gun shot wounds, the Will and all of its contents will surface. So it is better to discredit me now before there is a chance for the Will to go public. I would not be able to contest anything the department would have to say about me then.

Astonishingly, Mayor Hanson reportedly ad-

Wake Up and Die Right

---

dressed the city council with matters of the police department after being called on the carpet by councilwoman, Laura Raintree. Mayor Hanson said he'd be glad to meet with City Council about alleged police misbehavior.

(I think the mayor could see what was coming next and wanted to appear to have a clear conscience of what he had knowledge and to what extent he was involved.)

Hanson divulged that his hands were tied when it comes to disciplining rogue officers. He said he wanted to fire certain officers for some time, but when he tried, it was rejected by the city attorney due to lack of evidence. The city attorney didn't want to open Crestview up for a lawsuit.

Councilwoman Raintree spoke of the bad reputation Crestview had with rumored bad officers. Terminating them presented another problem, the lack of officers to protect the public.

"It's a corrupt department," Hanson said. "You're always going to split the baby and there's nothing we can do about it."

Hanson advised he is taking matters in his own hands to correct the problems.

(However, many of the city council had concerns that Hanson would be the first step in cleaning the police department. After all, he was the Police Commissioner. Rumors of his part of Casey Long's disappearance and death weighed heavily on their minds as well as police corruptions.)

Minutes where read from the last meeting where

Jones had spoken before the city council on record by saying, "Our officers' deal with a lot of stress. But more than 75 percent of our officers are doing a great job."

Councilwoman Raintree said, "75 percent wasn't good enough. I wanted a 100 percent!"

The Councilwoman called on Hanson to appear before Council to discuss misconduct allegations that have been lodged against his officers. Councilman Minor said the calls from concerned residents and the expected rise in crime as the weather warms, made him push for something to be done before the end of the month.

"I don't care if he attacks me or attacks the officers who are responsible for the misconduct," Hanson said in his best sounding standing on his soapbox voice. "But don't attack the whole department. This department does a lot of good things most of which you never hear of."

Another councilman blurted out "That's right, we don't hear about a "lot" of good things. We only hear about the same officers' misconduct over and over," he said in an accusing way.

The mayor went on to say, "A total of six officers have been accused of violating department rules since January."

"Since, January? It is only June and three of the accusations were related to theft, embezzlement and three other stem from more serious incidents like rape, murder and God only knows what else," snapped the councilman.

"The insignificant incidents you mention are Officer Carl Williams, who was suspended for three days for entering a bar while on duty to wish a woman a good luck on her divorce. He then saw an off duty detention officer talking to Williams ex-wife. The detention officer once dated Williams's former wife. Williams complained to three Horse Stomp County Sheriff officials about the detention officer, asking, "What's it going to take to get your attention? Am I going to have to take a baseball bat to him?"

"Your idea of discipline is placing him on paid leave and banned from carrying a gun after he was accused of threatening to kill himself in front of his estranged wife. He spent a week in jail for violating a civil protection order that his ex-wife took out on him the week prior to that incident.

He was then reprimanded more harshly for using foul language and discussing his estranged wife when he pulled over the ex-husband of his current girlfriend, Dina. Williams also went to the man's workplace while on duty to argue with him," said the angered councilman.

"Mayor Hanson, were you aware of Officer Emil Mora was investigated last month after deliberately dumping two guns given to him in connection with a drug transaction gone bad into a city sewer? Horse Stomp Sheriff's deputies found the guns during a recent drug investigation and learned about Mora dumping the guns. I am still waiting to hear the complete story in this matter", another councilman blurted out.

The mayor spoke up about having knowledge of three other officers that were being investigated. "Officer Jackson Bronsmann, was being investigated after he was arrested for domestic violence after a fight with his wife, Edna. She accused him of being intoxicated while on duty and answering calls while driving a patrol car.

More serious allegations were lodged against Officers Julian Sanders and Stedman Myers, both of whom are Sgt. Hanover's "gang" are now accused of sexual misconduct while on duty and are awaiting trial on civil and criminal charges. They remain on paid administrative leave. Their charges are very similar to Hanover's history of complaints in which I don't see documentation he was ever disciplined," said the councilman.

The lawsuit that Ben and I were pursuing against the department became public in 1992. Of course, no one in the department thought I would file it since I didn't have the support of Ben by my side. Little did the Crestview PD know, there was a bigger support team. There were good, law-abiding officers and support staff. However, it was the public that was my prevailing support. We went federal.

Several citizens started taking notice of the unusual practices of the department. On December 14, 1995, a federal judge ordered an investigation of the Crestview Police Department. After reviewing the federal lawsuits, my collection of tapes, documentation and the testimony of witnesses, the same federal judge in turn ordered the department dissolved and taken over by the Horse Stomp Sheriff's Office. Their actions ignited a chain of events that affected the decisions of the good officers within the Crestview Police Department.

By the time, further federal investigations were initiated, two years later the named officers were investigated for everything from sexual harassment/assault, discrimination, murder, as well as the death of my partner Ben.

For those two long years after Ben's death, I had to keep my wits about myself to stay ahead of the new corrupt officers. I worried about the new recruits that were in line to take the place of the next wannabe Hanover, Jones and Lester's of the department. My termination was litigated and I was awarded $500,000 when the federal court judge addressed the defendant's in my suit he looked austerely at them and their attorneys. The judge sat intently on his bench as each witness spoke of the grief the Crestview Police Department inflicted on their lives. Tears were shed by men and women as they gave detail accounts of their encounters with the rouge officers.

The city paid more than a $1,000,000,000 in just legal fees and settlements for claims against officers during that time, according to auditor's records.

I filed a separate claim reference to my phone conversation with my attorney, with Ben had been illegally recorded without my permission, I was awarded more than $100,000 in damages by a federal jury on this matter alone.

I was awarded an additional $262,000 in compensatory damages for invasion of privacy and unlawful seizure and $230,000 in punitive damages against Horace Jones and Bubba Bansheer. The jury rendered the verdict following a four-week trial before U.S. District Judge A. Dontanelli.

My suit alleged Jones ordered Bansheer to tape a phone conversation in which Bansheer told my attorney about it. I was able to encourage Bansheer to admit to doing phone tapping for the Mayor on Jones as well. That didn't set to well with Jones nor did it set well with the mayor when he learned he too was being recorded.

My suit alleged the men made the recording in an attempt to entrap, distort or otherwise create an impression those officers where out to get them and to blackmail them with personal information they had knowledge.

Odie Halbrook said the jury's verdict shows the claims of the Crestview police were not credible. Halbrook told me, Jones, who is now retired and Bansheer is now living in Florida were never charged with violating wiretap laws. Halbrook said that as far as he knows, no disciplinary action was taken against either man. He said he does not expect police will take any action against Jones, despite the verdict.

Judge Antonio Dontanelli was a former prisoner of war during WWII, was well known for not taking

Wake Up and Die Right

---

any guff from anyone. The judge had aged gracefully with white wavy hair; wire framed half glasses worn snuggly around the tip of his nose and look over them in disbelief as a defendant made a statement on the stand. Before the verdict was made in my case, Judge Dontanelli spoke dynamically and told the defendants that he highly suggested the city settle out of court before it goes broke. In his opinion, six million dollars would not be an excessive award amount for all those lawsuits pending. Odie Halbrook and the city attorney Boots Johnson spent an hour to reach the negotiated sum of money.

My case was the first to be settled and the city worried what the other twelve pending cases would cost them. It seemed the hell we where put through, was in turn bad Karma for Chief Jones, Sergeant Hanover, Lt. Lester and Jack, Corporal Slick Rutherford, Detectives Archibald Riddle and Rufus Odell and the other officers that followed their footsteps.

Six months after Ben died, Chief Jones was demoted to lieutenant and two months after that he was a patrol officer. Jones spent 30 years with the department only to have his retirement that of a new patrolman just out of the academy He has since been diagnosed with Lou Gehrig's disease and is living on his houseboat. A once shrewd man now has become humble and he and his wife, who suffers from dementia, now depend on the kindness of others to help them with daily routines. The investigation on Jones was going to give him some jail time but the courts gave pity to his disease that was so advanced that it made him a prisoner in his body.

Rufus Odell was diagnosed with prostrate and liver cancer. He was living an uncomfortable life, still relying on his former police partner. Archibald Riddle and Rufus Odell had to file for bankruptcy after leaving the department when they opened a septic tank cleaning service that failed. Rumors about their indiscretions went public and no one felt they could trust them to clean the shit out of their septic tank.

Prosecutors charged both of them theft and forging the signatures of twenty-eight officers on weapons and improperly keeping the weapons for themselves.

More than a hundred guns had been turned over to the department. The Georgia Bureau of Investigations filed the charges when they found the forged signatures of officers on weapons "buyback" forms indicating officers improperly bought confiscated weapons that should have been auctioned off after a court order, or they were either to be released to owners or for sale.

County auditors went into the evidence room for a standard audit. They found $200,458 in drug money that couldn't be accounted for. There was no documentation found to prove that 224 handguns had been destroyed. There was no effort made by the department to return the 182 weapons to their owners, as they were court ordered to do.

(When officers confiscated them by telling un-

suspecting tourist, "It is against the law to have a gun in Georgia)

Odell and Riddle left a sloppy trail of evidence to the weapons. The IRS was also looking into matters of their income, as they were living well beyond their means. Both former detectives have had their bank assets frozen, their elaborate homes, boats and cars have been put up for auction. Upon the aggressive investigation by the GBI they were educated that Sergeant Hanover was the leader of this ring since neither Rufus or Archie had enough common sense or could be sober long enough to mastermind such an elaborate scheme.

Sergeant Hanover was first charged with the rape of Willow Smith along with embezzlement after taking rent money for the apartment complex where he lived and worked part-time as a manager.

Prosecutors were confident the Georgia Bureau of Investigation was able to make a case on the theft of a gun, tampering with evidence in reference to Mr. Wilson Moore and extortion and criminal damage to Denise Connor's hair salon. GBI never stopped working on making their case against Hanover's additional sordid crimes that he seemed to elude prosecution. The IRS brought Hanover to his knees when they audited him while looking into Riddle and Odell's unexplainable fortune that was three times more than a Georgia police officer's income. Hanover found nothing is sacred when the IRS is involved.

The day Hanover was taken into custody, a

Horse Stomp County deputy called me and asked if I would like to be present when they arrest him on a federal warrant for gun trafficking. I felt it would be an honor as they arrested him while he was in uniform, during a traffic stop.

(Ben would have loved to see that.)

During GBI's investigation, they found in addition to the marijuana, cocaine, crack and pills on 1,326 cases where evidence disappeared over the last eight years. The Crestview Police Department could not provide documentation to prove they had destroyed the drugs as ordered by Judge Snodling.

Not long after the investigation started, Riddle's wife, Hortense, entered rehab for cocaine addiction. After hours of questioning her prior to her admission to rehab, she was asked where she got the cocaine. She became a state's witness against her common-law husband and Odell. Upon further investigation, they found Hanover, Lester, Jack and Mauzer's involvement and were awaiting trial on those charges.

GBI learned some interesting facts about Lt. Lester. One of which he had taken a plea to second-degree murder while working the Yukon County Sheriff's Department in Florida. He testified against his former police partner, Guy Gunter, in two trials, only served 3 ½ years in prison. His record had been expunged with the help of the FBI who used Lester's talents as a conniving and syndical informant.

Nearly 20 years after his first criminal case,

Wake Up and Die Right

Lester was ensnared with the Feds, once again turned state's evidence.

Lester was back in the familiar hot seat as a co-operating star states witness. He joined the Crestview police department in 1981. By 1985, he was living the high life, driving a Corvette and dating at least two women while giving into his other sexual needs to humiliate and control women he came across while working as an officer.

One woman he took an exceptional interest in; he states she drove him to temptation. (*As if, he didn't already have enough temptation*) She urged him to rip off drug dealers with her. He gave into her persuasion and indicated that his moral compass has been tilted since then. (*Odell and Riddle along with Hanover where the first of his drug rip offs.*)

Lester told GBI his first drug rip-off was back in 1985. Said it went smoothly, until his new partner, Sgt Hanover "went crazy" when he didn't find any money. He said Hanover shot and killed two people, one of which was the mayor's former lover, Casey Long. Lester said, Long was at the wrong place at the wrong time.

He confided that the mayor had already asked him to find a way to get rid of Casey. When Hanover took care of the situation by mistake, he embellished the murder by running over Casey's head and using the baseball bat. Lester said took the money from the mayor any way and decided to let Hanover take the fall for the actual murder if anyone was smart enough to put the facts together.

During the interrogation Lester initially refused to talk to investigators, but made a beeline for the district attorney's office when he heard Hanover, was about to testify against him. He was a shrewd man and wanted to make sure he got a smoking deal as he did with Guy Gunter case.

When it was time for Lester to testify against Hanover, he told some of the truth, but not the whole truth, under oath. He worked on sugar coating his part in the rip off and murders. He did his best distancing himself from the crime.

By lying, Hanover was acquitted but was then tried again in federal court a couple of years later. Lester testified against him again. Hanover was acquitted of murder but convicted of conspiracy.

(Lester was someone who has a remarkable insight into the criminal justice system. That is how he was able to stay ahead of investigators. He knew no one would expect a cop let alone a ranking official of the Crestview Police Department. That had been going on for years.)

GBI and FBI where appalled to learn that before testifying against Hanover in a public-corruption case, Lester was promoted to Internal Affairs and told by his then chief and the mayor, clean up the corruption. He did appear to be weeding out dishonest officers. Officers that he trained to be his cronies became over zealous and selfish. Lester turned the tables on them. So when officers were convicted of crimes, never had enough information against Lester to work a deal as sweet as Lester did

Wake Up and Die Right

with the district attorney.

One crony said he left a gift-wrapped present in Lester's patrol car. It was a small box stuffed with $25,000 in hundred dollar bills. It was stolen money; the officer gave as a protection gift to keep Lester on his good side. Lester took the money, applied it to other protection cash donations, and paid cash when he bought his burnt orange corvette he was known for driving around town. Over the next four years, Lester would take more than a quarter of a million in kickbacks and bribes.

He admitted he would look the other way as the corruption mushroomed out of control. His only concern was that he got his portion of the cut. He also helped his supervisors Chief Horace Jones and the mayor collect bribes. Just as the department was under investigation, Lester was about to plea guilty to a single count of organized scheme to defraud. He has already paid his restitution, about half of what he says he received. He kept the rest, unlike Jones and Hanover. Lester gloated that he thought of himself as a "man of integrity". The prosecutors laughed as he made that comment.

Lester was to be sentenced to two years in prison but was out on bond until sentencing. That was when he decided to take care of business with Justine Foxx, who just received her proceeds from her lawsuit against Lester. It was unfortunate that Lester won't be serving any time in jail.

Lieutenant Lester's repugnant lifestyle progressed further with a spiral spin to a darker side than first noticed. He snapped over the civil judgment that Justine Foxx got for the false arrest for the DUI. He had too much pride to have a women get one over on him. Still waiting for several more pending cases to go in civil court, the stress started to get to him.

The Horse Stomp County Newspaper reported Lester leaped to his death from the tenth-floor balcony of Justine Foxx's apartment in Pensacola, Florida where she had been stationed for a year. Her body was found strangled in her bed, where he left a suicide note blaming Ms. Foxx for his problems

I couldn't believe that someone who was pure evil as he was, die and not be able to get out of this situation as he has all the others. He was brought down because of a woman. Something he could not accept.

I saw the crime scene photos of his death. Lester's body was crumpled up as his left leg turned 380 degrees where his knee was broken. His left arm was severed from the forearm and his head was almost severed where it was cut while going through the windshield glass, ironically, of the victim's car. Oddly enough, I had a sigh of relief that he couldn't harm anyone else ever again.

The Foxx family attributed the tragedy directly to the failure to recognize or deal with Lester's abusive personality by the Crestview Police Department. Justine's death fell directly on the mayor and the Crestview PD, who had enabled him to do such heinous things for years.

Wake Up and Die Right

A representative for the Foxx family informed the press that they learned years prior to Lester's employment with the Crestview Police Department, he worked yet another Southern police department, which should have ended Lester's reign of terror as an officer. He chose to resign from that department than go to jail. Since he took a plea under the terms of a confidential agreement and his record was expunged, he did so that it would not undermine his previous department's integrity. The agreement was well thought out. Many wonder what type of bargaining went on behind closed doors and if anyone felt responsible for this decision.

Lt. Jimmy Jack had a tendency to lay low when the other motley crew where more obvious and blatant with their criminal acts. He had a secret. Well, he had many secrets but something he was able to keep silence for some time before it became known. Probably the only thing he ever did well as a serial bank robber.

Lt. Jack committed three robberies at two branches of Barnett Bank, twice in Georgia and once in Florida. At the first robbery, he showed a gun in his belt, it was believed by the teller to be a toy weapon. She refused to give up any money and thought it was a joke. When he couldn't convince her that he was serious, he left the bank on foot.

Then at his second attempt was at the same bank where he was successful and apparently got away with $100,000. Jack grew increasingly brazen, as he simply handed a note to the teller demanding money. Officials learned that he used some of the stolen money to apply towards the purchase a home for one of his girlfriends. He paid cash to pay off his car that had been repossessed just two weeks earlier.

At his third robbery, he waved a 9-millimeter gun at two bank employees, as he demanded cash in $20, $50 and $100 bills and was seen running into an alley, jumping into a small yellow car. Horse Stomp Sheriff deputies pulled him over in his mother-in-law's bright yellow Volkswagen beetle for expired plates just after a robbery. They found another $150,000 in a clear plastic bag on the passenger front seat in the car. The deputies also observed a blond wig, sunglasses pink bandanna and cowboy hat with snakeskin band used in the robberies. There was back up materials he thought may come in handy, duct tape, gloves and a black toy pistol.

Under questioning, Lt. Jack soon confessed in the two earlier cases in Georgia. He made statements to the effect that he was getting married again. Lt. Jack's friends were taken aback because he was already married. The Judge raised Lt. Jack's bail to $1 million, based on the allegations of pending charges. He blamed the police department for driving him to commit the robberies when he found that no other department was willing to hire him with his reputation of being associated with Lester and Hanover. He too was "black balled" from any other law enforcement jobs.

Lt. Jimmy Jack pending charges began when he

had to move into his in-laws' house when the sheriff's office took over the Crestview Police Department, thus loosing his job. He took out his frustrations on his wife, who tried to defend herself when he became infuriated with her cancer-riddled mother for whining from agony. He viciously beat up his wife, Billie Mae, when he threatened to kick her invalid mother out of her own home.

Billie Mae is now in a Savannah psychiatric hospital due to severe head trauma. The incident was so horrendous the neighbors said they could hear him screaming as he yelled the word "Bitch" with every blow to her head. The doctors' prognosis for Billie Mae is that she will remain in a vegetative state due to the massive beating.

Jack was convicted of aggravated assault and attempted murder on his wife. He also has pending auto theft charges where he stole the vehicle that the bank repossessed from him earlier that week. He is in prison and is now someone's bitch.

As for Slick Rutherford, he was used to throwing people in jail, but was the one who sat in a Horse Stomp County jail cell, stripped of his freedom and fired from his job when the "former" Crestview police officer was charged with stealing four-wheelers. He is now working in a convenience store after serving four years in prison.

(This is a joke to be charged with theft of four wheelers when the officers who have committed murder, rape and drugs are the ones charging him.)

According to investigators, Odell and Riddle

testified that they caught Rutherford who stole items from hunting camps in North Horse Stomp County. This all came to light when a stolen four-wheeler was recovered two weeks ago on the Florida border. Investigators managed to track the sales to Slick Rutherford. Rutherford's bond was set at $50,000 dollars.

Rutherford's downfall was when he was working part-time at Circle K as security while still employed as an officer. When the convenient store manager was counting the proceeds for the day, came across a $100 counterfeit bill. She notified Rutherford to make a report so that she can account for the $100 shortage.

Rutherford falsified a written report concerning the $100 counterfeit bill. According to court reports, Rutherford recovered the counterfeit bill but failed to log it as evidence, as required by department policy. Instead, he passed the bogus bill as change for one of the four-wheelers he sold to Sgt. Hanover.

Hanover met a beautiful 29-year-old female Petty Officer by the name Tallulah Green while handling a domestic dispute between her and an old boyfriend. Hanover was smitten by Ms. Green and over the next several weeks, Hanover exchanged telephone calls and text messages with her, subsequently gave her the phony bill, which she unwittingly tried to spend.

Deputy district attorney Fletcher said that when confronted as to where she got the money she pointed her finger towards Hanover, he in turn pointed to Rutherford who admitted he had falsified a report concerning the counterfeit money and claimed he had "mistakenly" given it to Sgt. Hanover, believing it was "another, legitimate bill."

Rutherford admits he made a horrible mistake, which ended up costing his career, so anything we do to him is sort of beside the point. He now spends most of his day restocking the freezer and telling stories of his days as a "super cop" to anyone who will listen.

He is still with Darla and tries to plays puppet master to Allie who has since moved out of state with her boyfriend just to get away from Slick's control over her. She just started to wise up to his games. Even though her infidelity caused the rift between her and Ben, she felt guilty about Ben's death and blamed herself. If it weren't for her lying to the magistrate judge about Ben assaulting her, the snowball wouldn't have picked up such momentum and he may be alive.

I always felt apprehensive of Allie's involvement in his death. I found it very strange that she received Ben's pension, life insurance considering the coroner ruled his death as a suicide. Most insurance companies won't pay out for a suicide when a person hadn't been employed for more than two years. Ben barely had eighteen months on the force.

I didn't think I would ever see any type of justice within this department in my lifetime. The only justice I never saw was the truth about Ben's death. Nothing ever came out about it. No one was charged. There was no logical reason for the alleged suicide. Even the manner in which he died didn't make since. I am sure he would have used his gun if he were going to kill himself. No one can explain the fact that he was moved after dying face down for several hours. Who would have moved his body and why?

My luck ran out that day when the bullet that hit me, was never recovered, after it ripped through my body. I am so tired. I can't fight anymore. My eyes are closed tightly. I lie comfortably under my champagne-colored satin comforter in the silence of the night. My thoughts are happy ones. My life has turned around because of the paths that my family and I have taken.

Life was hard for my parents and I seemed to have a parallel existence to my mother. I learned to stand up for myself because of it. That was something that my mother never seemed to have a chance to experience, except, when it came to her children. She died living the same old days repeatedly, until my father had passed away. She didn't have much peace in her life until her health deteriorated and had to be place in nursing home where she died weighing less than ninety pounds.

I have a feeling of euphoria whisking throughout my being. I feel like I can start over and learn from the things that destiny has put before me. I'm consumed with the memories of my mother, whose turmoil as a child made her a great mother and person.

Wake Up and Die Right

I learned that sometimes we have to endure both physical and emotional suffering to make us a better person. That suffering also is a big part of whom we are or who we may become.

I remember my wedding day to my soul mate Tom, who is a wonderful man I waited for twenty years before we became one. We entered a beautiful and long marriage. Regretfully, we missed out gracefully growing old together. Our lives were filled with laughter and tears, hopes and dreams for our children and grandchildren.

I'm looking forward to new changes and starting over, because things are going to be different. All the fears and sadness are behind me. I hope all that I have done in my lifetime will have some meaning for the next generation in my family.

Noticing that I am not alone in my thoughts, I hear the whispers of others as they reminisce about the good ole days. It is so faint but I can almost hear them, as they laugh about things from not so long ago. I catch myself as I start to smile with a feeling of love for the many friends that I made throughout my years in the military and as a police officer.

I have a warm feeling of peace and happiness as my body is lowered into the ground. You see, the doctors could not recover the bullet so long ago. They could not foresee that while lodged next to my heart, it would nick a major artery some twenty-five years later when I was involved in a minor traffic accident.

I found it eerie that I had a premonition around

the same time Ben died. In my dream he told me, we will meet again but it will not be in the near future. He said it doesn't matter anymore once you are on the other side. When it is my time, he will greet me. Only then will he tell me what happened to him the day he died.

Just as I feel my spirit no longer hovering over my body, I follow the light. There I met Ben as he takes my hand to greet me and escort me to my mother, waiting patiently with one of the brightest auras on cloud nine. I have so many questions. She smiled sweetly, and then gently place her index finger to my lips and in her loving voice tells me that now, I can start over again. This time I will get it right, a new life when I "wake up and die right".

The End.